Pr

Published in the United States through:
Goodnight Publishing
www.GoodnightPublishing.com

Cover art by Tricia Schmitt aka Pickyme
www.wix.com/pickyme/port

www.morgankearns.com

ISBN: 1-4609-2711-7
EAN13: 9781460927113

Visit www.MorganKearns.com to order additional copies.

His baseball cap was pulled down so low that his eyes barely showed from under the brim. His jeans should have been illegal, they were so tight, every muscle was visible as it flexed. And the Under Armour t-shirt fit him like a glove.

She swallowed. She would not drool.

Pathetic.

He tugged her to him and the towel pooled around her feet. He grinned, his dark eyes sparkling, and with large, muscular hands, he eased her against him, holding her close against his rock hard body. He smelled good; clean and male and ... mouth-watering.

The corners of his mouth lifted and tiny lines appeared around his eyes. As if he needed any more help being sexy.

Being so close to Grayson brought back every insecurity she'd ever felt. And she'd never been so aroused.

To Grayson: When you first came and asked for your story to be told, I said I was too busy. I'm so glad you were persistent. Jane is a lucky girl!

ACKNOWLEDGMENTS

A huge thanks to everyone who loved *Fade to Black* and asked when the next book would be in your hands. This is for you!

To Kathryn, Kim and Wanda, thank you!

To Tricia, thank you for a fantastic cover, girlfriend! I love it!

To Kari, I value your opinion. Thank you for being willing to offer it.

To Marva, thanks for telling me the truth, even if it's hard to hear! The novel is better because of it.

To Terri, I appreciate your friendship and your willingness to read anything I write—and your completely honest opinion of it!

To Trish, I couldn't ask for a better sister. Thanks for your two-cents, it's worth so much more!

To my four children, thanks for letting Mommy write and for telling everyone you know that your mom writes books. I love you!

Finally, thank you to my husband. You are my cheerleader, my lover, my best friend. I appreciate all you do to let me live my dream! My heart belongs to you, forever and always.

In It To Win It

Morgan Kearns

1

GRAYSON PIERCE WAS LARGER THAN LIFE—
and annoying as hell.

The man had been a thorn in Jane's side for nearly twenty years—if she counted elementary school, she guessed it was even longer than that—and he'd never been a bigger pain in her ass than in this very moment.

"Can you do that, Jane?" Dale asked from behind his desk.

Dale was the News Director for KHB—and her boss. His blue eyes were no nonsense and as he ran a hand over his thinning blond hair, Jane knew that his question wasn't up for debate.

Sweat coated her palms and she bit her lip. Jane wanted to say no. She wanted to say that there was no way she was going on the road to follow Pierce's team around the freakin' country while they played their way to the World Series. It was bad enough she had to report on how successful he was, but now, she was going to have to follow the jackass just to shove a microphone in his face so he could tell her how awesome he was.

She wasn't bitter though.

"Sure thing, Dale," she said through clenched teeth. "When do I leave?"

"You and Nate will head out tomorrow afternoon. First stop, Vegas."

"Okay, I'll go pack." She turned on her heel but was stopped when Dale cleared his throat. She paused in the doorway of his office and her already sucky situation got worse.

"Get an exclusive if you can. Anything nobody else has. There's a raise in it for ya."

"PIERCE IS HOT TONIGHT," THE COMMEN-tator said from overhead. "Swing and a miss."

Jane could clearly see Grayson from her van-tage point just inside the tunnel that led to the locker room. He backed out of the batter's box and tapped the bat against his cleats. A quick roll of his head on thick shoulders and he stepped back into the box, hefting the bat into position. The tip circled for a moment before stilling. The navy bat-ter's helmet with the large white *R* in the center was pulled down to his brows and his eyes were focused on the wind-up.

One more out—or one more run—and the team would be heading her way. Nate, her photographer and good friend, had the camera perched on his shoulder, waiting for the explosion of commotion that was only minutes away. He was all calm, cool and collected. Jane, however, had butterflies in her stomach.

Closing her eyes and sucking in a deep breath, she reminded herself that Grayson Pierce and his opinions no longer mattered. That hell called high school had been fifteen years ago. But she'd be damned if those scars didn't take eons to heal.

"...and a home run by Pierce brings in three! Rockets win by two."

Cheers and applause erupted, nearly shaking the walls of the stadium. *"Pierce. Pierce. Pierce!"*

The enthusiasm was enough to make Jane want to vomit. She swallowed hard and rolled her eyes.

In seconds large men flooded the space around her, making it suddenly seem like the walls were closing in around her. The smell of dirt, sweat and testosterone pushed her deeper into the tunnel until she was finally swept into the locker room. Nate was a big guy, easily as tall as any of the athletes with shoulders just as wide, and he captured b-roll to send back to the station.

Grayson, surrounded by his cheering teammates, entered and her heart nearly stopped. It had been years since she'd been so close to him and the effect he had on her was the same. Tears stung her eyes and she blinked. This was not the appropriate time to get emotional.

Come to think of it; *never* was the appropriate time to get emotional over Grayson Pierce. He didn't deserve her tears.

The one she recognized as Xavier stopped in front of her. His brows rose. "Hey, sweet thing. You lookin' for an interview?"

Instead of slapping him—which is what she really wanted to do—she stuck the mic in his face. "Great game."

"Thanks. Standing at the plate with men on the corners puts a lot of pressure on a guy, ya know?"

She bit down hard, grinding her molars to keep from rolling her eyes. "I can imagine," she said through gritted teeth, urging him to continue.

He did. "But doing it with a full count is enough to make you sweat." He chuckled and lifted his hat to wipe his forehead with the back of his hand. "It's a good thing I don't buckle under pressure. I thrive on it."

"You've had a decent rookie season—"

"Decent?" He laughed, looked over his shoulder and hollered, "Yo, Pierce, this chick says I've had a *decent* season."

In that moment Jane wanted to drop to the floor and dig herself a hole to hide in. The situation only got worse as Grayson lifted his chin and laughed. The sound was low and deep and—damn her straight to hell—sensual. He waded through the crowd straight toward them. Jane gulped and ignored the fact that he'd taken off his jersey. His navy uniform pants were so low on his hips she wondered if his cheeks would show if he turned around. His abs were damp with sweat and Jane felt the sudden urge to trace them with her tongue.

Which was absurd ... because she hated him.

Grayson's eyes met hers and he lifted a brow. *Damn!* Surely, he didn't know what she was thinking.

"Thanks for the interview," she mumbled, trying to get away without having to talk with Grayson.

Surely there was another ballplayer that wouldn't thrive on trying to humiliate her. No doubt when Grayson showed up that's what would happen. And she didn't need those kinds of problems.

The news industry was highly competitive and challenging, but being a female sportscaster made it all the more grueling. Most athletes were respectful. A high percentage flirted relentlessly. She'd been given more than one hotel room key—all of which were placed where they belonged ... in the trash.

Molly, her best friend since her college days at USC—Go Trojans!—insisted she wallpaper her bedroom with them. Or better yet, just hand 'em over to her. *She'd* be happy to *use* a pompous, egotistical man.

"Hey! Where you goin', darlin'?" A hand the size of a ham bit into her arm and roughly urged her to turn back around. She slapped Xavier's hand away.

"I am *not* darlin'. The name's Jane Alexander. If you'd like to stuff your testosterone where the sun don't shine, I'd be happy to put your ugly mug on TV. If not ... we're both just wasting our time."

Nate snorted, but didn't react further, professionally keeping the camera on the arrogant face that seemed momentarily stunned. But only momentarily.

"Listen, honey—" Xavier raised his hands in mock surrender. "—I didn't mean no disrespect."

"Listen, *honey*, if you can't call me Jane, then don't call me at all."

Xavier laughed and jerked his thumb in her direction—but the red tint to his cheeks revealed that he was embarrassed. "This one's a livewire. For real! Pierce, I think I'm in love."

Grayson finally made his way to stand before her. Those shoulders of his were even broader than she remembered—his body more toned with a wider chest, a narrower waist and more powerful thighs. The boy she'd known had become a delicious man. His dark hair was in a sweaty disarray, his cap having been removed, a dark curl rested against the tanned skin of his forehead.

He was sporting a goatee these days, trimmed close to his face, probably to hide the thin scar that she'd given him junior year. It was only fair; heaven knew that she wore enough scars from him. Hers were emotional—and still raw.

His heated gaze slowly roamed from her pink-painted toes, pausing at her hips and breasts, before coming to a stop on her face. Those perfect lips of his formed a smirk and her knees nearly gave out.

He stuck out his hand. "Hi. Grayson Pierce."

Wow!

Of all the reactions he could have had to seeing her after so many years that was by far the last one Jane would have expected. It hurt—an honest to goodness dagger to the heart—that there was no recognition in his dark brown eyes.

She glanced down at his hand, but didn't take it. She forced herself to make eye contact as she said, "Jane Alexander, KHB, can I get a comment on the win?"

His grin widened and he shouted, jabbing his fists into the air, "Rockets—all the way to the Series!" He winked at her. "And you can quote me on that."

"Pierce!" a male voice yelled. "I need you over here."

"Duty calls. I'll catch you later, Jane Alexander." He held her gaze for a moment longer than necessary before turning to stride off through the crowd.

"Let's get out of here," she told Nate, refusing to accept that her heart had been bruised yet again. Would she never learn?

MAN, IT'D BEEN GOOD TO SEE JANE.

She was just as beautiful as he remembered. Her shiny brown hair had highlights he didn't remember and was longer, sleeker than it used to be. It now hung just below her shoulders with just a bit of a curl at the ends.

Her eyes though, they hadn't changed a bit. They were the most intoxicating green he'd ever seen. Even after all these years, and all of his travels all over the world, Grayson had still never found a shade that could compare. The closest he'd found was the deep green of freshly cut grass, but that didn't have enough variations to be exactly right.

Grayson couldn't get over how sexy she was. That was new. Her body had matured into that of a woman. He'd not dared touch her because he was afraid he wouldn't be able to let go once he had her wrapped in his arms. And groping her in the locker room, in front of God and all his teammates would have just embarrassed them both.

Besides, it had been a long time since they'd crossed paths. He had a feeling that that was exactly the way she meant for it to be.

Yeah, how dense was he? She wouldn't even shake his hand. He'd felt like an idiot with his hand stretched out to her, hanging in midair. He guessed he deserved it.

Acting like he hadn't known her *had* been a pretty chicken-shit tactic, he had to admit. But standing there in front of her, he couldn't—just couldn't allow their reunion to happen in a crowded locker room.

Striding toward the elevators he shook his head, trying to clear it of the stricken expression on her face. He would make it up to her.

It had been ridiculously easy to get her room number. He felt like a letch, flashing a smile at the star-struck girl working the front desk. But that had been a means to an end and he'd learned a long time ago that Grayson Pierce could get just about anything he wanted. And a few things he didn't—like phone numbers and ladies underwear.

The elevator ride to Jane's floor happened in a blink, yet took a lifetime. He wanted to see her again. But then ... wasn't sure he did. He wanted her to smile at him the way she used to. The odds of that were pretty slim, he feared. The last few weeks of high school had been hell—and he wasn't even sure why.

When the *ding!* signaled he'd reached his destination, his heart jumped into his throat and he
suddenly felt sick to his stomach. He swiped a
hand over his face from chin to eyebrows and continued the sweep through his hair. Sucking in a
breath did nothing to calm his nerves.

The elevator doors started to close and Grayson
was surprised when his arm flashed out to stop
them. The doors retreated back into their pockets
and he stepped out into the corridor. He took two
steps forward, one back. Practically ran down the
hall, only to turn and stalk away. The back and
forth continued until he found himself standing in
front of her door. It was now his arm's turn to be
indecisive, rising and falling. Fist poised at the
door, only to be brutally shoved into his pocket.

Oh good hell! Was he a man or a mouse?

He lifted his arm again.

JANE SAT IN HER HOTEL ROOM, SURFING THE
internet for stats on the Rockets and the team they
would be playing in two days. She took a bite of
her room service hamburger and tried to concentrate on the graphs and stats that filled the screen
of her laptop. The colors and numbers blurred as
her mind kept returning to the exchange in the
locker room.

She'd changed since the days when Grayson
knew her. She knew that. She was no longer the
insecure little girl with braces and glasses, which
hid her uni-brow, and brown hair that was in a
constant state of frizz. The ninety's had not been
kind to her. But the twenty-first century came and
with it went 'Plain Jane', bringing straight teeth
and contacts, a monthly appointment with the sa-
lon for perfectly arched brows and John Frieda's
anti-frizz formula—and the boob job, not that she
ever told anyone about that.

Even her mother thought that college had magically made her breasts two sizes larger—and that was the way Jane was going to keep it.

Jane's parents had moved from the tiny town in Central Utah where Jane was born and raised and she had never gone back. Why bother? It was better to leave the past where it belonged—in the past.

Except now that painful past had come flooding back with a really sick sense of vengeance. She couldn't help but wonder what she'd done that made karma hate her so badly? She tried to be a good person. She'd never killed anyone or tortured any small, helpless animals. Surely, the spider in her room yesterday morning didn't count.

She moved her cursor and put KHB's web address into the browser, calling up tonight's newscast. She watched as her face appeared on the screen. She scrutinized every movement and was satisfied with her work today. Not bad. No notes to work on—except to keep her heart from pounding every time Grayson Pierce showed up.

Well, what do you know? It seemed that she *was* still the heartsick little girl whenever he looked at her.

Could she be more pathetic?

In a huff, she gathered her things and headed for the bathroom. A hot shower to wash away the frustration of the day was exactly what she needed. Too bad she couldn't scrub out the inside of her head and plaster a band-aid over the wound on her heart.

She groaned. She was not going to do this. She was here to do a job, not moon over whether or not Grayson remembered who the hell she was. She didn't care!

She stepped out of the shower and began to dry her hair with a towel. Standing buck naked in front of the mirror, Jane brushed out her hair and began to moisturize; first her legs, then her stomach and arms and...

A knock on her door made her jump. She grabbed a towel and wrapped it around her middle and went for the door, only to decide that it didn't cover enough, even if it was only going to be Nate. Especially if it was only going to be Nate.

Nate was happily married and wasn't afraid to admit how much he loved his wife, Roxie. The last thing Jane wanted was for word to get around that there was something going on between her and Nate. None of them needed the heartache that kind of rumor could bring—even if the gossip was completely unfounded, unsubstantiated, and untrue.

Another knock.

"Hold on," she yelled. "I'm coming."

Thankfully a big, white, fluffy hotel bathrobe hung from a hook on the back of the bathroom door and Jane shrugged into it, tying the belt as she opened the door and turned back into her room.

"I'm glad you're here. I've been thinking about the story and wanted to run some things—"

"Jane?"

She froze at the sound of her name. She knew that voice with a certainty that made her tingle from head to toe. Taking a breath to brace herself she turned.

"Grayson? What are you doing here?"

"May I come in?" he asked, dipping his Rockets hat covered head slightly.

She nodded, unable to find her voice.

He sauntered inside, closing the door behind him. She gulped not sure she liked the idea of being stuck in a hotel room with Grayson. His hands went up in submission. "I won't hurt you."

"I know," she answered softly. She knew he wouldn't hurt her—at least not physically.

She twisted the tie of her robe around her finger and waited for him to say something. His mouth didn't open. He just stood across the room and stared at her. She was going to show him the door when he rushed at her, wrapping his arms around her and swinging her around the room. The air raced from her lungs on a gasp. His arms held her to the hard planes of his body and she wasn't able to breathe. She heard the sound of his boot clunking into the door and the thud as it closed. Her heart was jumping around in her chest, but not because she was afraid.

"Jane, it is *so* good to see you."

She stumbled when he placed her on her feet. He kept hold of her hands and stepped back to arm's length, visually taking her in from head to toe.

"Man, you look amazing!"

"What are you doing here?" she asked the same question she'd voice when he stood in her doorway. Her mind swam. Why the hell was Grayson standing in her room? And why the hell had he wrapped her in a hug that turned her into a pile of goo? Not that she was going to complain any time soon.

His baseball cap was pulled down so low that his eyes barely showed from under the brim. His jeans should have been illegal, they were so tight, every muscle was visible as it flexed with his movements. And the black Under Armour t-shirt fit him like a glove.

She swallowed. She would not drool.

Pathetic.

He tugged her to him and the towel pooled around her feet. He grinned, his dark eyes sparkling, and with large, muscular hands, he eased her against him, holding her close against his rock hard body. He smelled good; clean and male and ... mouth-watering. She wiggled to get away from him—so she could think—and he released her.

"Sorry. It's just so good to see you." He shook his head, his face a mixture of elation and awe if Jane was reading it right. "I know I said that before, but it really is. I've seen you on TV, of course. You're really a great sportscaster. You actually know what you're talking about. So, do you like baseball?"

The guy was rambling, the questions spewing from his mouth like water from a faucet turned on full blast. Jane just stared at him. What else could she do? She'd dreamt of this guy once and he'd made her life miserable ... once.

Needing distance between them, she walked around the bed and stood on the opposite side. Grayson kicked at the towel, popping it into the air. He plucked it up midflight and tossed it onto the bed. The corners of his mouth lifted and tiny lines appeared around his eyes. As if he needed any more help being sexy.

"Whatcha wearin' under that bathrobe?" he asked suggestively.

"None of your business," she snapped, feeling unwanted heat under said robe. Her fingers unconsciously went to the tie, yanking it so tight she wondered if it was possible to be cut in half by the stupid thing. She glared at him. "What are you doing here?"

"Isn't it obvious? I wanted to see you."

"You *saw* me in the locker room earlier."

"Um, yeah, I was ... ah ... surprised." At least he looked contrite.

"You introduced yourself."

"I ... um ..." Muscles rippled as he lifted a shoulder in a shrug. When he grinned at her the chagrin on his face made her want to giggle. It was the same look she'd seen when they were kids. His eyes roamed casually over her face. "You're beautiful, you know that?"

"Yeah, so I've been told." She could almost taste the sarcasm, her only line of defense. She *had* been told that she was beautiful, but never by Grayson and she was not going to explore the effect that hearing it from him had on her.

"Hey, there's no reason to be that way." He took a step toward her and she willed herself to hold her ground. She would not be intimidated by him. "The truth is ... I didn't want things to be awkward while you were trying to do your job—and I was doing mine."

He ran a finger down her cheek and she fought a shudder. She was not going to let Grayson know how much he was getting to her. Hell, she wasn't ready to admit it to herself. His thumb ran lightly over her bottom lip.

"So ... is this a one-time deal or are you gonna follow me 'til the end?"

She blinked and gulped back her sigh. She snapped, "I am following the *Rockets*—not you."

That wasn't exactly the truth. Grayson was the hometown kid, who'd hit it big. Dale dreamed of stories like this, and unfortunately, it was Jane's job to chase this particular dream for him. Her hands tightened into fists and she jammed them into the pockets of the robe.

"But yes, I am to follow the team until you lose," she conceded softly.

"So you're with me until the end." He was so sexy when he was cocky.

"I guess so. Now if you'll excuse me, I've got an early morning."

His head dropped slightly as did the look on his face and he smoothed a hand over his chest. "I'd like to see you again."

"I'll be around." She strode past him and opened the door. "Good night, Grayson."

He took her not-so-subtle hint without protest and walked out into the hall. "Good night, Janie. I'll dream of you."

She didn't respond, mostly because the air had frozen in her lungs, and just closed the door. It took several moments of exaggerated breathing before the light-headed feeling left and her thoughts cleared.

This was impossible.

She couldn't do this. Being so close to Grayson brought back every insecurity she'd ever felt. And she'd never been so aroused.

Frustrated in more ways than one, she shrugged out of the robe and climbed into bed.

And, damn her, dreamed of Grayson.

2

THREE DAYS LATER JANE SAT IN A LITTLE BAR at the airport, waiting for her flight. A few minutes ago, Nate had gone to the men's room, leaving her alone. Both a good and a bad thing. With her laptop open she was typing out the script for her next report. Or at least she should have been.

Her mind however had other ideas: Grayson's smile; white teeth beneath the dark goatee. Grayson's butt enclosed in tight navy cotton. Grayson's eyes; chocolate brown with golden flecks near the iris.

Grayson's rejection.

She didn't know why the last thing surprised her. But it did and it stung! Hard as she tried, she couldn't get the memory of the latest cruel reminder out of her head.

Yesterday after the game the team came in celebrating another win, Grayson smiled at her as he raced past, surrounded by teammates. Every other reporter in the room spoke with him, except her—like he'd been avoiding her. And that pissed her off. Hurt her feelings too, but it was easier to just be angry so that was the emotion she concentrated on.

And that night she'd gone to the hotel gym, intent on punishing the treadmill. With her iPod buds deep in her ears, she ran. And ran. Her ponytail swished against her shoulder blades with every pounding step. She closed her eyes and lost herself in the hard beat of the newest Linkin Park song. She wasn't sure how, but she heard the soft swish and whir of the treadmill next to her powering on, followed by the steady thud of running feet.

It annoyed her that someone would choose the machine next to hers when the whole frickin' gym was empty. She cracked an eyelid and groaned when Xavier smiled at her.

"Hi," he said, his eyebrows jogging upward quickly.

"Hi." She looked him in the eye as she moved her thumb over the touchpad of her iPod, increasing the volume of her music.

He reached over and plucked the earpiece from her ear. "Hey! It's rude to ignore people."

"I don't ignore *people*, Xavier. Just you."

He put his huge hand over where his heart rested in his chest and acted wounded. "I just want to talk."

"So. Talk." She sounded breathless and hated the tone. It made her come across as enamored when in reality she'd run three-quarters of a mile.

Xavier smiled at her and found a pace for his own workout. "Did you know I'm only four away from the all-time top spot?"

"I didn't realize you were that close." She was surprised how easily, casually it was to talk to the jerk. Her animosity melted away as his face softened and took on the expression of a little boy.

"I'm totally stoked," he told her. His feet meeting the treadmill in a steady rhythm.

"I'd be stoked, too." To be in the same category as Babe Ruth *was* pretty awesome, but she would keep being impressed to herself.

His hazel eyes went lusty. "Wanna celebrate with me?"

And the jerk was back.

"I don't think so."

His laugh was deep and mocking. Xavier stopped his treadmill and glanced over her shoulder. She turned to see Grayson strutting toward them. She stopped her treadmill and considered running all the way back to her room. Sweat-soaked in grungy work-out clothes was not how she wanted to meet up with Grayson again.

Xavier raised a hand and shouted, "Hey Pierce, this little minx doesn't want a piece of me. Can you believe that?"

Grayson's dark eyes flicked from Xavier to her and back, humor sparkling in their depths. He appraised her from head to toe and smiled at Xavier.

"Those are the breaks, man." Grayson strode over to the free weights and made his selection. Sitting down he rested his elbow on his knee and began bicep curls.

Jane wasn't sure how to respond to his lack of … well, his lack of anything. She wanted to scream at him or slap him or … she wasn't sure. Jane liked knowing where things stood, no surprises.

She knew she had her hands full with Xavier. The guy had a reputation for being an ass to male sportscasters, and whenever he dealt with her he reached all new lows. She could handle him, though. It was Grayson she had a hard time dealing with because she never knew what she was going to get. He was one big question mark.

Coming back to the present, she stared at the blinking cursor in her nearly empty Word document. Her bag moved from the seat next to her and she reached out to rescue it from the clutches of the thief. Instead a warm hand covered hers. She looked up into eyes that were *way* too familiar.

"Grayson," she breathed. He looked better than she'd ever seen him, dressed in black Armani with a starched white shirt underneath. The first couple of buttons were opened, exposing the tanned flesh of his throat. She gulped.

GRAYSON STOOD, WAITING FOR JANE TO FIND her voice again. Her eyes looked him over from head to toe and he couldn't tell if that was a good thing or not. But man, it felt good to have that much of her touching him. He swallowed hard then returned the favor by taking an inventory of her as well. She was as gorgeous as ever; dressed in jeans and a white t-shirt, totally casual. Her brown hair was pulled up in a ponytail.

"Can I sit here?" He waved a hand toward the stool next to hers.

"It's a free country." She closed her laptop and shoved it into its case, taking no care for the bag or the computer. "I have to get going anyway; my flight is about to board."

As she stood, he reached out and snatched up her hand. Her hands were chilly and oh, so tiny. His engulfed hers and yet they fit perfectly together. Just like always.

"Will you have dinner with me?" The words were flung out into the open before his brain could catch up with his mouth.

"I can't."

"Yes, you can." Always a glutton. Inside, he was cringing as he threw his ego on the floor for her to crush beneath her flip-flop. Outside ... he rested a foot on the bottom rung of the bar stool and prayed that he looked the calm, cool, collected he didn't feel.

"No, I really can't. It's against the rules."

He smiled and felt a nervous twitch to his lips. He bit down on his bottom lip to keep it under control. "What rules?" he asked.

Her eyes narrowed and her lips tightened into a frown. "The no-fraternizing-with-the-athletes rule," she said the words in a *duh!* tone.

He laughed. "That's not a real rule."

She straightened her spine and hiked her bag onto her shoulder. "It's a personal rule. I have a reputation to uphold."

"Fair enough." He could respect her having scruples, but it didn't change the fact that it had been too long since he'd talked with her. The few moments in her room didn't count. "We could consider it a working dinner. We could talk—on the record.

WELL ... HELL! DALE HAD ASKED HER TO GET something exclusive, this could be her chance. But she couldn't trust herself with him. She would not let Grayson break her heart—again.

"I'm sorry. I can't. I really should get to my gate. Goodbye, Grayson."

He let her leave this time, for which she was grateful. Her mind still spinning, Jane looked at her feet, at a couple making out in a corner that was not nearly secluded enough, at ... She collided with a brick wall.

Okay, so it was only Nate coming back from the bathroom. She stumbled and he grabbed her by the shoulders, steadying her.

"Whoa! Where's the fire?" he asked with a chuckle.

"We need to get to the gate."

Thankfully Nate didn't argue. He silently followed her and then sat next to her at the gate where they would wait to board the plane. She looked at her watch and groaned. They still had at least twenty minutes before pre-boarding would start.

She liked Nate. He'd graduated from hard news to sports about the time she'd started. It was the unspoken rule around the newsroom that they were partners and good friends. They made a good team. He was the big brother she'd never wanted. He was protective of her and in a world of egos it was nice to have someone at her back.

Nate tugged a *Sports Illustrated* from his carry-on bag and flipped through the pages, settling on an article about ... Grayson Pierce.

Damn!

Jane opened her laptop bag and pulled the computer free. It caught on the corner and she tugged at the laptop. A curse slipped past her lips and Nate cocked a brow at her. He looked a little too amused for her liking and she glared her annoyance at him. His smirk grew into a grin. She shook her head and opened up her laptop, turning it on.

After a few seconds, the screen lit up and she began to re-read what she'd written before Grayson had so rudely interrupted ... and it took all of seventeen seconds to catch up.

Who was she kidding?

Her mind was in a jumble, making her worthless!

Closing her eyes and concentrating on the copy, she let her fingers type out whatever her mind told them and prayed she didn't come up with sentences like: Grayson is so hot. Grayson is so sexy. I want to have Grayson's babies.

"Ugh!" she groaned, slamming the computer shut.

"'Sup?" Nate looked mostly concerned, and totally confused.

"I can't concentrate, and it's driving me nuts!" She stood and paced up and down the little aisle between the rows of seats. "I'm gonna get a soda. You want one?"

He held up his can of Coke, looking at her like she had in fact lost her mind. "Nope, I'm good."

She nodded. "Okay, I'll be back in a second."

Nate muttered, "Get some Prozac, too" under his breath.

Jane had to admit his recommendation was probably a good idea. She needed *something* to calm her nerves. Maybe a little caffeine would do the trick.

The airport was busy, but not insanely so. There was only one near mishap when Jane was almost run over by some lady pushing a screaming toddler in a stroller.

Accident averted but still off her game, Jane strolled into a little coffee shop and bought a large cup. She walked over to the beverage stand and put the cup up to fill it with Diet Coke. A little further down and off to the side were the lids and cups and a dish a fresh, sliced lemons. She plucked one up, using the little silver tongs, and dropped it into the fizzing brown liquid.

"I thought you had a flight to board."

She cringed at the deep, sexy voice behind her. An entire monologue of curse words plowed through her thoughts as she considered whether or not she could pretend she hadn't heard him.

"Jane?" His warm hand came to rest on her shoulder.

"Yeah, I do have a flight to catch. Don't you?" She clamped a lid onto the cup and braced herself as she turned around to face Grayson. Not that the preparation did any good. He grinned and her heart screeched to a halt. Her knees went all gooey and she reached out to the metal counter for support.

"As a matter of fact—" He lifted his wrist to reveal a Rolex, complete with diamonds all around the face. "—I have about thirty minutes. Can we talk?"

"Sorry. I can't. Nate's waiting."

"Are camera guys doubling as babysitters now?"

Her eyes narrowed and she heard herself snort, much to her mortification. "No," she said, sounding like a child. She would have preferred a snappy comeback, but couldn't come up with anything profound so kept her mouth shut.

He gently wrapped his hand around her arm and led her to a cozy corner of the coffee shop. He offered her the chair facing the room and as she sat, he asked, "Can I get you something?"

"No, I'm good." She held up her drink, much like Nate had done a few minutes earlier. Although she doubted she'd perfected the you've-completely-lost-you're-freakin'-mind expression that donned Nate's face a lot lately. "Thanks though."

Grayson sat down in the chair and flashed another dazzling smile. Some of the tension seeped out of her, flowing down her body and out her toes to pool on the floor. She moved the straw around her drink, dunking the lemon and waiting for it to pop up again.

This wasn't awkward at all, she thought sarcastically.

They sat in uncomfortable silence; Jane studiously watching the lemon in her drink and Grayson drumming his fingers on the table.

"What have you been up to all these years?" he finally asked.

"Just doin' the sports thing. You?" *Good grief, next they'd be talking about the weather.*

"Baseball." He smiled, showing off straight white teeth and the tiny pale scar on his upper lip. It was barely noticeable under his trim-cut goatee.

She liked the facial hair, not that she liked it on any other guy. But for some reason it looked exactly right on Grayson's chiseled face. "It's kind of my life."

She thought of all the extracurricular activities—and media attention they caught—and blurted, "It seems you have more to your life than just baseball."

His dark brows pinched together, forming a V, and Jane could have sworn he flinched, but the reaction was so quick she wasn't sure. His face softened and he leaned forward, resting his large forearms on the table.

"There are a lot of facets to me," he said softly.

"Good to know." She stood, the chair screeching across the floor. "I should get going."

He reached out and snagged her hand. "It really was great to see you again, Janie. Maybe we can catch up in Phoenix. We're there for a couple of days. I'd love to buy you dinner and ... catch up."

"Listen, Grayson, I'm not the same girl you knew once..."

His dark eyes warmed and moved over her body slowly. The blatant heat in his gaze interrupted her thoughts for only a moment, before solidifying what she needed to tell him—if for no other reason than self preservation.

"I appreciate the invitation, but I want more than you can give me. *Catching up* would only be a waste of time—for both of us. Let's just say 'nice to see you' and leave it at that."

"What if I don't want to leave it at that?"

She laughed; the feeling built in her stomach and burst from her in a loud guffaw that caused more than one head to turn in their direction. A little embarrassed, Jane felt heat rising in her cheeks. She didn't voice another word, just gave him her back and walked away.

"You okay?" Nate asked as she plopped down in the seat next to him.

Soda splashed over the side of the cup where the lid wasn't on tight enough and Jane groaned. "Yeah. Fine. Couldn't be better." She plucked at the damp denim, brushing at the little brown dots that splattered her jeans.

"Jane." That deep voice saying her name made her insides go all mushy and her irritation spike.

"You have *got* to be kidding me," she muttered under her breath, then turned and smiled—okay, scowled—at Grayson.

"You left your purse in the coffee shop." He handed it to her. "I figured you'd need it."

She thought she heard Nate chuckle, and *knew* she had when his *Sports Illustrated* ruffled, covering his face from view. She would get even. Right now though, she had to get rid of Grayson ... again!

"Yeah. Thanks."

"Does my chivalry constitute dinner?"

"No," she said just as Nate asked, "You buyin'?"

She glared at the blond photographer—the guy who was supposed to have her back—beside her. Nate darted a mischievous grin at her before looking up at Grayson.

Totally unfazed by her attitude, Grayson offered his knuckles to Nate. "Of course. Jane, will *both* of you come to dinner with me? Please?"

She fought the urge to roll her eyes—and slap Nate silly—and nodded. "Fine. We'll *both* have dinner with you."

There was an awkward pause, then Nate handed Grayson his card. "My cell number's on there. Call us with the date and time."

Thankfully the flight attendant announced that it was time to board and Jane stood a little too quickly. Grayson reached out to steady her, those chocolate brown eyes of his staring into her Plain-Jane green ones.

"I'll call you," he whispered, his voice low with promise.

She couldn't break the visual contact that had magically turned into something much stronger. Her lungs burned with the need to take a breath. Her eyes burned with the need to blink. And the rest of her burned with the need to touch him, taste him, give everything she had to him.

"Thanks, my man." Nate slapped Grayson on the back, breaking the spell.

Jane could feel Grayson's eyes on her until she rounded the corner to board the plane. Then she was able to breathe. All those years ago she'd felt disoriented and flustered when around him, but now it seemed to be worse. And she couldn't afford that kind of distraction.

Nate settled into the seat next to her on the plane and turned to look at her. "What?" she grumbled.

"What, what?" Nate wasn't very good at pulling off looking innocent, and this time was no different. "I was just wondering why Grayson Pierce invited you to dinner."

"Us. He invited *us* to dinner."

"Yeah, I only get to come along because you need a bodyguard."

"No, I need someone to run interference." The words were out before she could censor them and Nate cocked a brow, his blue eyes suddenly much too knowing.

Nate was a great guy, but he was a guy. A very manly guy. He didn't want to hear the girly, emo crap. And she didn't want to share either.

"Look, Grayson and I have a past." His grin widened and she clarified, "We went to high school together, okay? Nothing more. And I want to keep it that way."

"Cool."

He was quiet, his large hands in a death grip on the armrests while the plane took off. His jaw opened wide, cracked and then his head moved on his shoulders, loud pops emitting from his neck. It wasn't surprising; it was his usual take-off ritual. Next he would stretch his legs—she smiled when he did—and press his arms out in front of him, stretching each out to its limit. Finally, he sighed and closed his eyes.

"You okay?" he asked.

"Yeah," she said, surprised. This *was* a deviation from the norm.

"If you don't want him around, I can make that happen." It wasn't said with arrogance, just cold, hard fact.

"Thanks, but I don't need a bodyguard."

His eyes opened. "I'm sorry about that. I didn't know. I've been told that I should think before I speak. And I didn't think ... well, I didn't think there was a history that sparked your hostility toward him."

"I wasn't *hostile*."

"Pretty damn close," he said with a smile. "Now excuse me, I've some sleep to catch."

As he closed his eyes, Jane had to smile too. Maybe having dinner with Grayson wouldn't be so bad with Nate watching her back. She opened up her laptop and, after only a moment's pause, she began to type. The story came easy this time. She quickly had it finished and closed her computer.

Carefully, she snaked Nate's *Sports Illustrated* and opened it to the story on Grayson.

3

"UGH!" JANE GROANED.

Clubs were not her thing, nor were sports bars or restaurants that catered to the loud and obnoxious. Yet, here she stood.

The lighting was low, the music was loud, and it was wall to wall people around the bar and on the small dance floor. It seemed the dress code was khaki slacks, button-down shirts or sundresses that showed off a lot of tanned leg, depending on your gender.

Jane suddenly felt underdressed in her jeans and Arizona Diamondbacks t-shirt. She'd worn the opposing team on purpose, wanting to send a statement to Grayson. Unlike her high school days, she didn't enjoy sitting on the sidelines watching him strut his stuff. Now, it annoyed her.

Nate leaned over to her and whispered, "This place is awesome!"

Annoyed and underdressed and over stimulated as she was, she had to agree ... the place *was* pretty awesome.

"Can I help you?" asked a feminine voice.

Jane and Nate turned in unison to see a girl. A beautiful girl with long legs plugged into platform shoes that made her nearly as tall as Nate. Her skirt could easily double as a napkin, and extensions that made her platinum blond hair brush her butt. The smile she offered was full and lush and she only had eyes for Nate. She batted her well placed fake lashes and slid her tongue over her bottom lip.

Nate didn't notice a bit of her attentions. Gotta love a happily married man! His head moved on his neck as he searched the crowd for Grayson.

He offered the hook- er ... hostess a slight smile and said, "Yeah, we're here to meet Grayson Pierce."

Her gaze slid from Nate to Jane as if she were surprised to find that someone besides Nate was standing there. Raising a perfectly arched brow her look said *"sure you are"* as loudly as if she'd screamed the words.

Jane squared her shoulders and ... didn't know what else to do. She could cause a scene and insist that she be taken to see Grayson, knowing full well that it wouldn't work. She could also gather her pride and leave.

She was about to do just that when Nate put a hand on her arm. It seemed that he wasn't deterred by the unspoken insult. "Is he here?"

"I can't verify that information." The hostess smiled at an older couple who'd just entered and, ignoring Jane and Nate, asked, "Can I help you?"

"Table for two," the guy said.

"Of course, right this way." And with that, she walked away, leaving Jane staring after her with her mouth gaping wide.

Nate snorted. "What a bitch! She's gonna feel really stupid when Grayson *is* waiting for us."

"This is ridiculous." Jane hiked her purse higher on her shoulder and stepped toward the door. "I'm outta here."

"Hold up." Nate's hand was huge on her shoulder. "I think the tide's gonna change."

Jane could hear the smile in Nate's voice and turned to see Grayson coming toward them, a sexy grin on his full lips.

"Janie!" He raised a hand in a wave.

Did the guy ever look bad?

Tonight he sported beige slacks that hugged his thighs and a navy button-down shirt. (Obviously he'd gotten the dress code memo.) The short sleeves showcased his muscular arms. His goatee was trimmed close, his cheeks clean-shaven. One dark curl fell over his brow.

Jane smiled, more at the gawking hostess than at the greeting itself. As Grayson swept Jane up in a hug and twirled her, the smile grew and she was honestly thrilled by the reception. She'd dreamed of being held tightly against Grayson's chest. Giddiness bubbled in her belly and when she giggled, she wrapped her arms around his neck.

He kissed her check as he set her back on her feet. Her knees were wobbly and she was grateful when he eased a protective, steadying arm around her waist. She fit perfectly, tucked against his side. He held out his other hand to Nate.

"It's good to see you again, man. Thanks for coming."

The two men shook hands and Nate looked nearly as giddy as Jane felt. His grin was cheesy, and she would have laughed out loud if she hadn't felt so idiotic about her own behavior.

What the hell had gotten into her? Had she forgotten that she hated Grayson Pierce?

Yes. Yes, wrapped in his arms, she had.

But now she did remember and with a graceful side step, she eased out of his hold. It felt oddly comfortable being around Grayson. *Way* too comfortable. Her insides warred; wanting to push him away and pull him close all at the same time. As she inhaled the scent that was exclusively Grayson, she decided to just go with her gut. If she ended up crying a river, so be it.

He glanced down at her for only a moment, his smile fading. "Nice shirt."

"Thanks. I got it at the Team Shop." She rubbed a hand over the snake logo on her chest and didn't feel quite so haughty now. The disappointed look on his face made her rethink her reason for wearing it. She'd wanted to make a point of not supporting Grayson, but now she saw it as the insult he'd obviously taken it for.

Would anyone notice if she just whipped it off and continued dinner in just her bra? Surely that would at least divert Grayson's attention.

His eyes dropped to the motion on her hand, he frowned but didn't comment. He waved an arm toward the crowd and took her hand in his other one. "We're right through here."

Even though she felt bad for dissing Grayson with her ill-conceived t-shirt choice, Jane couldn't resist the urge to look over her shoulder at the snotty hostess and smile.

Okay, she was gloating. Only a little.

Grayson led them past a bouncer, through a door into what looked like a banquet room, only smaller. Six tables lined the perimeter with a wooden dance floor in the center. Only one table was set—for three. They were the only ones here, the only ones expected.

"I hope this is okay," Grayson said.

"This is awesome," Nate said, pausing for Grayson's indication of a seating arrangement.

Grayson stood behind one chair and motioned for Jane to sit. She did and he took the seat across from her. Nate then sat next to her. All three of them flipped open their menus and began perusing their choices.

A girl appeared—this one with dark hair—dressed in the same short skirt and tight top as the hostess, notebook poised in his hand. "Can I get you something to drink?"

"Water's fine for me," Grayson said without pause.

Her black brows pinched slightly. "I would have thought…"

"Don't go dry on my account," Jane said.

Grayson looked at Jane like she'd slapped him. His eyes didn't leave hers as he said once again, "Like I said, water's fine."

"Sam Adams for me," Nate said. Somewhere in the back of Jane's mind she recognized that Nate was easing the prickly, awkward situation she'd created. But in the moment, with Grayson's eyes on hers, she hated herself for being so callous.

The waitress nodded and looked at Jane, who couldn't stop looking at Grayson. She was such a jerk! Chagrin ate at her. Grayson could order whatever he wanted. He was a grown man and didn't need to be reprimanded for ordering *water* for hell's sake. Good grief, what was wrong with her?

"And you, Miss?"

"Oh, um…" She glanced down at the menu, not that she really needed to, but it gave her something else to look at besides Grayson. "Diet Coke with lemon, please."

"Sure thing. Be back in a minute." And then she was gone.

Jane pretended not to notice the uncomfortable silence in the room, focusing on the black and white letters scattered across the menu.

"Which way to the bathroom?" Nate asked.

"Back out the door and off to your right," Grayson answered.

"Thanks."

Jane glanced up to see Nate's retreating back. *Damn him!* She couldn't believe he'd left her alone. But at the same time, she was grateful not to have an audience for the apology that needed to be offered.

In the uncomfortable silence, Jane peeked at Grayson over her menu. He sighed and closed his menu, pushing it away. His hands—his strong, long-fingered hands—rested on the table in front of him, his fingers weaved together. His head was tilted down, his eyes on his hands. He sighed, a dramatic rush of air leaving his lungs.

She softly began her apology. "I'm—"

"Jane—" he said at the same time.

They both smiled and he waved for her to go first.

She dipped her head in submission and said, "I'm sorry. It's really none of my business what you drink. And I had no right to give you a hard time for drinking *water*."

"It's okay." He rolled his head on his shoulders then scrubbed a hand over his face, his fingers smoothing the hair on his chin. "Geez, I don't think I've ever been so nervous on a date."

"Is that what this is?" she croaked. "A date?"

He shrugged and grinned. "I don't know what else to call it, but if that terminology makes you nervous then, by all means, call it whatever you'd like."

Fifteen years ago, she'd have given her eye teeth to be sitting across the table from Grayson—and not be tutoring him.

Her palms were sweaty, so she briskly rubbed them on her thighs, and couldn't believe what she was going to say next. She almost edited it, but instead confessed, "I have to admit I'm a little nervous, too."

She was grateful she'd wiped her hands when he reached across the table and took one, giving it a gentle squeeze. He smiled. "Why don't we both take a deep breath and promise to relax and enjoy our non-date."

"Deal."

Their drinks arrived. But Nate hadn't. Later she would note that the Sam Adams he ordered hadn't made it to the table either. Jane knew she should probably wonder where he'd gone, but with a white flag now flying, she couldn't bring herself to care. Especially when Grayson kept looking at her the way he was now.

His eyes sparkled as he took a long gulp of his water. He put the glass down on the table and lounged back in his chair, his arms crossed over his chest. He was perfectly at ease. And very sexy.

She hoped that she looked as comfortable. Or at least not as freaked out as she felt.

Their waitress showed up again. "Ready to order?"

Jane and Grayson both looked at Nate's still empty chair. Grayson shrugged. "Um, well, we're kind of waiting—"

"I can get his order when he gets back," she said, both statement and question.

"Okay," Grayson said, "I'll have a burger, medium well, American cheese, no onion." His eyes met hers and her toes tingled. "And can you throw some cheese on the fries, please?"

"No problem." She nodded and turned to Jane. "And for you?"

"Um..." Jane was still enamored by Grayson and she had a hard time thinking. The fact that he could order a cheeseburger shouldn't have her hanging on his every word, but she was. "I'll have the same. Thank you."

When they were alone again, Grayson smiled at her, making her insides go liquid. This was very dangerous territory. Every defense mechanism she had was screaming at the top of its lungs for her to get up and run away. Yet it was her damned traitorous heart, nearly pounding out of her chest that seemed to be making the decisions and kept her sitting exactly where she was.

"Geez! It's been forever. When was the last time we saw each other?" Before she could answer, he said, "When you blew me off for prom?"

All her warm and fuzzy feelings froze solid, as though an iceberg had floated into the room and settled under her chair.

She frowned and just stared at him. All of the progress they'd made was dashed. She knew it had all been too good to be true. He hadn't changed at all. He was still a jerk. And she still wanted to cry.

"I blew *you* off?" Her voice was quiet but strong. She made herself look into the golden brown depths of his eyes. With a heavy heart she told him, "This subject is totally off limits. I didn't want to discuss it then, and I sure as hell don't want to discuss it now."

ANGRY COLOR RUSHED INTO HER CHEEKS AND Grayson knew he had some serious damage control to do. Not that he blamed her for being ticked. He needed to remember that he didn't have to front with Jane. He'd been stupid to bring up a subject that was sore for both of them. Not that he understood why—on her part.

One thing he did know, if she walked out of the room, she was never coming back. And she would never, ever give him another chance.

As she rose to her feet, his hand flew out and grabbed her by the arm, his fingertips touching on opposite sides just above her wrist. "Please ... don't leave."

She shifted from one foot to the other and glared at him. Her fingers pushed the straps of her purse further up onto her shoulder and he thought she would leave him forever.

He stood and motioned to her seat. "Please, let's finish our dinner."

The debate went on in her head; he could almost see the arguments going back and forth behind her eyes. Finally she let out a sigh and dropped her purse to the floor.

He waited while she sat. She took a sip on her drink and kept her eyes from meeting his gaze. The sweet camaraderie they'd shared only moments ago was gone, thanks to his thoughtless comment.

"Look, I'm sorry. I know it was stupid." He shook his head, plowing his fingers through his hair. "It was a joke, Jane. A really poorly executed joke, but ... yeah. Forgive me?"

Her gaze met his and she smiled tightly. She sighed as if she were exhausted. "Listen, Grayson, I don't need, nor do I want your macho, I'm-king-of-the-world crap. Be straight with me. That's all I've ever wanted from you."

"Okay. I'll be straight with you, if you'll offer me the same courtesy."

"I always have."

They both nodded as if an agreement had been made. Tension still swirled in the air around them and he was afraid his next question wasn't going to help things. But, hard as he tried, he couldn't keep from voicing the question that had been racing around in his brain since the second she'd stepped back into his life.

"Do you have a boyfriend? Fiancé? Husband?" He actually cringed as he said the last word and she smiled.

That smile had always made his heart melt. When he knew her before the second tooth on the right had been twisted a bit, now it was straight and he kind of missed the endearing flaw. As he waited for her to answer his question with regards to her availability, he hated that Jane was witnessing him this way. He'd never felt so vulnerable ... and he didn't like the feeling.

"No. No. And ... no," she said with a laugh.

He let out his breath, surprisingly relieved to hear that she was unattached. He was relieved until she turned the tables on him.

"What about you?" she asked. "How many girlfriends do you actually have?"

That made him laugh too, although it sounded strangled to his ears. He shrugged and gave her the honesty he'd promised. "Would you believe there's not a single special girl in my life?"

"Not a *single* special girl? So there are what; ten, twelve, a baker's dozen?"

Her words were a slap, taking all the humor from the moment. His laugh cut off abruptly and he felt his smile morph into a grimace. "I'm not the guy the media wants to make me out to be."

He would have thought that, of all people, Jane Alexander would understand how the media could manipulate things to fit into any box they wanted. He hated that that was the man she knew.

"Sorry." She stirred the lemon around in her glass with her straw and chewed on her bottom lip. She looked adorable and, absurdly, he suddenly wanted to kiss that lip. He realized he was leaning toward her when she asked, "If they've got you so wrong, who are you then?"

He was just about to answer, had even opened his mouth to do so, when they were interrupted by the waitress delivering their burgers. "Can I get you anything else?"

Jane's eyes shot toward the door then to Nate's chair and he imagined her thinking, *Yeah, you can bring Nate back.*

He knew he should probably care that Nate had abandoned her, but he couldn't find one single ounce of remorse. Grayson was glad to have Jane all to himself. Their first few moments had been a little weird. He hoped that given a few minutes alone they would fall into the easy friendship they'd shared all those years ago—until life blew up in his face, for reasons he still didn't know.

Grayson glanced at Jane and she shook her head. "No, we're good. Thanks," he said, dismissing the waitress.

JANE COULDN'T HELP BUT WONDER WHERE the hell Nate had disappeared to. It didn't take *that* long to use the restroom. Least of all for Nate. He was a speed-pee'er.

Trying not to make the situation more bizarre, she opened the bottle of ketchup and dumped a huge glob next to her fries. She double-fisted her burger and took a huge bite.

Grayson was also chewing on his burger. He groaned softly and Jane giggled. He grinned.

"You like?" he asked after he'd swallowed.

"Um-hmm. Not as good as the drive-in back home, but good."

"Agreed."

The heavy beat of an eighties rock song started. It was one she recognized, one that, if she were home—and in the shower—she'd be singing every word at the top of her lungs. Her foot tapped under the table. His leg moved against hers and she smiled.

"I love these guys," he said, setting his burger on his plate. He wiped his napkin over his mouth and then licked his lips before taking a quick draw on his straw. "They're one of my all-time favorite bands."

"Def Leppard." She nodded, wiping her mouth with her napkin. "They're classic! And one of my favorites, too."

He drummed his fingers on the table and sang along with the chorus. Grayson had a nice voice. He always had. Pretty much Grayson could do anything he set his mind to. Jane, on the other hand, couldn't carry a tune in a bucket. Given that fact, she allowed him to finish the improvised concert ... himself, clapping when he finished.

She laughed and sat back in her chair, admiring him. His cheeks had a soft pink tone to them and she wondered if he was embarrassed by her praise. She didn't want to investigate the feelings of accomplishment that thought brought. She couldn't go there. Ever.

The conversation turned to music—a nice, safe topic—and she breathed a sigh of relief. His tastes were similar to hers. Although high school had been the late nineties, they both loved the hair bands of the eighties.

"Can you believe that I bought a fifteen cd set from an infomercial? It was a totally stupid purchase since I had all the songs on their original cds." He shook his head. She smiled at him and couldn't believe how relaxed she felt. "I guess the part about me being frivolous with my money is true."

She shrugged, understanding frivolous purchases. Her Achilles heel was books. She'd go without eating if it meant she could get a book from her favorite author on the day it came out. She laughed lightly. "At least you have the money to be frivolous with. You're not in debt up to your eyeballs, are you?"

She felt her eyes go wide and bit down hard on her tongue in punishment. The conversation had been going so well and she'd just asked a question she had no right to ask.

Instead of glaring at her and spitting a harsh reprimand—which she fully deserved—he didn't even look offended when he answered, "Nope."

He took another big bite of his burger and chewed. The muscles in his jaw flexed with the movement of his teeth. Jane forced herself to focus on her food and popped a fry in her mouth. It was really good; hot, crunchy and salty. She finished one fry and ate another two before finding the courage to talk to him again.

"Do you eat here a lot?" she asked between bites.

He shook his head, chewing until he finished the bite in his mouth. "I wouldn't say a lot. I do like to eat here and try to stop in when we're in town. It doesn't always work out that way, though. You like it then?"

"Um-hmm." She wiped the napkin over her mouth. "Good call on adding cheese to the fries."

"My mom says that cheese always makes it better." He laughed. His eyes softened at the mention of his mother. Jane also felt a slight tug at her heartstrings at the reference to Maude Pierce. "Cheese and butter. *If you feel the need to substitute margarine, then don't bother cooking.*" His voice had gone into a high-pitched, nearly perfect imitation of his mother's and Jane burst out laughing.

"I think I heard her say that once or twice with my own ears." Jane loved Mrs. Pierce. The woman was kind and, despite her beliefs of cheese and butter, was stick thin. "How is she these days?"

As soon as the question was asked, Jane prayed the dear woman hadn't died in some tragic twist of fate. She'd been healthy as a horse the last time Jane had seen her—a near lifetime ago.

Grayson took a drink of his water then wiped his mouth with his napkin. "She's good. She's still in Salina; working at the 5 and Dime." A panicked expression crossed his face and his eyes were vulnerable when he looked at her. "Please keep that off the record, Janie. The last thing I need is for somebody to print that my mother works because—" He used his fingers to form air quotes. "—I won't take care of her."

Jane wasn't sure what possessed her to do it, but she grabbed his hand. It was enormous compared to hers. She squeezed it gently, leaning across the table to promise with every ounce of who she was. "Don't worry, Grayson. Your secret is safe with me. I have no doubt that she refuses to quit because it'd put a damper on her social schedule."

His eyes met hers and there was a moment of ... of what? She couldn't be sure. Just a moment. A moment where time seemed to stop. A moment where she couldn't find her voice, couldn't blink, couldn't even take a breath. She wasn't sure if her heart beat.

He squeezed her hand and the spell was broken. But far from forgotten—at least for her. With his eyes still locked on her face, his lips lifted at the corners and he laughed softly. "I'm surprised that you remember her so well."

"I'm full of surprises," she said in a horribly breathless tone. Why didn't she just *tell* him how he affected her?

"Yes, you are." His eyes dropped to her lips.

Good grief, was it hot in here?

The evening had started out awkward and Jane had fought the urge to bolt, had actually been on her feet once. Now though, she was completely comfortable. In fact, never before had she been so comfortable with any guy.

But this wasn't just any guy.

This was Grayson Pierce.

4

"Come on, Jane, you can't stay mad at me forever." Nate was sitting next to her on the airplane. "And you can't tell me that you're upset I left."

After dinner with Grayson, and the battle over who would pay—he did—they'd come out of their inner sanctum to find Nate perched at the bar. He had gone to the bathroom, like he'd said, but then he'd not felt the need to return. He passed the time by plopping down on a bar stool.

"You were both laughing and I didn't want to intrude. You know you had a good time, admit it. I saw the way you looked at him."

"And how was that?" she snapped, forgetting that she wasn't speaking to him.

He grinned. "Like you wanted to eat him."

She scowled at him. "Crass much?"

"Not like *that*—or maybe just like that. Who am I to judge?" He raised his brows and smiled, showing all of his perfectly straight, white teeth.

Her eyes rolled without a conscious thought. "If you can't be serious, I'm going to go back to ignoring you."

"You looked at him like you liked him."

"So?"

"So, he was looking at you the same way. I didn't want to impose ... because it looked to me

like there was actually something to impose *on*."
One beefy shoulder lifted in a shrug. "At the airport, I really did think I'd have to run interference.
I also knew that Dale would love an exclusive with
Grayson Pierce, ass or not. I don't want you hurt
and was glad to play the bodyguard. But it took
about a second and a half to realize that I wasn't
needed."

Jane huffed, irritated ... because he was spot
on. Dammit!

"I was only out at the bar. It's not like I left you
without a way back to the hotel. Besides it gave
me some time to catch up with Roxie. She said hi,
by the way."

He was quiet for a few minutes then cleared his
throat. "Speaking of Roxie."

Technically, they'd been 'speaking of Roxie' a
few minutes ago, but she'd take any segue she
could get if it meant they didn't have to talk about
Grayson anymore.

"What about Roxie?"

"Her birthday's coming up," he said. Jane
waited for him to go on. When she just stared at
him, he finally said, "It's her fortieth."

Again Jane thought 'okay'.

"Anyway, I thought it would be nice to throw
her a surprise party."

"Yeah, that'd be great."

The flight attendant brought some peanuts and
a drink. Jane hated that they never handed over
the can. She sipped at her Diet Coke while Nate
opened a packet of peanuts and dumped the whole
thing into his mouth. His head was tipped back so
far, Jane was amazed the guy didn't choke on the
nuts. He was quiet while he chewed. Then he swallowed and guzzled the tiny cup of soda.

"Would you mind helping me with her party?"

"Me?" Jane asked, genuinely surprised.

She considered Roxy a friend, and vice versa. But they weren't the daily-phone-calls-just-to-check-in kinda friends. That was where Kate Spencer—or even Jordan's wife and producer, Olivia—fit in.

"You're perfect. She won't expect you throwing her a party. It'll be easy to plan because you and I are together so much. I mean, hell, we can even stop and look at cakes on the way to or from a story." He was sporting a grin that spread from one ear to the other. "So, will you do it?"

"Sure." She could solicit Molly's help if needs be. "No problem."

He was quiet for a few minutes then closed his eyes and went to sleep. Not wanting to be left alone with her thoughts, Jane laid her head on his shoulder and slept.

It was the tensing of Nate's shoulder muscles that woke her. She jerked back and looked at him. Every inch of him was preparing for landing. He gripped the armrests until his knuckles turned the color of chalk. The muscles in his jaw jumped as he ground his teeth. His eyes were clamped shut. The guy was stiff as a board. She wasn't even sure he breathed for the few minutes it took for the tires to kiss the asphalt.

Then with an exaggerated breath, Nate's entire body relaxed and he was once again calm. "What'dya say we get our stuff and get to the hotel?"

"Sounds good to me."

AN HOUR LATER, JANE WAS ALONE IN HER room. She took a quick shower and put on her favorite pajamas; bottoms that were pink and red vertical stripes and a matching pink tank-top. It was too early for bed, but she wanted to be comfortable. It wasn't like she had anyone she was trying to impress.

The knock on the door made her jump and cringe. Good hell, she was a mess. A clean mess, but a mess nonetheless. Running her fingers through her still damp hair that had somehow developed tangles since being brushed, she went to the door and looked out the peephole.

Disappointment made her heart stutter. It wasn't too far-fetched to think it would be Grayson.

The last time someone knocked on her hotel room door, it had been him. This time it wasn't. Nor was it Nate. Standing on the other side of the door was a hotel worker, holding a box. She opened the door until the chain pulled taut.

"May I help you?" she asked through the crack between the door and the jamb.

"I have a package for Miss Jane Alexander." He held the box up as if to provide evidence.

She was confused, her brows pulled tightly together. "A package?" She closed the door, slid the chain free, and opened it to accept the box. She mumbled a 'thank you', feeling a bit numb.

He turned and strode away before she could even think to offer a tip. Holding the box out in front of her like it might blow up, she kicked the door closed with her bare foot.

The package was the size and shape of the box her newest boots had come in. She padded over to the small table next to the window and put the box down. With a quick tug she released then ribbon then used the small pocketknife on her keys to cut through the tape that held the lid closed. She plucked at the white tissue paper, pulling it away from the contents.

Still confused Jane dragged a white Rockets jersey from the box. She turned it around and laughed when the navy letters across the back spelled *Pierce*. Clutching it to her chest she giggled, spinning in circles like a love-struck idiot.

Grayson hadn't been impressed by her Diamondbacks shirt. He'd not criticized then, but was obviously making a statement now.

She had to remind herself not to read too much into the fact that the jersey had *his* name on the back. Really, did she expect him to send one with Xavier on it?

Lifting the box from the table she noticed that it wasn't empty. There was a navy blue envelope at the bottom, nearly hidden by all the see-through white paper. The almost unreadable scrawl was one she recognized. She'd spent hours trying to decipher it during their tutoring sessions. With fingers that shook, she opened the card.

If you're with the team, you should look like you're one of us.
I enjoyed dinner. Can I see you again?
-Grayson

GRAYSON PACED AROUND HIS ROOM, TRYING not to drive himself crazy. His little present would be delivered to Jane anytime now. He didn't know what he expected; it wasn't like she had a way to get a hold of him. And there was no way in hell the front desk would help her track him down. Even they weren't sure which name he was registered under. Truth was … he wasn't sure *he* could remember.

When he'd seen her across the entry of the restaurant his heart had soared. The moment he noticed her shirt, his heart had dropped to his toes and his stomach rolled. She was making a statement by wearing the opposing team's colors, he got that. What he didn't get was her reasoning; did she really hate him? Had he really messed things up so badly all those years ago? He sure wished he knew what he'd done.

He guessed all would be known tomorrow. If she wore the shirt, that was good. If she didn't...? Well, he wouldn't think about that possibility.

He forced himself to climb into bed and turn off the light. Tomorrow's game was big, and he really needed to get some sleep. He closed his eyes, knowing damn well that his dreams would be filled with Jane Alexander.

THE NEXT AFTERNOON, JANE SPENT EXTRA time on her hair and make-up. By some miracle she had a navy tank top in her suitcase and put it on before tugging the white jersey over her head. She had never been so proud to have a name across her back.

The game seemed to fly by, despite the butterflies fluttering around in her stomach. Nate did his thing and she took notes so the story would come together easily when she delivered her report. This was game five and the Rockets' win meant they would be going to the playoffs.

As the team raced into the locker room, the masculine cheers and yells made her ears hurt. Grayson smiled when he saw her, his eyes twinkling as he slowly took in her appearance from head to toe and back up.

Heat flooded her cheeks and she hoped he didn't notice her blush. He stopped for only a moment in front of her.

"I see you got my gift." His fingers trailed down her arm, causing goose bumps to blossom in their wake. He squeezed her hand. "It looks good on you."

"Great game."

"Thanks."

And without another word, he slipped from her side, engulfed by the wave of people, high-fiving his way through the crowd.

She was aware of every movement he made and had gotten used to the way he almost avoided her. It still bugged her that other reporters got the best soundbites, but she was wearing his name on her back—just like he wanted.

FORTY-FIVE MINUTES LATER, WITH INTER-views done, Jane looked around the parking lot and waited for Nate to stow all the gear in the rear of the rented Explorer. She leaned back against the truck and bent her knee to rest her foot against the tire.

Xavier came out of the building and crossed toward them, instead of going to the high-dollar vehicles in the other direction.

"Lookin' good, Jane. Mmm-mmm-mmm! You look *real* good in Rockets' blue." He licked his lips, his finger made a circling motion. "Turn for me. Work it."

She didn't turn around. Didn't work it.

"Good game tonight." She'd hoped to change the subject to Xavier's favorite topic—himself.

But for the first time in his self-centered life, he refused to be distracted. "Come on, sweet thing, who's name you sportin'?" His hands were hard and rough as they grabbed her upper arms and tried to physically turn her.

"Let go of her," Nate growled. "Now!"

Xavier puffed out his chest like a rooster in a barnyard and dropped his hands to his sides, forming fists. Hazel eyes narrowed in challenge. He widened his stance, squaring off against Nate.

"Or what? You gonna start a brawl, big man? That'd be a good way to get yourselves—"

"Xavier!"

All three of them turned to see the coach scowling as he walked toward them. Xavier groaned. Nate breathed a sigh of relief and Jane decided she wasn't going to puke.

"Leave Miss Alexander alone."

Xavier ran a finger down her cheek and she refused to let herself flinch. She stood with her shoulders back, her eyes narrowed as they met his.

"No harm done, sweet thing. I just wanted to see if you belonged to me."

"I *belong* to no one," she snapped and waited until he backed away. Only then did she look at Nate. His hands were in fists, his feet wide, his every muscle coiled and ready to spring into action.

In that moment, she realized that Nate was ready to fight to protect her, just like any good big brother did for his little sister.

His breath was slow, controlled as he tried to slow his adrenaline. She turned and stepped closer to him, her hand extended. "Nate, are you o—"

"I knew it!" Xavier yelled.

She could hear the animosity in his voice, but wasn't prepared to turn and meet hostility that enveloped every other part of him. Every muscle was taut, his mouth curled up in a snarl.

"You're a Pierce girl! You see that, Pierce. The little reporter wants you."

She hadn't realized that Grayson was even around, but he must be if Xavier yelled at him. Her first reaction was to be embarrassed that he'd witnessed her humiliating exchange with Xavier, but then she spotted him crossing the lot. He walked with a swagger and she bit the inside of her cheek to keep from smiling in anticipation.

Grayson would set Xavier straight. She looked forward to seeing Xavier put in his place. But Grayson didn't come near her, didn't slow his pace. His eyes scanned her up and down and he licked his lips. He'd done the same thing in the locker room, but this time it felt different. This time he looked ... positively lecherous. Jane's skin crawled. Then he smiled; a gloat-filled grin.

"Add her to the list."

"What the hell?" Nate murmured behind her.

She'd been thinking that exact phrase with the exception of a more profane expletive on the end. Tears stung her eyes and she blinked violently to keep them at bay. Her heart clenched and her throat grew tight, making it hard to swallow.

She never should have trusted Grayson to protect her. Had history taught her nothing?

"Let's get out of here." Nate's touch was soft, strong, and supportive on her shoulder. "Come on, kid, let's get the hell out of here."

She didn't want to look up into his face, but found that's where her eyes went. Big mistake! His baby blues were sympathetic and kind, which only made the battle to keep her feelings in check that much harder.

"Come on." He took her elbow and led her to the passenger side. Once she was settled in her seat, he handed her a tissue. She wasn't sure where he'd gotten it, but it looked clean and her nose was running. Her cheeks were damp. She was crying.

When had she started to cry?

Had Grayson seen?

Would he even care if he had?

"Do you want me to go kick some ass?"

She giggled, a little blubbering sound that made Nate smile. She smiled, too. "No, let's just go home."

The team was off for a few days, then the National League playoffs would send them back out on the road. Jane was grateful for the reprieve. Her hatred for Grayson Pierce had been restored to its prior glory. She would never let him worm his way back into her heart.

Grayson Pierce could go to hell!

GRAYSON WATCHED IN HIS REAR VIEW MIRROR as Jane's SUV pulled out of the parking lot. He had to admit that she looked pretty damned good wearing Rockets' blue, and he really liked that it was his name across her back. Like a stamp of ownership. And Grayson wanted to own her.

The tires on his rental car squealed as he roared out of the parking space. Easing to a stop at the exit of the lot, he waited for an opening between cars then with a chirp of the tires he flew out into traffic. He opened his phone and called his agent, the man who got him whatever he wanted.

"What can I do for you?"

"I need a favor." Grayson relayed what he wanted which, surprise surprise, wasn't met with any kind of reprimand.

The man chuckled.

"Okay," Kevin said, "I'll have it delivered to your room in an hour."

"Make it thirty minutes and there will be a bonus for you." Money was the one thing that spoke volumes with Kevin. The man was as greedy as Grayson himself. That was probably why they got along so well.

"Thirty minutes then." Kevin paused for a heartbeat. "Because of the nature of your request, I ask that you try to keep it low key."

"Yeah, yeah." He hated when Kevin got all fatherly. Grayson had a father and didn't want another one. Kevin had one job and one job only ... to kiss Grayson's ass. "Give it a rest, Kevin."

THIRTY MINUTES LATER THERE WAS A knock at his door. The smile on his face grew. He had big plans for tonight.

Opening the door he stared at the girl standing in the hallway. She was exactly what he'd requested; thin with curves in all the right places, brown hair that rested at her shoulders. The eyes were wrong and the face was a bit thinner around the mouth, but she would do.

Oh, yes. She would do just fine.

Grayson had to hand it to Kevin, the guy was good.

Grayson opened the door wider to allow her entrance. "Please come in, Jane."

Her perfectly arched brows pulled together in the middle. "My name's—"

He silenced her with a press of his fingers to her lips. Her voice was wrong too. Which was okay, he had a gag that would cure that particular problem. He tried to ignore the irritation he felt building and forced a smile.

"Tonight, you are Jane ... and you will call me 'Master'."

"Yes, Master," she purred, coming in and closing the door behind her.

5

JANE WASN'T SURE HOW SHE'D DONE IT, BUT she'd survived the playoffs. The Rockets lost two games to three in the National League Playoffs. There would be no World Series for them this year. She couldn't say she was totally heartbroken over the outcome. Although she refused to examine the realization that she did feel bad for Grayson.

Sitting at her desk in the newsroom, Jane waited for her cue to head into the studio. Kate Spencer, KHB's main anchor, was currently delivering the news in the B segment. Hard news was the A segment, lighter stuff came in the B, weather C and sports in the D.

"Jane, I've got a call for you," Jordan called from the assignment desk.

If the newsroom was the central nervous system, then the assignment desk was the brain. Jordan told everyone where to go and what to do. At least for the news crews.

Sports kind of did their own thing, unless breaking news happened to a sports figure. Then she might get recruited to do the story.

"Who is it?" Jane asked, looking over the sea of cubicles to the red-haired man holding the phone up in illustration.

His shoulders lifted in a nonchalant shrug. "You wanna take it or not?"

Calls into the assignment desk weren't uncommon, but very seldom did a random call get put through to a reporter. Most were stopped at the front desk, bless Lydia's heart. If—and that's a big *if*—a call made it to the newsdesk, they were almost always stopped there. More a safety measure than anything.

There were a lot of crazies out there ... and they all wanted to get to know the people that were perceived as local celebrities. Little did they know every person sitting in the newsroom was an average, every-day schmuck just trying to make it through the day.

"Take a message," she told Jordan.

"You should take this one," he said stamping a veto all over her decision.

And her phone rang.

If he was going to put it through anyway, then why did he even bother to ask, she thought irritably.

She glared at him and glanced at the clock. Five minutes. She could spare five minutes, but literally only five minutes for the person on the phone.

"KHB Sports, can I help you?"

"Janie."

That one word, spoken by that one person in that low, sexy voice made her insides turn to jelly. Breath froze in her lungs. Self-preservation shouted at her to hang up. Instinct told her heart to start beating again.

"Janie, are you there?"

"What do you want, Grayson?" She was quite proud of herself that her voice was strong, with the right amount of irritation. She was also glad that he couldn't see her, because her knuckles were white as she gripped the phone. Her spine was straight and her teeth ground together.

"I wanted to apologize?"

"*You?* Apologize?" She laughed mockingly. "And just what exactly do *you* have to apologize for? You're the almighty Grayson Pierce. You don't owe anyone an apology, least of all me."

"I'm sorry," he whispered.

The words were spoken with such honest contrition that they were like a knife to her heart. She would not cry. She would *not* cry! She blinked as a tear slid down her cheek. Damn! Grayson had done some really shitty things over the years—but this was the worst.

The jerk thing she could handle. In fact, it fortified her defenses against him. When Grayson was kind, when he spoke sweetly to her, when he looked at her like he finally saw her as the confident woman she was ... well, that was when her carefully erected walls crumbled.

"I gotta go. I'm on air in ... shit!"

The floor director was waving his arms over his head. "Jane! Two minutes."

She hung up without saying another word to Grayson and, grabbing her mirror to check her make-up, headed for the studio.

"WELL HELL, THAT COULDN'T HAVE GONE worse," Grayson groaned to the emptiness around him.

He tossed the phone down on the granite countertop where it skidded down the surface, luckily coming to a stop before tumbling off the edge. He leaned against the wall, knocking his head a few times. Jane deserved an apology. And she sure as hell didn't deserve the firestorm that was going to land on her head tomorrow morning.

When he'd picked up the phone to call her, he'd meant to apologize. He'd meant to tell her what was brewing. Instead she'd misunderstood his intentions and lashed out at him. He'd heard the shake in her voice, which meant he'd also made her cry. He really was an ass!

Grabbing his keys he headed out the door. There was only one place that could bring him solace. He had responsibilities and he needed to take care of them. Daisy was due soon and she depended on him.

JANE REGRETTED ANSWERING HER PHONE, and wondered if she could avoid ever answering a phone again. Thankfully she'd made it through the sportscast without a single snuffle.

After watching her report and making sure that she came across as composed she gathered her things to leave.

"Goodnight," she said to Jordan, hiking her laptop bag onto her shoulder. He was on the phone and raised his hand in farewell.

"What's the rush?"

Jane cringed. She could hide her emotions from the world, from her co-workers and her viewers. Unfortunately there was one exception.

"Hey, Molly."

As Jane turned she came nose to nose with Molly, who stood with her hands on her hips. Her long blond curls tumbled down around her shoulders. Her brows rose for a moment before pinching together as she narrowed her eyes. "What's up?"

"Nothing." Yeah, not even Jane bought that.

"Wanna try again?"

"No." Jane slumped down into her chair and groaned.

"Lemme guess." Molly sat down on the corner of Jane's desk. "Grayson?"

Jane looked up at her best friend ... and hated that Molly knew her so well. "He called and I kinda ripped into him. It wasn't pretty."

"Why do you let him get to you? Never mind. I know." Molly shook her head. "Let's get out of here."

Molly and Jane lived in the same condo community. It wasn't a coincidence. They'd been friends for years and had purposely tried to land jobs at the same station. Jane did sports. Molly did weather.

But that wasn't the only way they differed. They were polar opposites; Molly was curly blonde, Jane straight brunette. Molly was stick thin with big perfect boobs. Jane had curves with ... okay, her boobs were pretty perfect *now.* Molly was five, four—if she wore four inch heels. Jane was five, ten in bare feet.

Different as they were, Jane wouldn't trade the friendship she had with Molly for anything in the world. Molly could practically read her mind, and freshman year she'd helped Jane heal and get over Grayson.

Molly stopped in front of Jane's driveway. And Jane smiled. It was good to be home.

The driveways and garages were all on the backside of the condos, down alleys. The front doors faced each other with a large grassy area separating the buildings. Sidewalks weaved around huge trees that shaded the entire area in the summer time. Now though they were more skeletal with a few wisps of stubborn leaves.

She loved her condo. It was a drive to the station, nearly an hour, but the price had been right and it was all hers. And Molly lived two doors down.

"I can come in," Molly said.

"No. I'm fine." She wasn't. But the last thing she wanted was to rehash her feelings for Grayson. Her unrequited, ridiculous feelings for Grayson. "I'll call you tomorrow," she said and got out of the car. She punched the code into her wireless garage door opener and waited for the door to slide up.

Her blue Mazda 3 sat alone in the garage and she hurried past it, shutting the garage just before she went inside.

It was dark. Not a surprise; it always was. Jane worked the ten, which meant she didn't leave the station until nearly eleven. She flipped on a light. Without thought she put her bag on the table near the door.

She went over to scoop up the mail where it'd come to rest after coming through the slot in the front door earlier in the day.

Phone bill, electric bill, a flyer for a free dinner (if you bought one, of course), and an envelope with only her name scrawled across the front—in handwriting she didn't want to recognize.

Her teeth sank into her bottom lip and she marched over to the garbage, depositing the un-opened card where it belonged. She didn't want anything to do with Grayson.

Really, she didn't.

Unable to move, she stared at the white envelope resting amongst the soup cans and ba-nana peel and empty Diet Coke cans.

Molly was right; Jane really should recycle.

She looked around her kitchen; the white cabi-nets and black appliances, the black and white checkered tile floor. Opening the fridge, she pulled out a bottle of juice and sank down into a chair at her black table. She picked through the rest of the mail, trying not to think of the elephant in the trash. She could almost hear the trumpet calling to her.

Finally she sighed and turned away, leaving the letter in the trash and went to bed.

Tomorrow. She would deal with Grayson tomor-row. Or not.

Hell, she didn't know how to react. She wanted to yell at him. She wanted to kiss him. She wanted to toilet paper his house, like she had in high school. She wanted to date someone uber hot and drive him crazy with jealousy.

Like that would happen.

Slamming a fist into her pillow she rolled over, huffing. Every time she closed her eyes, she saw Grayson's face. His gorgeous face with that arrogant grin that lacked any regard for her or her feelings. Sleep was not going to come anytime soon. She was too wound up. Television seemed like a safe alternative.

A press of the *on* button revealed ESPN and a report on … Grayson Pierce.

Would he haunt her forever?

She changed the channel, settled on a movie, leaned back against the pillows, and fell asleep.

THE NEXT MORNING JANE WOKE FROM A dreamless sleep. Refreshed and ready to take on the day, she stretched and headed for the bathroom. After washing her face, she looked in the mirror and frowned at the dark circles under her green eyes, not to mention that she looked pale— even paler than usual.

Not wanting to think about that though, she gathered her long brown locks in her hand and whipped them into a bun on the top of her head.

Dressed in shorts and a sports bra, Jane turned on the morning news and hit the treadmill. The steady pounding of her feet was a comfort. The television was on, but Jane's only thoughts were of the *thud, thud, thud* of her feet and the whirring of the treadmill. Her morning routine kept her centered; the thumping of her feet, the in and out of her breath.

After the escapade with Xavier and Grayson in the hotel gym, she'd avoided it like the plague. Which was probably best since the last thing she needed was to have pictures of her, half-naked on the internet. Stranger things had happened.

Her phone rang, interrupting her concentration. Her feet stuttered and she nearly found herself flipped off the back of the treadmill. She grabbed the handrails and jerked the emergency key out. The whirring stopped immediately and Jane ran over to grab her cell phone off the dresser.

"Yeah?"

"Hey. Are you okay?" Nate sounded strange.

"Um ... yeah ... are *you* okay?"

He chuckled. "I'm fine, but it's not my face on the cover of every tabloid in the grocery store."

"What? Why am I...? I'm nobody."

"But Grayson Pierce is definitely somebody."

"Nate—" She forced herself to take a deep breath and *try* to relax. Something about his tone and the few words he'd said had butterflies zooming around in her stomach. "—what the hell you're talking about?"

An exaggerated sigh whistled through the phone. "Roxie is a sucker for the tabloids. We get some that come to the house, but the others she goes out and buys. Every month." He sounded disgusted and Jane laughed. She never would have guessed that side of Roxie Hughes. "I swear half my salary goes to them."

"Nate." That one word from her brought him back on topic.

"Okay, so anyway, Roxie went to the store this morning and brought home three—or maybe it was four—magazines with your picture on the front."

"*My* picture?"

"Yeah, your picture. You and Grayson." She heard the turning of pages and knew Nate was describing what he was looking at. "Some of the pictures are just you, with the byline '*Who is Grayson's latest girl?*'. And you'll never believe which one's the biggest..."

"I don't wanna know."

He plowed on like she hadn't spoken a protest. "It's you and Grayson at dinner, when he hugged you. Crappy resolution. Probably a cell phone."

"Ugh!" she groaned and suddenly felt like she was going to hurl.

"No kidding. Sucks to be you, Jane."

"I thought we had privacy," she said more to herself than to Nate.

"I even made one of the pictures. Roxie's so proud." He sounded just as proud of this great accomplishment and Jane's fingers curled into fists.

"I'm glad you guys are enjoying your thirty seconds of fame," she snapped only to instantly regret it. "I'm sorry."

"We're cool. You have to admit that this is pretty freakin' awesome. I mean to be associated with Grayson Pierce ... that's just awesome."

"Nate, I don't want to be associated with Grayson Pierce. He's a jerk. Always has been." Even as she said the words she knew she was embellishing the story. Grayson hadn't *always* been a jerk. There were times when he was quite sweet ... and cute. No, cute wasn't the right word. Maybe he'd been *cute* in elementary school. By high school he'd graduated to hot and never looked back.

"Jerk or not, his popularity could really help your career. Not to mention what it could do for KHB if you could land an exclusive."

Jane snorted. "You sound like Dale."

"What can I say—" He paused and she could imagine his beefy shoulders lifting in a shrug. "—I'm a team player."

"How very noble of you," she said sarcastically.

He chuckled. "That's me. Excuse me ... I have to go buff my shining armor."

Jane laughed. Leave it to Nate to lighten her mood. His sense of humor was his most admirable trait.

Her doorbell rang and Nate said, "I wouldn't answer that."

Peeking out through the blinds from her upstairs bedroom verified that she would *not* be opening the door. "Oh hell! It's starting already. I never thought I'd hate damned reporters."

"Anyone we know?"

"Yeah, it's Clayton."

He laughed, really hard. Jane wondered if he had to wipe any tears away. Despite that she didn't find the situation a bit funny, she found herself smiling. Nate gasped and snorted, struggled to take a deep breath.

"Damn ... that guy will ... do anything ... for a story."

Clayton Tate, reporter extraordinaire, had managed to make the rounds of all the stations in the Salt Lake valley. He'd left KHB three months before Jane had come on board. She didn't like working with him on the rare occasion they crossed paths in the field. He had beady little eyes that focused on her breasts when he talked to her. Like most of the other guys she worked with, Nate despised the toe-headed weasel.

She took her time going downstairs, pausing to rub a hand over the back of the leather couch that formed a faux wall between the living room and the kitchen. She stared at her reflection in the television and pushed at the hair that had come loose during her workout. Slipping her phone into the pocket of her workout shorts, she took the dark brown fleece blanket off the back of the couch, unfurled it with a snap then refolded it and replaced it. Some might say she was stalling. Jane chalked her attitude up to patience.

Clayton obviously didn't share her patience, since he rang the bell three more times and had started to pound on the door. When she couldn't put the confrontation off any longer, she walked to the door where she took a moment to compose herself. Deep breath in through the nose, out through the mouth. Then she looked out the peephole only to see an eye staring back at her.

She squeaked and jumped back.

"Jane? Jane Alexander, I know you're in there." More pounding.

Jane shook her head. No wonder this guy couldn't stay at one station. He was a loose cannon, a real piece of work. TV-101 taught that you didn't piss off the person you were trying to interview. At least not right away ... and not without cause. Her not answering the door did not constitute cause.

Thud! Thud! Thud! Thud! Thud!

Ding-dong! Ding-dong!

Thud! Thud! Thud!

"Go away, Clayton!" she shouted.

"All I want is a statement on the pictures of you and Grayson Pierce."

"No comment."

"I'm not leaving."

"I said 'no comment'."

"Not good enough," he shouted.

"Get off my porch!" She kicked the door for emphasis. Her toes, propelled by inertia, met the end of her shoe and she winced. She jumped in a circle, doing her best to cradle her injured foot.

"Jane!" Nate interrupted the standoff.

She had completely forgotten that the line was still open and that Nate had been listening to the whole conversation via the phone.

"Jane! Jane!" Nate's muffled voice said from her pocket. She pulled the phone from her pocket and put it to her ear.

"What?" she shouted, too pissed off to even feel bad.

"Tell Clayton to get the hell off your doorstep or I'm gonna make his life miserable."

"Listen, Clayton, I only have one thing to say to you."

"Finally," he said.

"I'm on the phone with Nate Hughes right now. He says if you don't leave, he'll come and *make* you leave."

With her eye affixed to the peephole, she watched him cringe. "Fine. You can call off your guard dog. I'm leaving." He did, but not without kicking the crap out of the shrubs that lined the walk and slamming the gate that enclosed her tiny front yard.

"Thanks, Nate."

"You bet. I'll be by to pick you up at noon."

She hated needing a meaty guardian, but wasn't stupid enough to turn him down. "I'll be ready. Hey, Nate ... thanks for the heads-up."

"No problem. I always wanted to be a bouncer. Now I get my chance." She could hear the grin in Nate's voice and grinned too. The line went dead and she dropped her phone onto the kitchen counter.

Grayson's phone call and his apology suddenly took on a whole new meaning. As did the letter currently residing in the garbage can. She went to the trash and plucked out the envelope. Her hands shook as she opened it.

Janie,

I have to apologize. I tried to on the phone, but we were disconnected before I got the chance to tell you the reason.

It's come to my attention that a photo of our dinner together is going to be plastered on the covers of most of the tabloid magazines. It was not my intention and I hope that your life won't be turned into a whirlwind.

I would really like to see you again and apologize in person.

-Grayson

His number was included.

Maybe he hadn't told her the reason for his apology. She assumed it was for his actions—or lack thereof—in the locker room or in the parking lot or in the gym. It'd been weeks, yet the pain was still very raw.

Nate had been supportive, mostly because he didn't bring it up again—after the initial tirade that included an interesting variety of name calling. Jane had never realized that Nate had such an extensive vocabulary.

Due to the change in plans, Jane had to make a phone call. She hit the 'M' on her speed-dial and waited.

"Hello?"

"Hey, Molls."

"Hey. What's up?"

Jane regurgitated the events of the morning as Molly interrupted with phrases like, "Wow." or "Seriously?" or "You've got to be kidding me!"

When the story was over, Molly was stuck between a fit of giggles and utter silence. The sounds coming through the phone were muffled hiccups. Jane guessed she would have reacted the same way if the roles had been reversed. Wearing the shoes, the scenario wasn't a bit funny, but from Molly's moccasins ... yeah, it was frickin' hysterical.

"No problem, girlfriend," Molly said. "I'll see you at the station."

"Thanks, Molls."

"Hang in there."

Hang in there was right. Jane felt like she was dangling from a cliff by nothing but her fingernails ... and was quickly losing her grip. Just like the old days. She went back upstairs and started the task of getting ready for work.

As she showered, she visualized her feelings for Grayson washing down the drain with the soap bubbles. This was the end of the road for him. A person could only hurt her if she was willing to be hurt. She no longer was.

She turned off the shower, dried off and began the transformation on the outside. She blew her light brown hair dry and tugged at it with the round brush until every strand was straight with a slight curl at the ends. She added a little extra concealer, then dabbed and blended her foundation. Her green eyes twinkled as she applied her eyeliner, eye shadow and mascara. She finished her make-up with some neutral colored lipstick then headed for the closet.

Jane was just fastening her watch when her phone rang. The ringtone belonged to her mother. She debated letting the call go to voicemail but knew that Sheri Alexander was not going to leave Jane alone today.

With phone in hand, she closed her eyes and tried to sound nonchalant. "Hi, Mom."

"You're dating Grayson Pierce?" The question was appalled accusation.

"No."

"Go ahead, lie to your mother."

Jane's eyes squeezed closed tighter in frustration. "Believe what you want, Mom, but I am not dating Grayson. It's all—"

"He's not the same boy you went to elementary school with, Janie. In case you don't read the tabloids, he's kind of a ... a bad boy. And not in a good way. He likes his cars and his alcohol and his ... floosies."

"I know, Mom."

"You, my darling daughter, are not a floozy. At least I didn't think you were. But I guess if you don't want to listen to me, go ahead and date him. Just don't come crying to me when you end up with your heart broken. Because he *will* break your heart. Just like last time." She took a moment to breathe. Jane heard the air get sucked in and blown out—right in her ear. An exaggeration of her mother's frustration. "I swear don't know how Maude deals with his exploits. I really don't. It makes her look so bad."

Jane rolled her eyes. Maude Pierce loved her son and probably wasn't a bit concerned with how his actions may or may not make her look. Yet another trait that Sheri Alexander and Maude Pierce didn't share.

The doorbell rang and Jane relaxed. *Saved by the bell*, she thought. "Hey Mom, that's Nate. I have to go."

Another exaggerated sigh. "Okay, fine." And then the line went dead.

Jane opened the door. Nate was dressed in jeans and his heavy winter coat with the KHB logo over the upper right breast.

"You okay?" he asked. "You look a little frazzled."

"My mom saw the magazine."

He nodded that he understood, but didn't say anything else. He didn't need to; he'd been witness to more than one of her rants. "You ready?"

"Yeah, let's do this," she said, donning her red KHB winter coat.

THE STATION WAS BUZZING WHEN SHE AND Nate walked through the door. Nearly every face wore an innocent expression that screamed *guilty*. More than one person quickly shoved a magazine in their desk or under a notebook or … one idiot even threw their copy in the garbage. Only to retrieve it once she'd passed.

Nate sat on the corner of her desk and plowed a hand through his hair. "So, um … do you think … I mean … would it be okay…?"

She laughed and held her hand out, palm up. "Should I make it out to you or Roxy?"

He placed three magazines in her hand. "Roxy's fine. Unless you wanted to make one out to 'the best photographer a girl could ever want'."

Jane quickly autographed the front covers, addressing them just as he'd requested. "If these show up on *EBay* I will kick your ass."

At well over six feet with shoulders that nearly brushed door jambs, she didn't stand a chance in physical warfare, but he still had the decency to feign fear. He stood and lifted the magazines. "Thanks for these. You're a good sport, Jane."

"Ya know, this is totally ridiculous," she told him, rolling her eyes dramatically. "Nobody cares who I am, really. They only care that I might be banging Grayson."

He raised a brow and the corner of his mouth quirked. She glared at him, knowing exactly where his thoughts had just taken him.

"No, I am not banging Grayson. And don't want to be."

Liar, his look said.

"Go to hell, Nate ... and say hello to Grayson when you get there."

6

"...AND THE LAST THING I NEED FROM YOU is a location," Jane said to Nate.

They were driving along in the news vehicle; him driving, her in the passenger seat with a notebook in her hand. Nate didn't respond, although Jane knew he'd heard her. That was what Nate did when he was thinking. While his mind churned with thoughts, Jane went down her list.

Cake, check. Food—sandwiches (made by a sandwich shop)—check. Decorations—She and Molly had gone crazy at the party store.—check.

Finally Nate said, "Well ... I really want Gracie to be there."

"Of course." It was completely appropriate to have the daughter of the birthday girl attending. "So we should probably do a Saturday afternoon, huh?"

He nodded, but again drifted into his thoughts and fell silent. "I guess the park's out."

"Unless we want to freeze our butts off."

"Yeah." He chuckled. His glanced at her quickly out the corner of his eye before staring out the windshield again. "I don't suppose you'd like to have it at your place."

She turned in her seat and gaped at him. "You've seen my place. It's not near big enough for the shindig you're planning. Or the shindig *I'm* planning—according to *your* instructions."

"You're probably right. I guess we could ask Dale if we could use Studio B."

"That'd be real fun for the kids," she said sarcastically.

"Why don't we just do it at Chuck E. Cheese then," he retorted, the muscle in his jaw jumping.

She laughed and after a moment he did too. "It's not that hard," she said. "What's wrong with your house?"

"That is an option, but I'd rather not have to do it there." He slapped his forehead with his palm. "I know the perfect place."

"Where?" she asked as he whipped his phone out.

He pressed a button and the quick beeps of the speed dial rang out. With the speakerphone on, he popped his cell on the dash and waited for an answer.

"Hey, man," Rich Spencer answered.

"Rich, I need a favor," Nate said without preamble. "Can we use your house for Roxie's surprise party?"

There was a momentary pause. "You're asking the wrong Spencer, my man. You'd better ask Kate about that. I'm sure it'd be okay, but I don't wanna speak for her."

"Thanks." Nate disconnected while Rich was still talking. His thumb worked over the keys and pressed send then put the phone back on the dash.

"Hello?" came to soft feminine voice.

"Kate."

"Hi, Nate."

"Can we use your house for Roxie's surprise party?"

"Sure. When?"

Nate looked at Jane for the date and she answered, "A week from Saturday."

"Hi, Jane." She could hear the laugh in Kate's voice. "So you're the one who got wrangled into planning the party?"

"Yep, lucky me." The two of them laughed and Nate snorted.

Jane really liked Kate. She was kind and truly competent at her job. Jane knew too many anchors who sat back, doing nothing while the producers wrote everything for them. Kate was different, she wrote as much as she could. Along with the brains, Kate had beauty too. The girl seemed to have it all, Jane thought.

"So … Kate, we wanna do it in the afternoon, so the kids can be a part of it," Nate added.

"Oh, Jesse would like that. If you bring the decorations over the night before, I'll take care of it. Jesse would love to decorate."

"Um … well, I hate to do that to Molly. She's kind of excited about it."

Kate laughed. "That doesn't surprise me. I think Molly and Jesse would get along really well. Why don't you two come over first thing Saturday morning and we'll all do the decorating," she suggested.

"Sounds good. Thanks, Kate."

"Let me know if you need anything else. I've gotta run."

"Well, everything's settled," Jane told Nate, plucking his phone off the dash and handing it back to him. "I'll do the invitations tonight and mail them in the morning. I hope we're not too late."

Nate shrugged and eased the truck to a stop at a red light. "Most everybody knows already."

Jane shook her head. "I'm surprised Roxy doesn't know." She studied his profile. "She doesn't, does she?"

"No!" His head whipped around to glare at her. "I can keep a secret."

"No, you can't." Jane laughed and patted his arm. "That's okay, Nate, not everyone needs to have a mouth like Fort Knox. Besides it's your secret to tell."

"Speaking of telling secrets," Nate said. "What's up with you and Grayson?"

"Don't."

"Are you into him or not?"

"Not. Definitely not."

Grayson was the last man she should be into. But heaven help her, she *was* into him. She wanted him with an intensity that made her wonder if her brain had taken a vacation. And she knew that he wanted her, too. That knowledge was very dangerous. He had the power to hurt her, more than any other man on earth. But in order for him to do so, she had to let him. And she refused to give him that kind of power.

Keep telling yourself that, her thoughts chided. *Just keep right on lying to yourself.*

ROXY'S PARTY WAS TOMORROW AFTERNOON and with all the party preparations made, Jane was left with nothing but Grayson to occupy her thoughts. She turned on ESPN and watched as the guys debated the happenings in the day's sports world.

"Personally, I can't believe he's done it again," one said.

"You'd think he'd learn that there is no such thing as a closed door when you're an athlete."

A picture popped up on the screen. Jane was going to be sick. Her insides twisted around themselves and bile rose up in the back of her throat. It seemed Grayson *was* at it again. This time a hooker he'd bought had taken pictures with her cell phone. Thankfully, it wasn't too explicit. But it was still explicit enough to give the viewer a really good idea of what he had planned.

She found herself leaning into the screen, scrutinizing the picture. There was something that bothered her about it, something she couldn't put her finger on. But something bugged her. Something ... just not right.

Grayson was leaned back against the pillows with his arms behind his head. His biceps were sexily flexed. His brow was quirked and his smile promised all kinds of intimate acts. His eyes were looking directly into the lens of the camera. So ... he *knew* he was being photographed. What an idiot!

This wasn't like the time that she had been with him. Neither of them had known then. They certainly wouldn't have posed for the picture on purpose. Jane couldn't imagine that Grayson would be so stupid as to pose for this picture, knowing full-well it would end up on the cover of a tabloid.

Unless ...

Would he cast himself in a bad light to draw attention away from the pictures of her?

"In the interview," one of the sportscasters continued, "the prostitute says he asked her to call him 'master.'"

The three men laughed and Jane cringed. Another of the men, still chuckling, said, "He's a little full of himself, isn't he?"

Jane turned off the television. She didn't want to know any more about the story. She didn't want to know any more about Grayson. She knew all she needed to; Grayson Pierce was not the man for her—no matter what her heart kept trying to tell her.

"PUT A STOP TO IT, KEVIN!" GRAYSON YELLED into the phone. "I don't care what kind of favors you have to call in. But you need to fix this!"

"I did say that I wanted you to get publicity, I just didn't think you'd go that far." Kevin's laughter gave Grayson a pretty good idea that his agent wasn't taking the situation seriously, and that made Grayson's anger spike.

"Fix this, Kevin," Grayson snarled, low and deadly serious. "I don't want to see this anywhere."

What would Jane think?

He knew exactly what she'd think.

She'd think he was a womanizing jerk who requested his women call him 'master'. His fingers rubbed circles on his forehead and his teeth ground together.

"I want this fixed."

Kevin sighed through muffled laughter. "Okay, I'll see what I can do. But I can't see how this is necessarily a bad thing. I mean, the media loves when you're bad. They've nicknamed you the 'bad boy of baseball'. I love it."

"Yeah, well, I hate it. I've told you before I don't want to be bad." Grayson used his hand to rake through his hair. If he didn't stop he was going to end up bald. He picked up the bottle of Mylanta and guzzled.

"But you do it so well," Kevin said through another bout of unrestrained laughter.

"I pay you a lot of money to take care of shit like this, Kevin. Make it go away."

"I'll do my best, *Master*."

Kevin's sense of humor was not humorous and Grayson couldn't even voice a farewell. Instead, Grayson hauled back and launched the phone into the wall. It splintered into pieces of plastic and electronic crap. He shook his head. He was known for the tight rein he kept on his temper.

Yet another sign that he was losing it.

"Totally losing it," he grumbled, pulling out the broom.

JANE AND MOLLY PARKED IN THE DRIVEWAY of the Spencer home and began to unpack the back of Molly's pink and black Smart Car. With arms full of bags and boxes they waddled to the porch. Molly used a toe to knock on the door.

The door opened a bit and a little boy's face appeared in the crack. "Who are you?"

"Is your mommy here?"

"Mom!" he screamed, slamming the door. His muffled voice said, "Someone wants you at the door."

The door flew open again and Kate looked embarrassed, even if her son didn't. He stared up at them with big brown eyes focused on the stuff in their arms. His skin was brown and his hair was black. His face was rounded with baby fat. He wore khaki pants, a denim shirt and brown shoes and belt. He looked like a miniature man.

"Jesse," Kate said, "please say hello to my friends. This is Jane and Molly."

"Hi," he said, waving a chubby hand. He pointed a finger at Jane. "Which one are you?"

"I'm Jane."

Molly bent down, nearly toppling her party supplies all over the ground. "And I'm Molly. Can you help us put all this stuff up?"

"Oh, yeah!" He grabbed at a bag and hurried inside, dragging it behind him as he ran. He paused and turned around, waving at them. "Come on. Hurry."

Kate laughed and looked lovingly at her son. "I think he likes you."

It didn't take long to get the decorations up. Molly was a wiz with the helium tank that Rich had gotten and Jesse, perched on Rich's shoulders, made quick work of putting up the happy birthday banners. Jane had to remind herself not to stare at Rich, but couldn't seem to help herself.

Jesse looked nothing like his father. Rich, who was dressed just as his son, was so tender with the little boy. It was nice to see a man who adored his son ... especially when the son was so obviously not his, biologically speaking.

"So Jesse?" Jane asked when the two caught her looking at them. "How old are you?"

He looked down at his fingers, concentration on his face. The digits wiggled in the air, his lip between his teeth. Finally he held up four fingers. "I'm four. I go to preschool. My teacher is Miss Hailey. I can write my name. Wanna see?"

He didn't wait for a response; running out of the room to fetch what Jane assumed would be paper and something to write with.

He came back with a piece of white paper and a purple crayon. He plopped down on the floor and pressed the crayon to the page. His brows pinched together and his tongue stuck out the side of his mouth. The letters formed slowly, but they were legible. After he'd written his name Jane and Molly clapped.

"That's awesome," Jane told him.

He beamed and asked, "Can you write your name?"

"I can." She nodded, falling in love with him.

The first of the guests began to arrive; Roxy's parents, her brother and his wife, Jordan and Olivia. There were a few people she didn't know, but Kate—or Rich—did and made the introductions.

Rich pulled his phone out of his pocket and looked at the display. "They're coming around the corner. Places everybody."

Everybody raced around like chickens with their heads cut off. There weren't enough places to hide. Most of the people crammed into the kitchen or into the living room where they couldn't be seen from the front door.

There was a soft knock, followed by an insistent bell ringing that reminded Jane of Clayton's persistence. Jane heard the click of the door opening and a little girl with blond curls ran in. She was younger than Jesse, but Jane guessed by only a year or so. Her dress was red and was like overalls with straps that came up over her shoulders. She had a white blouse underneath with white tights. Her black patent leather shoes clomped as she raced in ... only to stop abruptly when she saw all the people.

Her face crinkled, her bottom lip started to quiver and then her mouth opened to allow the *bwaaaa!* to escape. "Mommy!" she screamed, turning on her heel to run back in the direction of her mother.

Jane couldn't see the entryway from her vantage point, but she could hear Roxy's voice say, "It's okay, baby. What's wrong?"

Roxy rounded the corner, the little girl with arms and legs wrapped firmly around her like a backpack fastened to her side, and when shouts of *"surprise!"* rang out, her reaction was surprisingly similar to that of her daughter's; her eyes filled with tears and her hand moved up to her mouth as her lip started to quiver. She murmured a soft, "Oh, Nate."

Nate plied the miniature Roxy from her mother and held the little girl tight against his shoulder. Nate's eyes scoured the crowed and when he finally spotted Jane, he flashed a smile and nodded slightly. Now that Jane had been given her kudos, Nate turned his full attention back to the frightened baby in his arms.

Jane saw his lips whispering next to the little one's ear. Blond curls bobbed in a nod, and Nate set her down on her feet. She popped a thumb into her mouth and reached up to take hold of Nate's finger.

Roxy weaved her way through the crowd. Nate did too with Grace in tow, until the two of them came to stand next to where she and Molly stood in the kitchen. Nate's knuckles bumped into her shoulder. "Good job, Jane."

"Hey, I helped," Molly said in mock chastisement.

Nate dipped his chin. "You both did great. I appreciate it so much. She was surprised. Did you see how surprised she was? I'm *so* gonna get lucky tonight."

"I'm lucky," Gracie said.

Nate yanked his daughter into his arms, hugging her tightly to his chest. He pressed a kiss into her hair. "Yes, you are, Gracie. You are very lucky. You're my lucky charm."

"Graaaaaa-cie!" Jesse screamed from across the house.

"Love you, Dad-dy." Grace kissed his cheek and struggled to get down. "Jessss-se!" she answered, deafening her father in the process.

Nate put her down and rubbed at his ear with his palm. "That little girl has a set of lungs on her." He watched with a smile on his face as she took off on a dead run, then his grin turned mischievous. "Just like her mother."

7

OVER THE NEXT MONTH, JANE WAS BOM-
barded by people who wanted to talk to her. Her
phone rang nonstop until Dale instructed the station receptionist to take messages (and there were
a lot of them). Even the calls on Jane's cell had
increased substantially. It'd gotten to the point
that if she didn't know the number, she didn't answer it. Not surprising, there were a lot of hang-
ups.

The whole situation was beyond ridiculous.

Nate was a good sport about the whole thing.
Before she'd teased him about being her bodyguard, now the statement had become a self-
fulfilled prophecy. More than once he'd had to get
between her and someone wanting a statement,
someone who wouldn't take "no comment" for the
only comment they were going to get. He'd actually
introduced Clayton Tate's back to the wall of a
building downtown.

A trip to the grocery store had produced a total-
ly-off-her-rocker groupie creeping around in fruits
and vegetables. "Holy cow! I can't believe it. You're
... you're you."

Jane looked over her shoulder, hoping beyond
all hope to find another *you* behind her. There
wasn't. "Can I help you?"

"Oh! Oh!" Her head whipped around in search of something, Jane couldn't be sure what. The girl finally grinned. "Please. Wait right here."

"Okay," Jane said, knowing full well that she was going to dart as soon as this crazy girl walked away. She raced to the dairy department for some yogurt and milk so that she could get out of the store before...

Someone cleared their throat behind her. Jane grimaced, knowing darn well who it would be.

"You didn't wait," the girl pouted.

Jane didn't say anything because she wasn't sorry she hadn't waited and any other excuse would have been lame.

The girl had her hands on her hips, her clothes in disarray. She held out her hand and Jane squeaked. Part of her wanted to bust up laughing until she pee'd a little; the other part of her was completely mortified.

"Will you please give these to Grayson?"

"No!"

The girl's hand moved closer in an insistent jerk. "You have to."

"Actually, no. I don't."

Seriously, this girl was trying to get Jane to give Grayson underwear. Not that Jane was sure it could be called underwear. It was the tiniest scrap of nylon she'd ever seen.

"I'm sorry, I can't," Jane told her.

The hopeful expression on the girl's face flashed into one of fury. "Who the hell are you anyway? You're not even that pretty."

Jane just shook her head and walked away ... as quickly as she could without breaking out into a full-on sprint.

It was all unnerving. And sure as hell gave her a new perspective of being hounded by the paparaz-zi. She now understood the reasoning behind celebrities hitting the guys chasing them around with cameras.

GRAYSON WANTED TO HIT SOMETHING, PRE-ferably the jackass who'd taken the picture of him and Jane and sold it to the highest bidder.

She refused to take his calls and it was pissing him off. He'd apologized—or tried to—but she didn't want to hear anything he had to say. Now her phone rang once or twice and went to voice-mail.

He didn't leave a message.

He wasn't a loser.

His phone rang and he jammed a finger at the button to answer the call. "'Lo?"

"Grayson, it's Kevin." Grayson's agent sounded giddy. "My phone has been ringing off the hook since those mags hit the racks. Good job, my friend."

Grayson rolled his eyes and ground his teeth together. "How can I help you, Kevin?"

"I was wondering if you'd give me the name of the young lady in the pictures and let me release a statement to the press."

"Absolutely not!" Grayson saw red. "You are to stay away from her."

"It wouldn't take very much to figure out who she is, Grayson. I know she's a reporter. Think of what it could do for her career to be—."

"Her career is just fine." Grayson's hand tigh-tened on the phone and it squeaked a protest. "I'm warning you, do not push this."

Kevin blew a frustrated breath through the phone. "I'm just trying to do what's best for you."

"What's best for me is to leave Ja- —" He bit down on his tongue. He'd been so careful to keep her identity as quiet as her local popularity would allow. He was pretty sure that the entire state of

Utah knew her, but he wasn't going to make her national news. "Leave her alone, Kevin. The subject is closed. I've said all I'm going to say about it. *Leave her alone.*"

"Okay. Okay, I'll leave her alone. Can you give me something else for those vultures to chase?"

"Isn't that what I pay you for?"

Before Kevin could say anything he ended the call and made another. There was more than one way to accomplish his apology.

THE LARGE GLASS DOORS THAT SEPARATED the newsroom from the lobby opened and in bobbed an enormous arrangement of multi-colored tulips. As Jane admired the flowers, the vase floated closer and closer until it stopped next to her desk. Wrinkled hands with pink nails pushed the vase until it came to rest on the corner with a soft thunk.

Lydia, the gray-haired receptionist, smiled. "I know you said to hold your calls, but these aren't exactly a call."

"No, they're not." *They're gorgeous.* "Thank you."

Jane was entranced by the yellows and reds and pinks and whites. There were even ones that were more than one color. She glanced up just in time to see Lydia give the flowers one last appreciative glance before she headed back the way she'd come.

Jane sank down into her chair and stared at the flowers. She was almost afraid to open the card. If this was yet another ploy by a reporter for a statement she would scream.

"Look at you. Girl of the hour," Molly giggled as she rested her behind on the corner of Jane's desk. "Who are they from?"

"I don't know."

Molly tsked her tongue, dipping her head to sniff some bright yellow petals. "What do you mean you don't know?"

Jane waved toward the flowers. "I haven't opened the card."

Molly raised a brow and quirked the corner of her lip. Jane knew that her friend was trying not to laugh. It really was ridiculous to be afraid of the flowers and the stupid card that accompanied them.

"Don't you dare laugh at me!" She huffed and plucked the card from the plumage while Molly walked away—laughing.

The card was full-sized, not a little one that normally accompanied flowers. And the handwriting said that these had been picked out personally.

Jane,

I'm sure your association with me hasn't been pleasant, and I'd love more than anything to make it up to you. I tried to call, but just got voicemail. I don't know if you're avoiding me or if it's your defense against the world.

She could almost hear his soft, low chuckle that indicated he was nervous. And the image in her mind's eye made Jane smile.

I hope it's the world you're avoiding.
Call me.
-Grayson

She really shouldn't.

She knew she shouldn't call Grayson.

More to the point, she *knew* she shouldn't *want* to call Grayson. But she did. And as she dialed the number he'd provided, her heart thumped wildly in her chest and her fingers shook. She ended up having to dial the number three times before she got all ten digits punched in the correct order.

"'Lo?"

"Grayson?" she asked, suddenly afraid he'd given her the wrong number. Wouldn't that be a great joke?

"Jane!"

Nope, she had the right number.

"I'm so glad you called."

"Thank you for the flowers." Her voice sounded distant, and she was grateful to pull off the non-chalance—even if she was shaking like she'd been dumped out of a blender's frappe cycle.

"Tulips are still your favorite, right?"

Suddenly she couldn't breathe. Her chest felt tight and her eyes stung. He'd remembered her favorite flower. That was so sweet. So very, very sweet.

"Jane, you still there?"

"Yeah. I'm here."

Her thoughts tumbled around in her head and she couldn't manage to hold on to one for longer than a moment before another swooped in and assaulted her. Grayson made no sense; one moment he was flirty and handsome and remembering her favorite flower, the next he was aloof and almost cruel.

"I can't do this." She'd meant to only think the words and didn't realize she'd spoken them until he responded.

"Can't do what?"

Crap. She was glad when that word stayed in her head.

"This." Her hand waved between her and the thin air where she imagined he'd be standing if this conversation were happening in person.

"Grayson, I appreciate the flowers. They're very pretty. But I need you to stop contacting me."

"Why?" He sounded genuinely confused and that infuriated her.

"*Why?* Come on, Grayson. This back and forth is giving me whiplash. I can't do it anymore. Okay? My *heart* can't do it anymore."

"I want to explain."

"What's to explain? When we're alone you're charming and captivating and completely adorable, then when other people are around, you're … well, if I'm being perfectly honest, you're an ass. It's so bad that even Nate's noticed it. I'm done. Don't—"

"That's not me."

"Oh, that's original," she snorted.

"There is a reason for all of that. Come spend a week with me."

She laughed; a hysterical sarcastic laugh that caused tears to gather in the corners of her eyes. "Seriously? You really expect me to come spend a week with you."

"Think of it as an exclusive."

"You can take your exclusive and shove it where the sun don't shine!"

"I'll call Dale."

Well, hell. Dale would jump all over an exclusive with Grayson.

Her eyes narrowed and she glared so hard an intern ducked back into the bathroom. "Listen, Grayson, I don't know what kind of game you're playing, but I'm not willing to lose my career just so you can pull one over on Plain Jane."

"Janie. Oh, my sweet—"

"I'm not—"

"—Janie."

"—your sweet anything!"

"There is no game." His voice was soothing, like fine chocolate. A warm fuzzy feeling started to build in her belly and it reinforced her need to put him at an arm's length. "I only want you to know who I really am."

"I know who you—"

"Baby, you don't know shit about me."

"Which is just about all I want to know!" Her head pounded, her heart throbbed and her anger soared. "Just drop the charade. It's not doing either of us any good. If you want a glowing package with my voice telling the world how wonderful you are, then ... fine. I'll do it. Over the phone. We can use stock footage, heaven knows we have plenty."

"That's not what I want. Well, it is. I *do* want you to tell the world how wonderful I am. But what I want, Janie, is for you to say it because you actually believe it."

"Ain't gonna happen." She'd meant to say the words under her breath, but his sigh signaled he'd heard her.

Grayson's voice was quiet when he spoke next. "I promise you will never be in any danger and you can leave any time you wish."

"If it's only me and you for a week—" The thought made her stomach flutter, and she wasn't sure if that was a good or a bad sign. "—how am I gonna get my exclusive interview?"

"Have Nate come the last day, and you can interview me. On camera. Any questions that I haven't already answered, you can ask. Nothing off limits."

"Wow." She was just about to chomp on the hook he dangled. Just about. "You're really gonna trust me with questions like ... how many women have you banged—this week?"

He chuckled softly. "Not that you could put that on TV, nor is it any of your business—" She was just about to throw his *nothing off limits* back at him when he said, "None."

She scoffed, a loud snort that vibrated in her own ear.

"Believe it or not, Janie. I promised to tell you the truth and that's what I'm gonna give you. I haven't *banged* a single woman ... this week."

Her mind started spitting out questions, questions that she suddenly had the desperate need to have the answers for. "Okay, you want me for a week. Fine. If I discover one lie, one single, little itty, bitty white lie, I'm gone. I will *not* promise to be kind in the final interview. And I will *not* sugarcoat the story."

"Okay."

"Let me talk to Dale and I'll—"

"Don't worry about it. I'll call him." She could hear the smile in his voice and her fingers tightened around the phone, the plastic cutting into her palm.

"Damn you, Grayson Pierce. Damn you straight to hell," she said to no one because he'd already disconnected the call. At the same time, she looked over her shoulder and saw Dale pick up his phone and smile.

She busied herself by staring at the empty Word document she was supposed to be typing words into. Her nails tapped on the keys. Her teeth nibbled on her bottom lip. And she wasn't surprised when ten minutes later her name was said over the overhead speaker, asking her to come to Dale's office.

In that moment, she had never hated Grayson more. How dare he! Actually she knew the answer to that. Even though they'd made a deal, he wasn't giving her an option for an out. By calling Dale himself, Grayson made sure that Jane would show up ... for their week. Her stomach did another flip and it had nothing to do with standing on the threshold of her boss's office.

"Jane, please come in." Dale waved a hand at the chairs in front of his desk, taking a sip of his Coke before leaning back in his chair and popping his feet up.

Jane didn't say a word. Not that she could. Her heart was in her throat. Her stomach was full of butterflies and she had to breathe deeply through her nose to keep from vomiting all over Dale's floor. And she didn't even know what that pain-in-her-ass had said to her boss. She could guess though.

"I got an interesting call just now."

"I can imagine."

Dale's blond brows pinched together, but he just pressed on. "It seems Grayson Pierce wants to give KHB an exclusive interview."

"Really?" She put in a little too much sarcasm to come off as truly surprised, and Dale noticed.

"You're not surprised?"

"Grayson might have mentioned something about the possibility of an interview."

His blond brows met his hairline, which was quite a feat since it was receding. "And you didn't jump on it?"

"I ... well ... I guess..." She'd be damned if she was going to lay out her painful past with Grayson on her boss's desk for further humiliation. "I told him I'd do it."

Dale sighed and leaned forward just enough to grab the Coke can and take another swig. The can met the desk and sounded like a gunshot in the quiet room.

"This could be really big, Jane."

"I know. I'm going to do it." Her lack of enthusiasm was bothersome to Dale, it was written all over his face.

He nodded; his mouth was so tight that little lines appeared at the corners. "He has stipulations for this exclusive."

Oh goody! He'd only named one in their conversation—that she come alone.

"He wants one week," Dale said.

No surprise there.

"A week in the life of Grayson Pierce, if you will. He has asked that you meet him in the parking lot of North Sevier High School day after tomorrow."

"No."

"No?" Dale's brow rose again and he stared at her like she was crazy.

"No, I mean ... I ..." She sighed, knowing she was beat. *This just keeps getting better.* "A week, just me and Grayson." Did her voice really just squeak?

"Yeah, just you. His second stipulation is that during that time there is to be no contact. No phones. No computers. No PDA's. No communication to the outside world ... for the entire week."

"Are you frickin' kidding me?" she shouted. "And you agreed to those terms?" *'Cause she sure as hell hadn't.* "What if he's a lunatic just wanting to get me alone ... for an entire week?"

Dale smiled. And now, she hated her boss.

What? Was she just some little puppet who had *manipulate me* written on her forehead?

"Grayson explained that you went to high school together."

"Yeah, so?" She sounded like she was twelve and would have been embarrassed had her adrenaline not been in control.

"So—" He slid a little metallic device across the desk. "—this is an alarm. If you need anything, you just press this red button and it will send a message to Nate's cell phone. He will be going with you."

She felt a tad better. She still didn't like the idea of being stuck with Grayson for a week. "Have you *been* to Salina, Dale? It's a blip on the map with one stoplight in the whole town. Don't you think someone will notice Nate?"

"He and his family will be in Richfield. Close enough if you need them but still far enough away to avoid suspicion."

Obviously Dale didn't know how small towns worked, especially this tiny cluster in Central Utah, but she wasn't going to argue him out of sending Nate.

"Besides, if someone does see him, he can say that he's just there early—with his family. Grayson said that at the end of the week, you could do the interview on camera. He's met Nate, right?"

She nodded.

"So it wouldn't be too far-fetched to think he's there for the taping of the interview," Dale finished.

Wow! It'd been only minutes from the time he'd hung up with Grayson until she was sitting in Dale's office. She had to admire Dale and his quick thinking and even faster planning. It would have taken her more time to get this all figured out. She just hoped that Nate was up for it.

But why wouldn't he be?

Nate was always up for an adventure. And Roxie was up for getting an inside scoop on what might appear next on the front pages of the tabloids.

Jane wrapped her fingers around what would be her only link to the outside world during her time with Grayson.

Dale leaned forward, resting his forearms on the desk. His light blue eyes scrutinized her. "Make me proud, Jane."

"I always do," she said, standing to leave his office.

As she made her way through the newsroom toward her desk, her mind replayed through the conversation she'd had with Grayson. He was up to something, she was sure of it. She couldn't figure out what just yet.

This had prom written all over it.

Jane had been beyond excited when Grayson had asked her to the Junior Prom, their senior year. With her mother in tow, they'd gone to the local dress shop and picked out the perfect dress. It was peach with an empire waist that flared out until the hem fell to just above her knees. The sleeves—what there were of them—wrapped around her upper arms, leaving her shoulders bare. Her mother had insisted on getting the matching wrap to keep her warm—and because her arms were 'a bit flabby'.

Jane had had other plans for staying warm. Plans that included nothing more than cozying up to Grayson.

Three days before the dance, Jane was walking down the hall at school and overheard a couple of Grayson's teammates razzing him.

"...You can tell us, man. Why Plain Jane?"

"You had to have lost a bet, Pierce."

"Yep," Grayson grunted.

And with that one word, Jane's entire world shattered.

"You look like the four men of the apocalypse just rode into your yard?" Molly asked.

Jane glanced up into the very blue eyes of her friend. "You have no idea how right you are."

A lot of years had passed since the sad truth was revealed, but her emotions were still raw when it came to Grayson. It didn't matter how good-looking he was, nor did it matter that her insides turned to Jell-O when he looked her in the eye and smiled.

There was no way in hell she was going to let Grayson Pierce destroy her this time around!

8

"Damn, it's cold, Jane mumbled as she stepped out of her Mazda 3. The shock of leaving her car and immersing herself in the chilly night was more like leaving a warm bath only to jump into a frozen pond. A shiver wriggled up her spine and she stuffed her hands deep into the pockets of her coat, using them to pull the warmth closer around her. It was the only barrier she had and by darn she was going to use it.

Another icy breeze blew, lifting the edge of her coat and licking up her body. The cold stung even through the denim that covered her legs. She stomped her feet to keep the blood flowing to her toes and clamped her teeth together to keep them from chattering.

It was the second week in December and, despite everything she kept telling herself about the boost this would give her career, she really did have better things to do. Christmas was right around the corner and she had yet to purchase a single gift. Not that she was overly concerned with that fact. She didn't really do Christmas and there were a total of three names on her list.

In her opinion that was three names too many. She wasn't a big fan of the holidays.

Sniffing and stomping, Jane continued to wait. She hated waiting. And it was totally rude that he would make her wait in the first place. Not that she should be surprised. She rubbed at her running nose with a gloved hand, thankful it wasn't any colder or she might have to resort to sticking tissues up her nose to stop the flow.

The weather was fairly mild for this time of year. No snow on the ground, only remnants remained in the form of snow banks on the perimeter of the parking lot and around the light poles.

She kicked at some chunks of ice that had fallen from the mound of snow she'd parked next to. A snowball the size of a golf ball rolled down and Jane crushed it under her boot. The soft crunch was surprisingly satisfying. A small smile tipped her lips and she began to look around at all that had changed ... and so much more that hadn't.

The campus where she'd gone to school fifteen years ago was the same. The same buildings, the same black asphalt with faded yellow lines. Jane suspected it had been repaved in the time she'd been gone, not that it looked like it now. She guessed the trees were a little bigger.

The baseball field where Grayson had made a name for himself had gotten lights—that was new.

She stomped her feet again trying to shake some of the icicles out of her blood. Damn, she was pretty sure that she was going to turn into a Popsicle.

How long had she been standing here anyway?

She considered looking at her watch. But that meant exposing her wrist to the elements, and she wasn't willing to do that. She'd been smarter if she had stayed in her car with the engine running. But she didn't expect to have to wait for heaven-knew-how-long for Grayson to show up.

Maybe that was the joke. Maybe he wasn't going to show up. He'd leave her freezing to death. Then at her funeral—after she'd been unthawed—

Grayson and his friends would sit around and laugh about how pitiful Plain Jane was.

She was looking out over the football field when the crunch of tires on salt and roar of an engine signaled that someone had shown up. She tried to pretend that her heart hadn't just skipped a beat or that the air hadn't frozen in her lungs. So the latter could be the weather.

Yes, she couldn't breathe because it was just too damn cold.

Intentionally keeping her back to him and acting as though she hadn't heard the click as his door opened or the thud and crunch of his feet meeting the pavement.

"Janie?"

The deep rumble of his voice made her knees go weak. Not wanting to fall flat on her face, she locked her knees and straightened her spine. Which wasn't too hard, since she was pretty stiff already.

"Who else would be standing here freezing her ass off, waiting for you to grace her with your presence?" She turned around to glare at him as he circled around the Jeep—one of the new four-door kind. Black, of course—to match his heart. "Never mind, don't answer that."

The grin that spread across his face made her even more grateful he didn't begin listing the harem of women who might have eagerly been freezing their asses off.

He was heartbreakingly handsome, even in his fluffy black parka and black knit hat. His muscular legs were covered by jeans that disappeared into a pair of thick-soled winter boots. He had dark scruff that covered his entire jaw.

Jane would consider growing a beard too, if it meant keeping her face warm. She snuggled her chin down into the scarf she had wrapped around her neck.

"Hop in." He opened up the passenger door and heat rolled out.

Jane could almost see the billows of warmth rushing out to embrace her. Her first instinct was to crawl inside and blast the heater until she melted all over his floorboards—and not in sexual need. Just literally unthawed, leaving nothing but a puddle behind. But then she glanced at her car and asked, "What about—"

"Trent'll take care of it. You remember Trent?"

"Yeah." She nodded, of course she remembered Trent. He'd been Grayson's best friend. Apparently still was. Jane felt her eyes narrow in the suspicion she felt everywhere else. Trent hadn't taken part in the antics that devastated Jane's seventeen-year-old self, but Grayson had. And it wasn't too far out of the realm of possibility that neither of them had grown up.

"He bought the mechanic's shop. He's got a tow truck," Grayson explained.

"He's gonna tow my car ... where, exactly?"

"He'll bring it up to my place later tonight." He studied her face and apparently her apprehension was written all over it because Grayson used a long finger to draw a cross over his heart. "I promise, Jane. No games. No tricks."

She still wasn't convinced there wasn't some hurtful ulterior motive behind this whole trip, but had gotten to the point where cold was seeping into her bloodstream. And she didn't want to be cold anymore.

Reluctantly Jane climbed into the cab of the Jeep while Grayson popped the trunk of her car and pulled out her suitcase. She noticed that her laptop conspicuously didn't make the leap.

As he settled into the driver's seat and put on his seatbelt, she shifted toward him. "I'm ... uh, I'm gonna need my computer ... to take notes."

He took hold of her hand and pressed a quick kiss to her knuckles. "I'll give you a notebook and a pen ... to take notes."

Rocks and frozen debris exploded in an arc behind the rear tires as Grayson lay on the gas and maneuvered the Jeep out of the parking lot. There was only a slight fishtail before Grayson had complete control. He went down First North and turned right onto State Street, which was also US Highway 89, and headed south out of town.

Familiar locales flashed by—as much as they can *flash* when the vehicle is zooming at the break-neck speed of forty miles an hour. The smile that crept to her lips actually surprised her. Jane hadn't realized she'd missed the sleepy little town, but she had. There were some really good memories attached to the place. The old drug store. The 5 and Dime. The drive-in—burgers, not movies.

"Before I go home, we have to go to the drive-in." Her stomach grumbled at the thought of the greasy burger with a side of even greasier fries.

"You know, I've been all over the nation and have yet to find a better burger than right here at home. I won't let you get out of here without having one, okay?"

"Okay."

And just like that, they'd fallen into an easiness that scared her. Jane knew that the man sitting next to her had the power to break her heart all over again. She also knew that no matter how many times she warned herself, every time he looked at her and flashed that grin of his, she melted.

The scenery changed from businesses to circa early twentieth century homes that were only reminders of past generations to sagebrush—and the occasional cow. She recognized every square inch of the landscape but this wasn't the way to the Pierce house.

But *duh!*—She caught the motion of her hand moving toward her forehead and was grateful it hadn't made the connection. Her realizations needed to stay inside her head—of course he'd moved.

Mr. Pierce—she realized that she didn't even know his first name—had died in a mine accident when Grayson was about five or so. After that Maude Pierce had raised her only son by herself. She'd done a fairly decent job. It wasn't like Grayson ended up behind bars with a cellmate named Bubba. At least not yet. With the insane life he was leading, there was still time.

The house Grayson grew up in had been small, but well-maintained. The local church group saw to it that the Pierce's received anything they needed. And the Boy Scout troop took turns keeping up with the yard until Grayson was old enough to do it himself. Then, though, his friends would show up to help him mow the grass, milk a cow or re-shingle the roof.

That had been a sight. The entire baseball team had shown up and eventually shucked their shirts, hammering away while the sun bathed their backs. Needless to say, Jane hadn't been the only girl in the town to notice. Thankfully it hadn't been Jane's car that crashed that day. She smiled, remembering the dent in the big ol' oak across the street.

"You okay?" Grayson asked from beside her.

The question startled her. Well, not the question itself, but the fact that he'd spoken. She was so lost in her thoughts that she'd forgotten this little rollercoaster-ride down memory lane had someone else with his arms and legs inside the vehicle at all times.

"Yeah. It's just changed so much." Which was a lie. The fields were the same; covered with patches of snow with rolling hills that eased from one pasture to the next. They'd left Salina and were heading toward the turn off for Aurora. "Where are we going?"

"My ranch is only a little further."

"Your ranch?"

She didn't expect him to have a ranch. A ginormous house with voluptuous maids, maybe—maids dressed in those little black and white outfits, complete with low necklines and obscenely short skirts, who bent over to pick up napkins and crap—but a *ranch*?

With her luck, it was like the *Chicken Ranch* in that musical with Dolly Parton and Burt Reynolds. If one singing whore came down the front steps of his *ranch*, she was leaving. End of discussion!

"Do you have any *chickens* on your ranch?"

He shook his head, obviously missing the reference. "No. No chickens, but I do have twenty head of cattle and six horses—almost seven," he said, his lips lifting in a proud smile. "Daisy is due to foal here any day. It should happen while you're here. You ever help bring a life into this world?"

It wasn't until her tonsils began to dry out that she realized her mouth was hanging open. "Uh ... no."

"No? Not even kittens or puppies?" He looked at her, she guessed he was surprised, but his face was hidden in shadows.

"Nope."

"Well, then, I really do hope that I get to introduce that awesome experience to you."

"Great." She didn't sound thrilled, she didn't feel it either.

Her mind was suddenly bombarded with images of blood and birth and ... *ew*! Her nose crinkled in disgust and she wondered if she could get out of Grayson's idea of a great time.

The silence between them was only disturbed by the soft music playing on the radio. It had been years since she'd listened to country music. It was yet another part of her life she wanted to close the door on. But just like the familiar buildings, the country crooner made her feel nostalgic.

More than nostalgic, she realized. It was like she was home.

That made her pause.

She didn't want to feel comfortable, not with Grayson sitting next to her looking like a million bucks and smelling even better. Not with the way her stomach fluttered and her heart hammered. And she certainly didn't want to feel like she'd come home.

Her condo was home. KHB was home. Salina, Utah was *not* home.

"It's okay if you're not interested, Janie. But it is something I'd love to share with you. I have a lot I want to share with you."

Yeah, right! was her first thought, quickly followed by *and I want to share it all with you.*

They pulled off the main highway and bumped along a dirt road, filled with mud and car-eating potholes. A few miles later revealed a gate with a large *P* amongst the wrought iron deer and elk. Grayson pushed a button on what looked like a garage door opener clipped on his visor and the gate slowly swung open.

"I'm gonna guess this is your ranch?"

"This is the west end of it, yes." He accelerated to ease the Jeep through the open gate, and then waited on the other side until it was completely closed again. A few cows came to greet them, mooing a happy greeting. "It's dinner time," he said.

She watched as the bovine sea parted only to move in behind and follow them as they drove over the cinder covered road. Even though it was freezing outside, Jane couldn't resist rolling down the window to touch the rump of a heifer that was walking right alongside. The cow didn't react, except to turn her head and moo.

"They're pretty comfortable around people," Jane noted.

"Yeah, they see a lot of me."

She felt her brows crinkle and she turned in her seat to look at him. "But how can ... I thought you were on the road a lot."

"Yeah ... well, I am." His fists had tightened on the wheel and the muscles in his jaw jumped and he very blatantly didn't look back at her. "If it's okay, we'll go to the barn first."

Okay, so obviously he didn't want to talk about going on the road. Which meant she did—really bad! What was he hiding? The question was going to drive her crazy. The time to ask her questions would come though, that much he'd promised as his end of the deal. She would bide her time and bite her tongue. For a few days anyway.

A fork appeared in the road. Off to the left was a roofline that was decked out in Christmas lights which twinkled all bright and cheery in the darkness. Jane couldn't see the whole house because of the low rolling hills and wondered if more 'Joy to the World' would greet her when she could.

Grayson took the right fork and in a matter of seconds another roofline appeared, followed quickly by an entire building. The barn. It was big and red with a black, shingled roof—white x's over the doors and all.

Grayson stopped in front of said doors. "You can wait here if you'd rather."

"That's okay. I'd like to help." *Help?* Where the hell had that come from? She wasn't a cowgirl. Never had been, even when she'd done 4-H and had taken care of a lamb.

Grayson smiled at her and got out. As she stepped out, she slipped on some ice. A gasp—and yes, a squeal—escaped and she grasped for anything to keep from meeting the ground in what was sure to be an inelegant display. Her hands fisted into the soft down of Grayson's parka and his strong arms wrapped under her armpits, pulling her against him.

His breath formed little white puffs that mingled with hers. He held her close and she let him, basking in his warmth, in his strength, in him. It felt good to stand so close to Grayson. Too damned good.

In that moment, it was as if time stood still. Neither of them moved. Surely she imagined that Grayson's eyes had darkened, that his lids dropped dreamily. And he wasn't even now leaning close. He definitely wasn't going to kiss her.

Except that he was.

And she was going to let him.

Her own eyes drifted closed and she tipped her chin to give him easier access to her lips. Wrapped in his arms she was heated from the inside out and as his mouth touched hers she darn near burst into flames. His lips were warm and soft and firm—and everything she'd ever imagined.

His hold tightened and she slipped her hands up around his neck, sliding her fingers into the short wisps of hair that weren't covered by his knit cap. Every part of him scorched her. She couldn't get close enough, and the way he held her against him implied he felt the same.

Another quick brush of his lips across hers, then a kiss pressed to each cheek and the tip of her nose brought an end to the intimacy, although the moment still sparked with desire. He rested his forehead against hers and his breath sawed from his lungs. The heat of his breath and the cold of the night made the action visible, puffs forming in quick succession. Jane liked seeing that he was as affected by their kiss as she was.

"Oh Janie, I've wanted to do that for a long, long time." His thumb stroked over her cheek. "I love your freckles. Always have."

As cold as she was his words iced her to the bone. *Always have. Always…*

"Don't." She pulled away, almost jerking herself out of his hold. The last thing she wanted was for Grayson to pretend that there was more between them than there was. He had the gall to pale a little under his cold-reddened cheeks. She put her hands on her hips and glowered at him. "You promised no games."

"You're right, I did."

He backed another step away from her and even though she'd pushed him away she felt his retreat with a sting that made her heart sink and her eyes burn. She was grateful when he turned his back to her and walked into the barn seconds before her feelings leaked out of her eyes and tumbled in streaks down her face.

Rubbing the sleeve of her coat over her freckled cheeks, Jane followed Grayson knowing that there was little hope of leaving this week with her heart in one piece.

WOUNDED PRIDE TENDED TO HURT WORSE than a punch to the jaw. A broken heart was more excruciating than any broken bone. Grayson knew both from firsthand experience. Knew both thanks to the woman who had once again pushed him away.

Their kiss, their first kiss, had been perfect. When he'd initiated it, he wondered if she would gasp and slap him. Instead she'd responded, wrapped her arms around his neck and even played with his hair. He loved when women played with the hair at the base of his neck. But knowing that it was Jane's nimble fingers weaving amongst the strands had done very pleasurable things to his body.

She'd melted against him. She'd kissed him back. For a moment, she'd been his.

He wasn't sure how telling her that her freckles were adorable killed the mood. But it had, just as if he'd doused her with a bucket of cold water. That was what he needed now. He needed a cold shower—in a bad way.

Wounded pride aside, his body was still hot. More than hot—he was nuclear!

The moments he'd spent with her on the road had proven that he was still attracted to her, but after tasting Jane, just a small, miniscule taste, he wanted her with an intensity that made him nuts. The feelings he'd thought might have been diluted over the last fifteen years were fully concentrated and stronger than ever.

Grayson wasn't too proud to admit to himself that he'd loved Jane in high school. He'd loved the insecure, nerdy girl. He'd never thought she was plain, he'd thought she was beautiful—in a girl next door kind of way. He saw through the braces and glasses and acne. Back then, in his mind's eye, he pictured what she'd be as a woman—as his wife.

His imagination hadn't come close.

The grown-up version of his Jane was drop-dead gorgeous! He wanted to feel her long hair spread over his bare chest. He wanted to swim in the depths of her seafoam green eyes as they darkened with desire for him. He wanted to melt into her soft luscious red lips. He wanted lose himself in the soft curves of her body.

He wasn't delusional enough to try to convince himself of anything else—he wanted her.

Grayson wanted Jane.

9

THE SMALL STOP AT THE BARN HADN'T HELP-
ed Jane's out of control emotions. After their kiss
and her accusations, he'd left her standing alone
in the cold. Instead of following him inside, she left
him to do what needed to be done, climbing back
inside the Jeep to wait. She'd felt a little irrational
for the way she'd snapped at him and pushed him
away. But she couldn't bear the closeness.

He was gone for ten minutes or so before he
came back out and climbed behind the wheel. His
face was drawn up tight, an emotionless mask.

"Is everything okay?" Jane asked softly.

He nodded but didn't look at her. "Yeah, I think
Daisy's about ready."

He didn't say another word as he drove them
over to where some troughs were set up in the
middle of an empty pasture. He angled the Jeep to
use the headlights, hopped out of the Jeep and
unlocked a gate that stood between the cattle and
their food source.

Grayson grabbed a bale of hay, each hand
wrapping around a piece of baling twine. With an
ease that surprised Jane he carried it over to the
troughs. He reached into his pocket, producing a
large pocket knife. A few quick slices and the hay
was ready for distribution.

As Grayson used a pitchfork to spread the hay
Jane found herself wanting to see him do this

same act in the summertime, when the sun would reflect off his sweat-dampened skin.

She'd barely gained some control of her overactive imagination when Grayson opened the door and climbed behind the wheel. A swipe of his hand removed his hat and he got out again to shuck his coat. His movements were jerky and frustrated. He chucked the coat and hat into the backseat, slid into the driver's seat and put the Jeep into gear.

The cows were coming from every direction as he turned the Jeep around and drove to the house.

The glimpse of lights Jane saw earlier were only a fraction of what actually adorned the house. Trees and bushes twinkled in reds and greens and whites along with the bright white bulbs that glowed on the roofline.

By the décor on the outside, Jane shouldn't have been shocked by the inside. Walking in the front door, Jane noticed two trees decked out from trunk to top and every needle in between. She spotted the mistletoe hanging over the doorway and quickly stepped out from under it. Like she needed to make that mistake again. Things had been painfully awkward since he'd walked away from her and into the barn. She liked the idea of kissing Grayson but knew that it was a really, really bad idea.

Given the agonizing silence, the situation had disaster written all over it! It was going to be a very long week.

"Did your mom do all this?" she asked, motioning to the decorations.

"No way." He helped her out of her coat and hung it on the coat tree next to the door. When he turned he was smiling and the tension had melted out of his shoulders. And melted out of the room. "I love Christmas. It's my thing."

She laughed. "Christmas and baseball."

He chuckled softly. "Yeah, Christmas and baseball. Come on, I'll show you to your room."

She followed him up the stairs, careful to not grab too tightly on the garland that was wrapped around the railing. He pushed open the first doorway on the left and set her suitcase next to a chest of drawers. His hand motioned toward a door off to the right. "There are clean towels in the bathroom. Let me know if you need anything else."

"Thanks."

"Why don't we go down and get a bite to eat."

"Sounds good."

He led her back down the stairs and into a beautiful kitchen, complete with marble countertops, stainless steel appliances and hardwood floors. He waved an arm at a stool. Jane pulled it out and climbed onto it. Using a fingertip to trace a natural line in the smooth marble, she watched as Grayson stood with the refrigerator door open. His shoulders were back to being tight.

Good grief, he was making her tense too!

Quietly she slipped from her stool and walked to him, putting her hand on his shoulder. He jumped and whirled around to face her, the fridge door closed with a pop. She smiled, at least she hoped she smiled, it felt more like a snarl.

"It's okay, Grayson. I'm not really that hungry." Just then her stomach growled and she groaned.

He smiled, an honest-to-goodness smile, one that showed off his dentist's expertise. One dark brow rose. "You may not be hungry, but I am. And, with Daisy being so close, it's going to be a long night. How about a sandwich?"

"A sandwich sounds great. Can I help?"

He nodded just a bit, pointing at a white door in the middle of the chocolate brown wall. "Bread's in there. I'll grab everything else. Ham or turkey?" he asked, opening the fridge again.

Dinner was quick and easy. Turkey sandwiches, chips, and some baked beans that Jane had also plucked from the pantry. Neither of them said much, which was okay with Jane. She wasn't sure what to say.

She volunteered to do the dishes and watched as Grayson grabbed his jacket just before heading for the door. "I'll probably be out all night. Make yourself at home."

As she looked around the kitchen, she knew just how much she wanted to be at home in Grayson's home. She quickly cleaned up from dinner and then made her way up to the room Grayson had given her. Jane sat on the edge of the bed and reflected on the last few hours.

Her emotions had run the gamut; excitement, intrigue, desire, and an overwhelming fear of losing her heart to Grayson. And did she mention desire? She had to hand it to him; Grayson Pierce was one hell of a kisser.

Not that that fact was an earth-shattering newsflash.

The man *was* full of surprises, though. He lived on a ranch in the middle of nowhere. *He had horses and cows, for hell's sake!* His home had been the most surprising of all. Jane wasn't sure what she'd expected, but it wasn't this.

The house was large, alright. That had been expected. The wrap-around porch filled with rocking chairs, the metal roof that probably sounded really cool in a rain storm, and the ten-foot oak double doors hadn't been. Nor had the high ceilings and slip-peeled wood poles covered in Christmas garb that supported the second floor.

The living room was filled with simplistic furnishings. Nice—really nice, top of the line but simple. Four beige leather La-Z-Boy recliners formed an arc in front of an enormous plasma television perched on a walnut stand. Three small end tables separated the chairs. Grayson's chair was the one just left of the middle table, Jane noted. The remote control and a Coke can rested closest to that chair.

Running her fingers over the soft worn leather, she thought of Grayson; the way he'd kissed her and then stormed away, busying himself in his work as a distraction. He'd been into their kiss, she couldn't deny that. Physically, at least, he wanted her. But she didn't want a quick tumble, adding herself to the list of anonymous women, who'd been loved and left by the great Grayson Pierce.

She wanted more from him.

As she'd looked around from the rough light oak floors to the expensive television, she realized she wanted it all. Not the possessions. She worked hard and made good money and was doing just fine all by herself. But she didn't want to be all by herself anymore.

She wanted the happily-ever-after.

With Grayson.

No, she didn't. She really didn't.

The rumbling of a diesel engine brought her back to the present. She stood up, making her way to the window. She pushed the red gingham curtains aside and looked out. Just as promised Trent was bringing her car. He stepped out and made quick work of unhooking the little blue car from his tow truck. He didn't dawdle, didn't even look at the house. He just left, his taillights fading from sight.

Jane looked out into the darkness. From her vantage point, she could make out the lights coming from the windows of the barn. That's where Grayson was—and where she unexpectedly needed to be with a vehemence that frightened her.

With jerky movements, evidence of her self-imposed need to hurry, she searched for her keys. They were in the side pocket of her suitcase. Tucking them into her jeans pocket, she changed from her light sweater into one that was fluffy and thick and warm, and all but ran down the stairs, grabbing her coat just before she dashed out into the cold.

Stars twinkled brightly, the sky cloudless. Grandpa used to tell her that a cloudless sky meant the night was going to be "cold as a witch's tit". As her own body reacted to the chill she laughed softly. It certainly was cold tonight. Thankfully, her own breasts were warm beneath her clothing.

She drove the short distance to the barn and wondered if she was doing the right thing. But before she could talk herself out of going inside, she climbed out of the car. The barn door opened silently. Jane wasn't sure why she expected it to squeak and didn't even realize she had until the silence surprised her. The sight inside though completely flabbergasted her.

A gold palomino mare—Daisy, Jane assumed—lay on her side, panting. Grayson knelt at her side, rubbing his hand over her swollen belly and saying soothing things in a kind, low voice. Every muscle in the horse tightened and Grayson reacted quickly, bending his head to Daisy's ear. Jane could see his lips moving and wished she could hear what he was saying.

As Daisy relaxed a bit, she nuzzled his leg with her nose. She whinnied faintly and swished her flaxen tail against the clean straw. Long lashes dropped over the huge brown eye that was visible and Jane noted that this horse trusted Grayson wholeheartedly. With her life.

Jane hadn't noticed that she'd taken a step forward, but Daisy had, twisting in the direction of her approach. Grayson's head jerked up only a fraction of second later. His expression was confused followed quickly by recognition.

"I didn't expect you," he whispered.

"To be honest, I didn't expect to be here." She closed the door and warmth wrapped around her like a blanket.

He made a motion to stand, but Daisy seemed reluctant to let him leave her side. Jane held up a hand, encouraging him to stay where he was. "Is it okay if I...?" she asked, motioning toward him. The last thing she wanted was to make Daisy uncomfortable.

Grayson ran a hand over Daisy's neck, whispering, "It's okay, girl. She's a friend," as he did so. When he looked up at Jane he smiled. "Come on over. Just go slow."

Jane walked so slowly that the short distance seemed to take forever. She shrugged out of her coat and laid it over the side of the stall then in a deliberate unhurried motion she knelt beside Daisy. Easing her hand out, she ran her fingertips over the hard stomach. It moved and Jane gasped.

Grayson chuckled softly. "I think she's ready to have this over with."

His hand moved toward Jane only to yank back and get shoved almost violently into the pocket of his jeans. The plaid flannel sleeves of his shirt were rolled up, showing off his muscular forearms. His dark hair stuck up in wild disarray. The shadow of his beard darkened his cheekbones. Totally sexy.

"Why ... I mean, it's okay that you're here, but I don't understand—"

"You did say that you wanted to share this with me, right?"

"Yeah. Hell, yeah." He studied her, his eyes moving slowly, intently over every inch of her face. "I'm sorry. I guess I was distracted when I came out here. I totally forgot that you'd never ... Shit. I'm sorry, Janie."

"It's okay." She watched in amazement as her fingers moved out to push his hair off his forehead. The motion touted a familiarity that should have sent her running for the hills. Instead those damned fingers traced his brow, traveling down the prickly hair on his cheekbone, coming to rest on the soft whiskers of his goatee.

His breath was warm on her fingers. Hers had stopped in her lungs, suddenly unwilling to go neither in nor out. Her heart however was pounding violently within her ribcage. Her thumb moved over his top lip, moving around one side of his mouth, his chin, then the other side of his mouth, stopping on the small scar on the upper left side of his lip.

In a movement she didn't anticipate, he pulled her thumb into his mouth and gave it a quick hard suck. Her eyes widened and she was sure that she looked like a deer about to get plowed over by a semi. That was what she felt like.

She was in very dangerous territory.

They stood in a moment suspended. Both of them staring into the eyes of the other. Neither of them willing to move and break the spell. His tongue swirled around her thumb and heat spread up her arm, through her torso and down her legs until her entire body felt like it might spontaneously combust.

Thankfully, Daisy doused the inferno before it could catch.

With ease she jumped to her feet, paced around the stall. Her belly tightened and Daisy gave a small snort. Grayson grabbed Jane by the hand

and backed both of them away from Daisy, who dropped to her knees and onto her belly. She rolled from one side to the other then rested for a moment, breathing heavy.

Jane watched in awe. "Shouldn't you call the vet?"

Grayson chuckled. "Nah. Daisy and I will be able to handle it. If there's a problem, I can call the vet. I gave him a heads-up."

Another contraction brought a tiny hoof and white leg into view. Daisy once again stood, pacing in a circuit around the stall. The fresh straw crunched under her hooves. Her front legs dropped and the rest of her followed until she once again rested on her belly.

Grayson moved quickly to the rear of the horse and waited until the muscles of Daisy's belly squeezed the little one, pushing it out. Grayson grabbed the front legs and tugged with the contraction, assisting with the birth. The little body slid free, coming to rest amongst the straw that was very similar in color to the new horse.

Jane was overcome and tears flowed freely down her cheeks. She didn't bother blotting them away. It wasn't like Grayson would notice. All of his attention was on Daisy and her baby.

Daisy turned her head around to sniff at her young. Their noses met. Jane sniffled. Grayson's eyes flicked upward for a split second then he let her have her privacy. His notice didn't diminish the overwhelming emotion of the experience he'd shared with her. She'd never been so happy that she'd done the unexpected and just done what she wanted. The old Jane would have stayed tucked away in the bedroom where he'd left her. She wasn't old Jane anymore.

"I'm gonna be a while, if you wanna go back up to the house."

"I'll wait," she said, wondering just how long *a while* was going to be.

Grayson nodded and began working with the horses. Jane leaned against the wall and slid down until with her back against wood and her legs outstretched. She pulled her jacket to cover her like a blanket.

The last thing she remembered was Grayson brushing Daisy and telling her that she was a "good girl".

Jane wondered whether the horse was a colt or a filly. She'd forgotten to ask and, in this very moment, she was too tired to voice the question.

GRAYSON'S ATTENTION SHOULD HAVE BEEN completely devoted to the horse he was brushing. He was just going through the motions though. His thoughts were on Jane. When she'd started to cry, it had taken every ounce of control he had not to rush to her and gather her up in his arms and comfort her.

He'd never seen Jane cry. He knew she was capable of tears, everyone was. Jane was a tough girl. At least that was the façade she put on for the world. Back in the days when she'd been his tutor—even though he was acing the class—the mask had cracked a bit. She wasn't stuffy. She wasn't the kind of girl who wanted to sit on the sidelines and pretend the world passing her by didn't matter.

Grayson believed he knew Jane Alexander.

And he wanted to give her everything.

He ushered Daisy and her new colt into the other stall and closed them in, then went to work on cleaning out the soiled straw. When the chores were complete, Grayson stood and admired Jane.

She was dead-to-the-world asleep, her back against the barn wall, her feet stretched out in front of her, crossed at the ankles. Her chin was lowered, resting on her chest. She had her jacket over her upper body to protect her from the slight chill in the air. Her lashes were a dark crescent against her pale cheeks. Her freckles were more obvious than when she was awake. Her lips were parted slightly. She looked so sweet, so innocent.

Unable to resist any longer, Grayson silently sat down next to Jane and eased an arm behind her, guiding her sleeping body against his very awake one. She sighed and relaxed, snuggling into him. Her head came to rest on the sweet spot between his shoulder and his pectoral and her arm draped around his middle.

He tightened his hold, closed his eyes and dropped his head to rest on the top of hers. He then fell asleep with a big ol' smile on his face.

Life didn't get any better than this.

JANE WAS HAVING THE BEST DREAM. SHE wasn't sure how many dreams she'd had last night—four, five … a dozen?—and Grayson starred in them all. This latest one felt so real. She could actually *smell* him; a combination of straw and horse and man. The musky scent caused her cognitive mind to pause.

Beneath her ear a heartbeat was strong. There was a slight pressure on the top of her head. Her fingers moved to form a fist around the sheet under her hand—which seemed to rise and fall in a steady rhythm. Then the entire bed moved—and moaned. The side came up in a wave, crushing her against a hard unforgiving shore. Her eyes flipped open and her mind came on track in a flash.

"Grayson," she squealed.

Holy crap!

It hadn't been a dream—at least, not this part of it.

They were still in the barn. The stall where, what seemed like only moments ago, Daisy and her baby had been was now empty, fresh straw on the floor.

"Where...?"

"The next stall over." Man, his voice was sexy first thing in the morning; deep and full of gravel. His grip loosened, but not completely. She liked that he still held her against him, yet gave her the option of getting up. She didn't, nor did she want to. She snuggled deeper into him, he squeezed her gently. "Did you sleep okay?"

"Yeah, I did." Actually she hadn't slept that well in a really long time. Not that she would think about that. It wasn't like she could make Grayson her new pillow every night from now on.

"I hope you don't mind, but you looked so cute I didn't have the heart to wake you." He didn't bother to give her the how's and why's of their current entwined state. "You hungry?"

"Starving."

He stood and offered her his hand. When she was on her feet, he tugged her against him. "Thanks for your help last night. I'm glad you were here." He tipped her chin with his forefinger and pressed a chaste kiss to her lips. "Let's get some breakfast."

It was in that moment she realized she was done.

She'd fallen head over heels.

Her heart, every single red and white blood cell, belonged to Grayson Pierce.

Heaven help her!

10

AFTER BREAKFAST THEY PARTED WAYS TO shower and get cleaned up. Jane had just finished dressing in jeans and a black and pink argyle v-neck sweater when a knock on the door made her jump.

"Come in," she hollered.

The door cracked and Grayson stuck his head in. He grinned. "You ready to go?"

"Yeah." She pulled her hair up and stretched a rubber band around it. "Where we goin'?"

"To town. Since you haven't been home in a while then you've missed all the changes."

Jane laughed and shook her head. "Because Salina is such a growing metropolis."

He rolled his eyes, his head jerking toward the door. "Come on. I've got a lot planned for today. And I promise you've never seen the Salina I'm gonna show you today."

It was her turn to roll her eyes and the motion made his grin. She grabbed her camera off the dresser and headed out the door, fast on Grayson's heels. He may have vetoed her ability to capture moving pictures for her piece, but he couldn't stop her from getting still ones.

Okay, so maybe he could … but he didn't make a move to take the camera from her.

"I've been thinking," Grayson said as they climbed into the Jeep.

"And just what have you been thinking about?" she asked, wondering if she really wanted to know.

"Well, Daisy's colt needs a name."

"My grandpa always just named his animals what they were. Ya know, cat or dog or ... horse."

Grayson laughed. "Your grandpa was a very creative man. But I was thinking of something else."

"Like what?"

"Alexander," he said.

Jane felt heat rise in her cheeks and knew they were flaming with a blush.

"It seems only fitting that the little guy be named after the woman who welcomed him into the world. What do you think?"

What did she think?

What *did* she think?

She thought she didn't like any of this. She'd been hanging with Grayson for only a few hours and she was already invested. She didn't like being invested with a love-'em-and-leave-'em man.

"It's your horse," she all but snapped.

Nonplussed, he smiled. "Yes, he is. And I'm going to name him Alexander, so I can always remember the night of his birth."

Jane didn't need a constant reminder of last night. Sleeping curled up in Grayson's arms would forever be embossed on her soul. She would never forget. Ever.

Jane had been so intent on the conversation—and lost in her thoughts—she hadn't paid attention to where they were going. Grayson pulled into the dirt parking lot of the Redmond airstrip and stopped. The 'airport' could be described as an asphalt strip, a dirt lot for parking and a windsock. There was a plane here now—that was a new addition. As was the 'hanger' which consisted of a corrugated metal structure just big enough to shelter the little plane.

The Jeep eased to a stop and Grayson turned it off. She looked at him with a brow raised in question. He smiled and reached over to tap her lightly on the tip of the nose.

"While you were off getting a college degree, I got my pilot's license."

Hopping out of his door, he was around and opening hers before his words sank in. "Wait a minute," she said, "you're gonna fly us around in that thing?"

"Yep."

Her head darted around so fast, in search of fuel stations, she nearly gave herself whiplash. "What about fuel? I mean you can't just fly on a wing and a prayer."

"Trent takes care of that for me. He takes care of a lot of things for me."

"Because he's your friend?"

"Because I pay him really well." He grabbed her hand and led her toward the plane. "And because he's my friend. There isn't another guy alive I trust more than Trent."

Jane felt like she was in some kind of really surreal dream. She was sitting in a plane with a headset over her ears and the only person that would hear her if she spoke into the microphone at her mouth was Grayson. They were at the end of the airstrip and the engines roared in protest and Grayson urged them airborne.

Jane's stomach jumped as the wheels lifted off the ground. She wasn't afraid to fly like Nate was. She smiled as she thought of how he'd react to this experience. He'd probably start crying like a baby.

When the plane leveled out, Grayson reached over and took her hand from where it was white-knuckled on her lap. "You okay? You're not afraid to fly, are you? I guess I should have probably asked. I didn't even think—"

She squeezed his hand. "I'm fine. I have to admit that I'm a little nervous ... but that doesn't seem to be anything new when I'm around you." As soon as the words left her mouth she wanted to suck them back and then bite down hard on her tongue for confessing too much.

He chanced a quick look at her and Jane thought she saw hurt in his eyes. "You're nervous around me?" he asked when his eyes were locked on the front windshield again.

"No. Of course not," she lied. "We're just a couple of old friends catching up."

"We're more than old friends, Jane."

Not wanting to let the conversation progress any further on the track it was going, Jane blurted, "Do you think you could take Nate up in this thing?"

The muscle in his jaw jumped, but he didn't react further to her derailing the conversation train. "Sure. Would he like that?"

"No." She laughed out loud, a guffaw that ricocheted around the cabin. Grayson started to chuckle too. Jane's sides ached and tears ran down her cheeks. "He hates ... to fly," she gasped.

"I don't understand. Why would you want me to give him a ride?"

"He gets all freaked out whenever we get on the plane. He cracks every bone in his body. He rolls his head on his neck." She giggled some more and used a hand to stifle it. "He has a whole ritual he does for take-off and landing."

Grayson's expression hardened, the muscle jumping in his jaw. "You seem to know a lot about your photographer."

"We spend a lot of time together," she answered. "You did know he's happily married, right?"

His face softened a bit. "I didn't know."

"I planned Roxy's birthday party." The next words burst from her mouth before she could censor them. "Believe me, Nate Hughes is not the man I dream about at night."

The corner of Grayson's mouth quirked and his brow rose. He glanced over and his eyes twinkled with mischief. "Who *is* the man you dream about at night, Janie?"

Sweat broke out on her brow, under her arms and between her breasts. She cocked a brow at him and grinned back, challenging him.

"A girl has to have secrets, Grayson. That's one secret I'll never tell."

TWICE HE'D STRUCK A NERVE WITH JANE. Both times Grayson had to nearly bite his tongue off to keep from forcing her into furthering the conversation. He knew that he made her nervous. Hell, she made him nervous, too. Every time she was near him, he forgot how to speak in full sentences and his thoughts turned to the things he wanted to do to her—with her.

He flew in the direction of the Redmond Lake, which was nothing more than a pond that grew wider with the spring run-off. The thing that made it famous amongst the local teens though was the submarine races. More than one of his buddies had been busted by local law enforcement while making out with their girlfriends. Grayson had managed to avoid that kind of embarrassment.

She laughed and pointed down. "Oh my gosh! It's really not very deep, is it?"

"No. Have you ever been there?"

"Who hasn't?" she answered, a little too defensively.

"You?" he guessed.

"I have too." Still on the defense.

Color seeped up into her cheeks, making her even more adorable. She was always beautiful, but man, put jeans on those long legs and pull all that brown hair back and Grayson fought the need to drool.

She was still looking out her window when she admitted softly, "I went swimming there a couple of times when I was a kid, but never to make out."

She sounded so disappointed. He, on the other hand, couldn't be happier about the fact that no other guy he knew had kissed her lips.

Or had they?

"Who was your first kiss?" he blurted.

She whirled around in her seat and stared at him, open-mouthed.

"I'm just curious." He shrugged. "Mine was with Lizzy Mortenson in second grade."

She laughed a little, the soft chuckled made louder through his headset. She looked at him and made a point to roll her eyes with added exaggeration. "That doesn't count. When and with whom was your first *real* kiss?"

"Last night," he heard himself say without a second of pause.

The smile died on her face. Her entire body went stiff and she settled back in her seat, turning to stare out the window. By all appearances she was relaxed, but Grayson could tell by the set of her back that she was far from it. She was rigid with tension and it had been two little words that slipped from his tongue that had done it to her.

He would not apologize for them. He meant them. Kissing Jane last night had been better than any other kiss prior to it. Unwilling to push her further he continued to fly around their small community. There was no need to point anything out; she knew all the landmarks as well as he did.

Eventually she would learn to trust him. He hoped.

THE RODEO GROUNDS IN SALINA LOOKED SO small. The cemetery where her grandparents were buried looked so peaceful. She would like to see it in the summertime when the grass was green. They flew over the high school and Jane could see the faded white lines from a long ago played football game.

There were so many memories that accompanied this town. Good ones ... and bad ones. Mostly they consisted of wanting the boy who didn't realize she was alive except for the brains that would help him ace whatever class he needed help with. Back then, she'd jumped at any chance to spend more time with him, even if they were only talking protons and neutrons or subjects and verbs.

Before long they were back at the airstrip and with expertise Grayson brought the plane to a safe landing. Jane stood at the doorway of the hanger and watched as Grayson did a final check of the plane and locked everything up. He dropped the padlock and it clanked against the metal it kept secure.

He walked toward her with long, purposeful strides and Jane's heart jumped up into her throat. She was frozen where she stood, her eyes locked on his. He grabbed her hand in his and tugged her against him. She went willingly, although a little stiffly. She loved the feel of his chest, so hard and solid, against hers. He pressed a quick kiss to her forehead.

"Did you have fun?"

She nodded, holding tightly around his waist. He was so warm. She leaned her head against his shoulder and reveled in the feel of having him so close. When the time came for her to walk away, it would be moments like this that she would cherish forever.

"Where are we going next?" Her voice was shaky and she inwardly cringed. There was no reason to give Grayson more ammunition to use against her. It was bad enough that he was making forward statements like his first real kiss being the one they shared last night. She hadn't been able to figure out what kind of game he was playing. She had to admit that whatever it was, he was playing it really well.

"I was thinking we could stop by the drive-in and get some burgers."

"You're gonna let me eat in your Jeep?"

"Hell, no," he said with a laugh. "They've added a new dining room for people who don't want to eat in their cars or take their dinner home."

Ten minutes later they were seated *inside* the drive-in. He led her to a table that was tucked back in the corner, which wasn't visible from the door or from the windows outside. Of all the tables in the place this one was the most secluded.

Jane wondered for a moment if he was embarrassed to be seen with her. Her stomach flipped; it was high school all over again. She was just getting ready to excuse herself to go to the bathroom when Grayson reached across and took her hand.

"This is my usual table." He squeezed her hand reassuringly, and pointed to a small plaque that read: 'reserved for Grayson Pierce'. "Most people are good to just leave me alone, but sometimes an out-of-towner strolls in and thinks they can interrupt my dinner because they need my autograph. That's when Bailey added some extra walls to hinder the view of this table."

"Why would he...?"

Grayson laughed and shrugged. "He just likes me, I guess. But what's not to like?"

"I've been asking myself that same question," she muttered.

Dinner went fairly smoothly. She and Grayson talked about everything—and nothing. Bailey made an appearance, making sure that they were happy with their burgers. The now-elderly man still stood over six feet and was built like a brick shithouse. His abdomen was now soft and had a paunch, but his shoulders were still wide enough to warrant going through doorways sideways.

"You remember Jane Alexander?" Grayson said.

Bailey stood back and stared at her. "My, my, you are truly a beauty," he said. Jane blushed as he continued to stare. "You are now as beautiful on the outside as you always were on the inside." He turned to Grayson. "She's too good for you, my boy."

"I know," Grayson said, smiling.

"It's good to have you both home. Dessert's on me. Apple or cherry?"

"Cherry," she and Grayson said at the same time.

Bailey grinned, shooting an approving look between them. "I'll send it right out."

BY THE TIME THEY GOT HOME, JANE WAS exhausted, not necessarily physically either. Emotionally, she was drained. She and Grayson had fallen into an easy togetherness that both thrilled and terrified her.

Both of them changed into pajamas and plopped down into a chair in front of the TV. Grayson reached across and plucked her hand out of her lap. His hands were much larger than hers—

and so much warmer. A fire crackled romantically in the fireplace. The lights from the tree twinkled brightly. They sat in companionable silence, until finally Grayson released her hand and shot to his feet. His fingers formed a fist and he cursed under his breath.

"What's wrong?" Her adrenaline shot through the roof.

He spun his arm in the shoulder joint like he was a big, handsome windmill. "My damn arm's asleep." He sucked a breath in through his teeth in a hiss, and then massaged his upper arm.

Then the remodeling began.

Grayson lifted the tiny table from between their chairs and put it against the far wall. With no effort at all he moved her recliner until it was side by side with his. He eased her back into her chair and sat down himself, taking her hand in his once again, as if nothing out of the norm had happened.

Jane though couldn't get over what had happened. He'd literally rearranged furniture so that they could sit closer. And yet it still wasn't close enough for her.

They watched KHB's ten o'clock newscast. After the weather, he yawned. "Is it okay if I turn it off?"

She nodded. "Yeah. I'm kinda tired."

"What do you want to do tomorrow? I know you haven't been home in a while. Is there anything special you want to do? Anything you want to see … from the ground, I mean?"

His question surprised her. She didn't have any idea what she wanted to do. She'd assumed that Grayson had their entire time together planned out. Obviously not.

"Um … I don't know. Can I get back to you in the morning?"

"Sure thing." He stood and offered his hand. She took it, and hand in hand they went up the stairs. He paused outside her door. There was not enough oxygen on the planet as he stared down at her. Only their hands touched, but she felt the heat from that minimal contact through her entire body.

"Good night, Jane. Sleep well." He lifted their joined hands and kissed the top of hers. He heaved a sigh and dropped her hand. "I have to stop there or I'm afraid I won't be able to stop."

And with that, he turned and went in the door down the hall.

11

JANE WASN'T SURE WHAT TO THINK OF GRAY-son's final comment before he left her standing alone outside her bedroom door. Confused—and totally aroused—she went inside and closed the door behind her. Dousing the lights, she climbed into bed and stared at the dark ceiling.

She was all too aware that only a few feet down the hall Grayson was attempting to sleep as well. Or maybe he drifted off as soon as his head hit the pillow. She doubted it though.

There was no denying the chemistry between them. His statements were blatant and obvious, even if she was too chicken to believe them.

He wanted her.

Jane just wasn't sure for what.

When they were alone, he said all the right things. Did all the right things. But when she wasn't looking, when she wasn't expecting it—and they had an audience—Grayson turned into a man she didn't know. A man she didn't *want* to know.

She wanted to trust him. Heck, she wanted to do way more than just trust him. She wanted to leave her bed, walk down the hall and climb into his. And do a whole lot of *not* sleeping.

Was that the thing that would cause the change in him again? She had heard of more than one man who was charming right up until the 'I do's'. Was Grayson not very good at maintaining the good guy façade, letting it slip?

No, she decided. Grayson was a good guy. Wasn't he? Was there a trigger for his bi-polar act? She shook her head. As far as she could tell there was no real trigger that brought it on.

Thoughts tumbled in her mind until at some point her eyes closed and she drifted into dreamland.

+++

SHE WOKE THE NEXT MORNING WITH THE sheets wrapped around her legs and most of the pillows lying on the floor.

She hadn't slept *peacefully* last night.

As if the sheer force of wills it took to keep her eyes open wasn't a good enough indication. She stretched and tried further to convince the rest of her body that it was time to wake up.

She had no idea what to put on the itinerary for today. What would they do? What did she want to see?

The questions had just crossed her mind when she knew exactly where she wanted to go. She hurried to get showered and once again dressed in jeans—she liked her jeans—and a white, long-sleeved t-shirt.

The scents of bacon and eggs made her mouth water as soon as she'd opened her bedroom door. She hurried down the stairs, hearing the pop and sizzle as the food cooked. She paused in the doorway that led into the kitchen and admired the view.

Grayson stood at the counter, his back to her. His butt filled out the jeans he wore. Apron strings hung down from his waist, tied in a sloppy bow.

"What can I do to help?" she asked.

He turned and she burst out laughing at the big red lips with the phrase 'kiss the cook' written in white across the black apron. His gaze dropped to the object of her amusement and a smile spread to his lips.

"Instead of laughing, why don't you do what it says?"

By the cocky gleam in his eyes, he thought he was extending a challenge she wouldn't take. He was wrong. She walked right up to him and, with a hand on each cheek; she kissed him full on the lips. What she didn't expect was for him to wrap his arms around her and pull her close. He deepened the kiss, his tongue slipping between her lips. He tasted of mint and desire.

She wanted to lose herself in the kiss but, as Grayson last night, she couldn't start something she couldn't finish. Grudgingly she pulled away from the kiss and gave him a quick, chaste one to soothe any hurt feelings. Before he could comment on her retreat, she said, "How can I help?"

He motioned toward the fridge. "Can you grab the orange juice and the butter, please? And the bread from the pantry?"

She did as he asked then she went about the task of making toast. Grayson's kitchen was awesome; it was well lit and modern and useful. Jane's own kitchen was tiny. It worked, since she usually only cooked for one—and the oven was only used to bake cookies (the frozen ones from the dairy section).

KISSING JANE WAS SOMETHING THAT GRAYson would never, ever be able to get enough of. He loved having her in his arms and her lips against his. He'd been half teasing when he all but told her to kiss him. Never did he imagine she would. The girl was really good at it, too! Even now his body was still trying to recuperate.

Grateful for the apron that concealed just how much he was affected by their kiss, Grayson put the bacon and eggs on plates and slid onto the stool next to where Jane was seated at the counter. She held out the plate that held the toast and he peeled a piece of the top. It crunched between his teeth, the melted butter oozed onto his tongue and he nearly moaned out loud.

"You like?" she said with a laugh.

"You make good toast."

"Yeah, I'm a gourmet chef." She smiled and lifted a forkful of eggs to her mouth.

"No, seriously. Not everybody can make toast."

She swallowed. "It's kinda hard to mess up bread and butter."

"You'd be surprised," he told her.

They ate in companionable silence. When her plate was empty, Grayson drained his glass and asked, "Do you know what you want to do today?"

She nodded, looking shyly at her plate. He reached out and took her hand, squeezing it gently.

"Jane?"

"It's been years since I've been home." She chewed on her lip and Grayson waited for her to continue.

Minutes ticked by.

Grayson had to bite on his tongue to keep from urging her to say something. Whatever was going on in her head wasn't ready to make its way through her lips. Hard as it was, he waited. And waited.

She kept her eyes diverted from his when she spoke again, "I'd like to visit ... my grandparents."

A tear slipped from her eye as she blinked. Grayson knew why she was emotional and he knew where her request would take them. He wanted to pull her into his arms and comfort her pain away. It took nearly more self control than he had to keep from doing just that. Or from wiping her tears away.

"Of course." He squeezed her hand again, thankful that he was able to at least touch that much of her. Then a thought occurred to him. "Would you...? Jane?"

For the first time in many long minutes she looked at him. Her green eyes glistened with unshed tears, making the color even more vivid. She looked so fragile, so very vulnerable that Grayson wanted to protect her—forever.

"Would you rather ... go by yourself?" he asked quietly. "I can wait here, if you'd be more comfortable—"

"No. I'd like—" She rubbed her cheek with her napkin. "You asked what *we* should do today. Me and you. Unless you don't want to go."

He put an arm around her shoulders and pulled her into him. She leaned against his shoulder. Her body was stiff against his. He gently rubbed her back and she relaxed into his hold.

"Jane, I would be glad to take you to the cemetery. Which one?"

"Pioneer Cemetery. That's where Grandpa wanted to be. It's where his grandfather is buried." She chuckled a little and wiped at her nose. "I think he was a little nostalgic."

"Most old people are," he said, and she smiled. Her eyes flicked up to his and they twinkled with her amusement. "Why don't we get this all cleaned up and we can get out of here."

"Sounds good," she said, getting up and gathering the plates.

WHEN JANE BROKE DOWN SHE'D EXPECTED Grayson to run or make fun of her. Instead he'd been so tender that the tears nearly overwhelmed her. His strength emanated through his hand into hers, supporting her in ways she couldn't explain. She was grateful for that support—and she would need it again this afternoon.

They stood side by side, doing dishes. There was a fancy schmancy dishwasher, but both of them had decided that doing them by hand would be more fun.

Actually Jane wasn't sure how much *fun* the task was. It'd been a chore when she was growing up. But right now, with Grayson doing the rinsing, she enjoyed it—even with the tense unspoken mood swirling around them.

Jane hated the down-in-the-dumps feeling that hung in the air, especially since she'd caused it. She bumped his hip with hers and grinned when he returned the gesture. Pulling his hand from the rinse water, he put it on the back of her neck, soaking her shirt from the inside out.

She squealed and slapped at him with her wet hand, leaving a perfect handprint on the front of his shirt.

"Oh!" he yelled, cupping his hand and dousing her with the warm water.

In a flash she flipped the faucet on and fisted the nozzle. The water rushed out and sprayed in his face. He roared and Jane laughed, waving the water up and down to cover him. He advanced on her, stalking her. She backed up until her back met the counter and she was at the end of her hose. The water was still spewing from the faucet, covering the floor, the counter—and them.

With his arms holding her tightly against him, he turned off the water and kissed the tip of her nose just as a drop of water slid down her cleavage.

She was still giggling when he kissed her again. This time on the lips. Her body reacted immediately to him. She wasn't alone though, she felt that he was affected as well. He heaved a long sigh and held her away from him. His gaze dropped to her chest and he grinned.

Water and white make a bad combination.

Her bra was clearly visible through the damp fabric, her nipples poking through the lace. She blushed. He smiled even wider. She used her arms to cover up. He handed her a dishcloth and she covered her chest.

"I'd be happy to help you get dried off," he said through a smirk.

His willingness to help made her stomach flutter. If she didn't get out of here, she might take him up on his offer. "Thanks, but I think I can handle it myself."

FOR A SPLIT SECOND, WITH WATER DRIPPING from his nose, Grayson wondered if Jane was going to let him help dry her off. He saw the moment of indecision flash through her eyes, but it had lasted only a second.

As he watched her leave the room and heard her footsteps retreating up the stairs Grayson was finally able to breathe again. The playful side of Jane made her all the more attractive. He would live to make her laugh like that again.

Today's outing didn't have much potential of being a laugh-fest.

He hurried up the stairs, his thoughts on the woman behind the door he rushed past. He changed as quickly as he could and was waiting in his recliner when her bare feet padded down the stairs. She held her shoes and socks in her hand, her fingers curled in the heels of her Skechers. Her toes were painted a faint pink that reminded him of sea shells nestled on a white sandy beach.

"Ready?" she asked, plopping down in the chair that had become hers.

"Yep, just waiting on you." Her perfectly arched brows rose and he smiled. "But I've already waited fifteen years, Jane—" Her gasp was almost silent and Grayson didn't even so much as pause in reaction. "—I can sure as hell wait a few minutes while you put your shoes on."

She didn't react other than to bend over and begin tugging the white cotton over her feet. Her shoulders were tense though. When he'd asked her to come, and when she'd surprisingly agreed, Grayson decided that he was going balls-to-the-wall. Jane was the woman for him. He'd known that years ago. He was going to do something about it now.

Grayson Pierce didn't like to lose.

When it came to Jane he was in it to win it all. To win her.

She stood and brushed invisible dirt from the thighs of her jeans. "Well, you don't have to wait a moment longer. I'm *finally* ready."

Grayson's brain didn't register that he'd moved until he was up, out of his chair, and had Jane in his arms. His face was a breath from hers.

"I would wait until the end of time for you, Janie." He kissed her lightly on the lips. She sighed into his mouth and Grayson's self-control held on by a thread. He broke their kiss and rested his forehead against hers.

Jane stood still as a statue, her arms around his waist, her forehead against his, her eyes closed. He raised a finger and stroked her cheek. Her skin was so soft and he loved that she wore little make-up when it wasn't needed for work. When she was doing her job, her freckles were barely visible. Now, he could see every one of them.

He was just about to press his lips to those freckles that dusted her nose when her eyes flicked open and she sighed again. This time it sounded frustrated.

"We can't keep doing that," she muttered under her breath.

The words were like a dagger through his heart, but he buried the hurt and said, "Sure we can. Let's go," he added before she could start a discussion on the pros and cons of their kissing.

As far as he was concerned there were no cons, but was pretty sure Jane didn't see it that way.

When they were buckled into the Jeep, Grayson started the engine and headed in the direction of Pioneer Cemetery.

THE GATES OVER THE CEMETARY WERE FAMiliar to Jane. As a kid she'd loved to come with her parents and run through the headstones, finding ones that had names that she recognized. She knew exactly which ones belonged to her people. She knew Grandma Annie was Grandpa Alexander's mother. She knew the story of how Grandma Annie and Grandpa Caleb had come to the Salina.

The cemetery was a big rectangle with roads that cut it into smaller rectangles. Grayson drove to almost the exact center and stopped. He shifted into park and cut the engine. He didn't say anything, neither did she. Her throat was tight. Her eyes burned with the need to cry.

She wasn't sure why she was reacting the way she was. Her grandparents had been dead for years. Some days, though, she missed them so much; her grandpa's words of wisdom—*"Keep the shiny side up, oily side down,"* he'd say, waving from the porch while she got in her car—and Grandma's cooking.

A tear slipped from the corner of her eye and she brushed it away quickly, embarrassed. She reached for the door handle and Grayson cleared his throat.

"I'll just stay here," he said quietly. She looked at him and he smiled, jerking his head in the direction of the door. "It's okay, I'll be right here if you need me."

His eyes were so kind and understanding another rush of tears pushed at the dam in her tear ducts. She shouldn't be so emotional. What the hell was wrong with her?

"No, I'd like you to go with me," she heard herself telling him.

He smiled and opened his door. He was around at her door, helping her out before she could come up with a good explanation as to why she didn't just agree to leave him in the car.

When his hand curled around hers, swallowing it in the strength of his grip, she was grateful he was with her. She hadn't thought this would be as hard as it was turning out to be.

He held tight to her hand as she led him over the frosty crust on the dormant grass. Her feet moved of their own accord, knowing the way. Jane and Grayson walked past headstones that had been in the cemetery since its inception, big ones that were a monument to the person resting beneath it.

When they finally stopped in front of her grandparents' headstone, Jane was numb. But not from the cold.

She didn't deal well with death.

Grandpa used to tell her that *"there are only two sure things in life; death and taxes."* She was pretty sure Grandpa hadn't coined the phrase, but knew that it was true. However sure as they were, Jane hated both; death had a way of ruining your day ... and taxes, well taxes just sucked!

Grayson squeezed her hand. "You okay?" he asked softly.

She nodded, not trusting her voice. She let go of his hand and went down on one knee brushing her gloved fingers over the marble that told the birth, death and marriage dates of the people she loved. A tear slipped down her cheek and hit the marble, making a dark spot.

"Tell me about them," Grayson said, dropping to his haunches next to her.

"You knew them," she answered, unable to look at him.

"Not the way you did," he said.

Jane wanted to protest. When her mouth opened, though, she told him about Grandpa's theory on marriage. "He used to tell me," she said then dropped her voice to mimic her grandfathers, *"'You should always remember one thing, Janie, my girl,'"* he'd say, *"you can marry more in five minutes than you can make in a lifetime."*

Grayson chuckled. "I'm loaded, ya know."

Jane did know and ignored yet another thing that made him perfect. "Grandma just laughed at him and would tell me, *'That's true, dear. But instead you* should *marry for love and live happily-ever-after. That's what I did.'* Then she would kiss his bald head. They were so in love, even to the end. Did you know that Grandma only outlived him by a few months?"

"I heard that," he said. "I'm sorry I wasn't here for the funerals. It was during the season and I was on the road."

"I know," she said. It had been the only way she'd been comfortable enough to come to the funerals.

"Tell me more about them," he prompted.

They sat on the frost-covered ground and Jane told story after story of her grandparents. She laughed as she spoke. Her heart felt lighter, *she* felt lighter. They weren't touching but Jane had never felt closer to a person in her life. She stood, surprising him, and took his hand.

"Come on, I wanna show you the rest of my family tree."

She led him through the cemetery, telling him the stories she'd heard from the time she could walk the circuit of stones. "Grandma Annie was supposed to marry someone else, but she ran off and married Grandpa Caleb as soon as she turned sixteen. Can you imagine?" She turned to him, her hands planted on his chest. "I was so not ready for marriage at sixteen. I guess they did things differently back then. Anyways, Grandma Annie and Grandpa Caleb took his horse—which was about all he owned—and went to City Hall in Gunnison and got married. Their parents were *pissed*. In fact, hers disowned her."

"And his?"

"I'm sure it wasn't pretty. I do know that they weren't exactly thrilled, but eventually they accepted the marriage and helped them. Caleb's father gave him a corner of the family farm and told him that now he had a wife and needed to provide for her. They worked hard ... and made it."

Grayson nodded, his eyes intense when he looked her full in the face. "Marriage is hard work."

"Yes, but it's easier when you have the kind of love they had. My family is known for fighting for true love, Grayson. I come from a long line of happily-ever-after."

The corners of his lips lifted and he kissed her lightly. "I wouldn't ask you to settle for anything else."

12

When Jane woke up the next morning all she could think of was the events of the last few days. She'd gone from hating Grayson—or pretending to hate him—to acknowledging that she'd never stopped loving him and never would. She was adult enough to admit her feelings to herself, but there was still too much water under the bridge to voice them to him. She still wasn't sure she could trust him, especially with her heart.

She stretched and sighed. She felt light as a feather. The smile on her face grew until her cheeks hurt. She peeled back the blankets and started to get ready for the day. All the while remembering...

Last night after they'd come home from their adventures, they'd had a quick dinner and then settled into the recliners to watch some TV. She'd been surprised when he tossed her the remote.

"Pay-per-view channels are in the one-hundreds. Pick out a movie."

"You're pretty brave."

"Hey, I'm not such a guy that I can't do a chick-flick once in a while."

But Grayson was a guy, a very, very handsome guy, who did very dangerous things to her heart. She flipped through her choices and clicked on a horror movie. She hated horror movies. They scared the bejeezus out of her. The movie started and her heart matched the *thump, thump, thump* of the theme music.

Two minutes into the movie the scary dude jumped out with his chainsaw and Jane shrieked, jumped, and popcorn fell from the sky like snow.

Grayson chuckled and reached over, pulling her into his arms, into his lap. "Come here, baby, I'll protect you."

She didn't doubt that he would protect her from monsters and things that went bump in the night, but could he protect her from … him?

Another roar of the chainsaw and Jane opened her eyes to discover she was fully entwined in Grayson's lap. Her fingers gripped his shirt. His arms held her firmly against the strength of his body. With her head against his chest, the steady beat of his heart was a comfort and her eyes drifted closed.

She'd awoken to the gentle jostling as he stood. She shifted, expecting him to set her down. Instead he'd cradled her closer to him and murmured in her ear, "It's okay. I've got you."

Once her head was on the pillow, he pulled the covers up over her and kissed her softly, chastely on the mouth. "Good night, baby. I'll see you in the morning."

It felt like they were a married couple, except that she still slept in the guest room. He didn't offer to change that fact, and Jane wasn't sure how she'd react if he did.

Was that what his game was? To make sure she was so hot for him that when he offered to slake her need, she'd jump at the chance.

Well, Jane would not jump. No matter how hot she was, she promised herself she would not make that jump.

Not that she was delusional.

Grayson would never let things get that far.

She was just coming out of the shower when a knock on the door made her jump and cross her arms over her bare breasts. Thankfully the door stayed closed, but Grayson's voice did come through it.

"Dress warm, baby. We're gonna be outside most of today."

"Okay," she yelled back, allowing her arms to drop only when she heard his footsteps on the stairs.

She dressed quickly—and warmly—and met Grayson in the kitchen. It was rich with the smell of breakfast. As she rounded the corner the kettle squealed. Freshly squeezed orange juice sat in a pitcher on the island, as did two bowls, two spoons and two glasses.

Grayson smiled when he saw her. "Did you sleep well?"

"I did. Did you?"

Something flashed in his eyes; desire, regret? He nodded. He poured some water into a larger bowl and began to stir, slow at first, then quickly.

"I did. Are you hungry?"

He was on the other side of the island from her, wearing his 'kiss the cook' apron. She sat on a stool and put her feet on the footrest. He took her bowl and scooped some Cream of Wheat into it. She fought the cringe and smoothed out her expression when she felt her nose wrinkling. She hated Cream of Wheat. Her mother had made her choke it down when she'd been a kid. It was like eating paste.

Yes, she had eaten paste in kindergarten. To be honest, the paste had more flavor.

Grayson put one bowl in front of Jane and one in front of the stool next to her. He came around the counter and sat down. He started shoveling the food into his mouth. He paused, spoon midair.

"You okay?"

"Yeah, fine." She braced herself and lifted her own spoon to her mouth. Her gag reflex was already preparing to purge the food from her system. She slipped the spoon between her lips, swallowed and ... sighed in bliss. "What did you do to this?"

His brows furrowed. "What do you mean?"

"It's good. I mean, really good. What did you do to it?"

He laughed and took a big bite. "A little butter ... and sugar. Lots and lots of sugar."

After her first spoonful, Jane didn't speak again until the spoon scraped the bottom of the empty bowl. "That was delicious."

"Thank you." Grayson winked and pointed to his apron.

She leaned across and kissed him on the cheek. "My compliments to the chef."

They made quick work of the dishes and she followed Grayson to the front door. Grayson put a vest over his long-sleeved flannel shirt and tucked a jacket under his arm. Jane put on her coat, but didn't zip it up. They were both wearing winter boots and Grayson put a scarf around Jane's neck, using it to pull her into a quick kiss.

She liked the familiarity they'd developed. But it scared her to death.

Before she could dwell on it for long, she was being led out the front door. Stepping outside caused Jane to pause. Instead of Grayson's Jeep waiting to whisk her away to destinations unknown, an enormous gray Dodge Ram was attached to a horse trailer with matching paint job.

"Where are we going?"

"It's a surprise," he told her. "And we have to do it today because a big storm is blowing in tonight." It wasn't the tone of his voice that made her skeptical; it was the wide grin on his face. He hadn't shaved this morning and the dark stubble along his jaw made his already breathtakingly handsome face heartbreakingly gorgeous. She wanted to feel the rough rasp of his whiskers against her hands, her lips ... every inch of her body.

She shook her head and climbed into the big truck. It had a bench seat. She imagined herself sliding over and sitting right next to Grayson, his arm behind her as they cruised through town.

Maybe she *was* delusional.

Neither of them said much—probably because Jane was too lost in her disturbing imagination—as they drove up Willow *Crick* Canyon. It'd been a long time since she'd heard creek pronounced crick, even longer since she'd been up the canyon. Grayson drove as far as the snow would allow, then unloaded the horses.

Jane got on a chestnut colored mare. Grayson fixed some padded chaps around her legs. "There are warmers in these. You should be nice and toasty. Let me know if they get too hot." He tugged at the one on the other side. "I have something up the canyon that I really want to show you. But you give the word and we'll turn around, okay?"

She nodded, even more curious than she was before. As Grayson got on his horse, Jane patted the neck on her own horse and asked, "What's her name?"

"Georgie," he said with a shrug. "That was her name when I got her. She's a good horse, really gentle."

"And his?" she asked, motioning toward the buckskin horse with his black mane and tail that carried Grayson.

"This is Zeus. And he can be every bit as ornery as the dude he's named after." He patted Zeus on the neck and clucked, putting his heels into the horse's flanks and headed out.

Grayson was right; she was toasty warm with her padded chaps and parka. He'd given her a black hat that matched his. She wondered how many he had in his stash of winter clothing. She was just about to ask when he stopped. She'd been alone with her thoughts, asking a question here or there, for the most part of the ride. She hadn't even realized that nearly an hour had passed.

He dropped from his horse and walked over to help her. It had been a mild winter and the snow only came halfway up her calf. He tossed the reins over a branch and took Jane's hand in his. He led her through a maze of trees. "It's right over here."

She loved these trees; quakies, they were called by Utahans. Aspens, the rest of the world called them. They were known for their white trunks and vibrant green leaves that snapped with the breeze. She missed that sound now.

In winter, the branches were bare, stretching toward the sky like skeletal claws. The trees were also used as a form of graffiti. Lovers ventured up the canyon to carve their initials in the white bark that turned black, making the words stand out.

One held the mark "*K.H. + S.K.R. '70*". Another said "*Tim + Kris 4ever*".

"This way." His grip tightened on her hand. He was walking like he knew exactly where he was going. And in fact he did. "Close your eyes," he said, stopping suddenly. She did and then his gloved hand covered them. "I've gotcha. Right this way."

He helped her as she shuffled around to where he wanted her, holding her up when she stumbled over something. She heard him take a deep breath and felt it, damp and warm, on the back of her neck as he exhaled.

"This is it."

Whether he spoke to her or himself, she couldn't be sure. His fingers dug into her arms through her coat. He took a step closer to her and his front met her back. She sensed his nervous tension; it almost crackled in the air around them. His anxiety made hers spike to a nearly nuclear level.

His lips brushed her ear. "I've always wanted to be honest with you. The time has finally come to do just that."

She swallowed hard, but the knot in her throat made it hard to breathe. Did she really want the truth out of Grayson? She wasn't sure she wanted to hear that he didn't find her attractive. Or that he'd asked her to prom to humiliate her in front of their classmates.

On second thought, she didn't want to know.

She was just about to explode when he took his hand away and whispered, "Open your eyes, baby."

She wanted to—and at the same time, she really didn't.

What if this was bad? She was good at the whole ostrich impression.

Her fight-or-flight instinct raged. And right now, as she stood with Grayson at her back, she wanted to run. Run away from him. Away from this sick game he was playing. Away from the heartbreak that was going to devastate her at any moment.

"It's okay, Janie. I promise. It's okay."

She wasn't sure whether it was his heartbeat or her own that was erratically pounding away. Actually, as his arms reached around to pull her back to his front, she realized it was both of their hearts, thudding in worried unison.

But why was he worried?

She slowly, hesitantly opened one eye … then the other. She meant to look up at him in question, but couldn't make her gaze move from the sight before her. There, on the tree in front of her, were words she couldn't wrap her mind around.

"Grayson loves Jane"

Grayson loves Jane?

Grayson loves Jane! Those three words were from a fantasy. This couldn't be reality. She even reached up to pinch herself—and it hurt.

She wondered where the punch-line was. Where was the audience who was going to, at any moment, jump out and point and laugh as Grayson reneged on this declaration?

She wrenched herself out of his hold and glared up at him. His chocolate eyes studied her as her hands made their way to her hips and her feet parted to stand in defiance. She hoped she looked formidable, because inside she felt ... broken.

"I'm out of here!" She stalked passed him, making sure to ram her shoulder into him. It hurt—not that she'd give him the satisfaction of rubbing it—and hoped that it hurt him too. "I don't know what kind of game you're—"

In a flash she was no longer walking. She was suddenly airborne, twisting and turning in midair. The flight instinct turned to fight in an instant. She squirmed and slapped and punched and...

It wasn't until Grayson kissed her that she stopped. She didn't want to fight that. She wanted to get lost in him.

Suddenly, he dropped her to her feet, still holding her close. She could feel every inch of him through the many layers of clothing that covered them both. He kissed her lips, her forehead, her eyes, her tear-streaked cheeks. Once again he led her to the tree—their tree.

"Look, Jane." From behind her, he reached out and traced the characters encased by a heart. "You keep accusing me of playing a game. I'm not playing, sweetheart. I've never been playing. Look at the letters."

She did look, with her eyes and with her fingers. She traced over the letters, noting how they were a dark black among the stark white. Every swipe of her fingers seemed to carve the letters into her heart. Her vision blurred and her nose began to run. She sniffed.

"When...?" she asked.

It hadn't been recently. The tree couldn't lie. New carvings were thin lines that grew wider and darker as time went by. The words *Grayson loves Jane* were almost an eighth of an inch wide and black as night.

Her fingers trembled as she traced over the letters again. "When ... did you...?" She turned to face him, wanting to see his face when he answered her next question. "Was this somebody's idea of a joke?"

He tugged his glove off and shoved it into his pocket. His fingers were warm as they stroked the side of her face from temple to chin.

"No joke. Senior year, I carved this the week before prom. I planned on showing you then, but you cancelled and I..." His voice broke and he cleared his throat. "Why did you cancel on me, Janie?"

His eyes were glossy and full of such unashamed honesty that caused her own to sting anew. She leaned into his gentle touch and decided on the truth. "I heard you, Grayson. I heard the real reason you asked me to prom."

His brows pinched and he shook his head. "The *real* reason? I don't understand. This—" He waved at the tree. "—is the *real* reason. I have been in love—"

She stopped him by putting her fingers to his lips. "You lost a bet, Grayson. I heard you admit that you asked me ... because you lost a bet." Her

voice wobbled and her cheeks turned into miniature riverbeds.

"Jane, I don't know what you heard." When she
opened her mouth to argue with him, he held up a
hand to silence her and continued. "I don't doubt
that you heard what you think you heard. Nor do I
doubt I was stupid enough to say something like
that, not knowing that you were in earshot. I was
too chicken to admit to anyone how much I loved
you ... because I didn't know how you felt about
me. But it's true. I loved you then. I love you now.
And I've loved you for all the years in between."

She took another look at the declaration carved
for the world to see and turned to look at him, de-
fiant. "Prove it."

Did he ever!

He kissed her hard on the mouth. It was almost
a punishment in its intensity. His arms shifted
around her and pulled her tight against him. His
hands moved down until they cupped her rear and
fitted her against his groin. There was no mistaking his reaction to her and it seemed that that was
the way he wanted it. He was proving his attrac-
tion to her. But love?

"I love you," he whispered, spreading kisses to
the tender skin below her ear. "I love you," he re-
peated, nudging her collar away from her neck
with his cold nose. "I love you," he shouted, sending critters scurrying for cover.

She giggled, her entire body melting against
him. There was nothing she wanted more right
now than to feel those hot mind-bending kisses all
over her body.

"Let's go home, love." He shook his head and
chuckled softly. "I have wanted to call you that for
so long. Man! It feels good to know that you know
how I feel about you." He stopped abruptly and
took hold of her upper arms, his hands firm even

through the fluff of her coat. "Please tell me you feel something for me. If you don't love me *yet*, I'm willing to help you see the light."

"Well, I ... It's not that I don't love you, it's just—"

"I can wait," he assured her. "As long as you know how much I love you." He laughed again, a loud bark. "I love you, Jane Alexander."

He picked her up in his arms and spun around, holding her tight. He seemed sincere. Very, very sincere.

In this moment, though, she couldn't bear to consider a future with Grayson. Because if that future didn't come to pass, it would obliterate her only hope for happily-ever-after.

And from what she could tell, talk was cheap.

.

13

GRAYSON WALKED THROUGH THE HOUSE like he owned the place. Because he did. He loved all the perks his reputation brought. Take this house for instance, or the Mustang he drove or the sexy sportscaster that would soon be standing in front of him.

Jogging up the stairs he stopped at the first doorway. A smile spread to his lips when he heard the bathtub turn off. He thought of all that ivory skin, pink from the heat and damp from the water, and got hot himself. Using the palm of his hand he shifted things around beneath the denim at is groin and wasn't sure he could wait for Jane to be ready before he slaked his need—the first time.

Patience was not his strong suit and by damn he'd been more than patient with her. It was time for her to give him what they both wanted.

Silently he twisted the knob and slipped into her room. Soft splashes sounded from the bathroom and he sauntered through the bedroom. He leaned against the jamb and licked his lips.

Holy hell, she was beautiful.

Bubbles covered her most tempting parts, which made the scene before him even more erotic. One of her long legs was propped up on the side of the tub. Her toes painted a pink that was only a shade or two darker than her own skin tone.

He wondered if she'd let him suck them.

JANE TRIED TO TELL HERSELF THAT STAYING in the bathtub, buried to her ears in bubbles, was only to warm up from their ride. She knew she had to talk to Grayson. He'd been brave, confessing his feelings for her, and she was a coward. She needed to find her big-girl panties and be honest with him.

She wasn't sure she could though. Mostly because she wasn't exactly sure what her feelings were. She was well aware of how she wanted to feel about him. But there were too many loose ends, too many unanswered questions to commit to him.

When her fingertips and toes began to prune painfully, she unplugged the tub and stepped out onto the plush brown rug. The air in the bathroom was thick with humidity, which was really an accomplishment since she'd left the bedroom door open. Jane wondered if she could simply open her mouth and drink her daily supply of water.

She dried her hair and was just wrapping the towel around her torso when a masculine clearing of the throat brought her head around. Grayson was in the doorway, leaning against the jamb with his arms crossed over his chest, and he was leering. His eyes were flat as they roamed over her body. She shivered and it wasn't because of the cold. The hair on the back of her neck stood on end. Her smile died on her lips.

"Lookin' good, Jane," Grayson said.

GOOD ENOUGH TO EAT, HIS THOUGHTS CONTINued. He planned on devouring every delicious inch of her—starting with those edible pink toes and working his way up.

She clutched the towel to her chest until her knuckles whitened. It was too late. He'd already seen those perfect boobs. Some doctor had earned every pretty penny. Maybe Grayson would send him a bonus—and a thank you note. The MD hadn't expected to be doing Grayson Pierce a favor, but that was the way of things, wasn't it?

His tongue snaked out and licked his lips as he imagined that it was Jane's soft skin he tasted. He eased up from where he'd been leaning against the jamb and cracked his knuckles. He smiled at her and her frown deepened. Her eyes narrowed and she tipped her head to one side. Her mind had recognized the difference. In that moment, he knew that *she* knew his secret.

Not that it mattered.

He would take her whether she wanted it or not.

He was Grayson Pierce and the world—and this exquisite woman—belonged to him.

ALARM BELLS BLARED IN JANE'S HEAD. THIS whole scenario was wrong on so many levels Jane couldn't begin to name them all. Except that they all centered on the man standing in the doorway. She scanned the room for a weapon. *How easy would it be to get the towel rack off the wall?*

He stepped toward her and she stepped back, bringing her against the counter. His grin was victorious as he moved closer. Closer. And even closer.

She could feel the heat of him. He smelled like sweat and liquor and lust. A dangerous combination. A combination that was so *not* Grayson Pierce. When he invaded her personal space, Jane put her hand on his chest, pushing him away, and was startled by the rate of his heart. There was no increase, no violent pounding. Just a slow and steady thumping that meant he was in total control of his emotions.

"You need to leave," she informed him.

He laughed, a low, mocking bark. "I'm not going anywhere, sweetheart. Everything in this house belongs to me—including you."

"I don't think so," she said, surprised at how calm she sounded.

"But it does." He ran a fingertip over her cheek. "How would feel about getting my name put on your back permanently. I don't like the idea that you can take off my jersey when you feel like it."

"Get out!" she screamed.

"No." His expression was tranquil as if he didn't have a care in the world. His eyes were flat and emotionless as his hand moved down, quick as a shot, and roughly dragging her towel away from her body. He licked his lips ... and that was when Jane verified what she'd already known. No scar.

Considering that she was standing naked as the day she was born, her voice was surprisingly calm as she said, "You're not Grayson."

That made him stop short. He actually stepped away from her and grinned, rubbing his goatee. "Sure I am."

He was certainly close. But *close* only counted in horseshoes and hand-grenades. "No. You're not."

His dark eyes narrowed, sparking with animosity. "What is it about Grayson that makes you *think* I'm not him?"

"You. Are. *Not*. Him!" she screamed as he reached for her. She jumped back, crashing into the wall behind her. The towel was on the floor at her feet, but reaching for it would make her vulnerable. Taking her eyes off of Grayson—or whoever the hell he was wasn't an option. "Don't you *dare* touch me!"

He advanced, rubbing his hands together. "Oh, I'll do more than simply touch you."

"Derek!" a voice growled, low, serious, dangerous. "Back away!"

And then *he* appeared—the softer, truer version of Grayson Pierce. The *real* Grayson Pierce.

She blinked, her eyes darting from one Grayson to the other. Her heart would know him anywhere, even as her mind tried to piece together the double-vision.

Derek's eyes raked over her body in a way that made her feel dirty. She reached down and yanked the towel from the floor, clutching it to herself. A thousand questions whirled through her head, but now was not the time to ask them. Because A; she wasn't sure she could find her voice, and B; she didn't want to miss anything by interrupting the confrontation.

"You need to leave, Derek," Grayson spat. His hands were in fists at his sides and the muscles in his jaw jumped violently. "You need to get the hell out of my house. Now!" he roared, grabbing the front of Derek's shirt and yanking him into the bedroom.

"We had a deal." Derek held up his hands, and used a tone that suggested Grayson was the volatile one.

Maybe he was, Jane thought as Grayson's hands uncurled, only to once again form fists.

"Yes, we *had* a deal. It's done. Over. I don't want you living my life anymore. I'm gonna live *my* life, *my* way from now on."

"Hey, I didn't realize she was off limits," Derek said with a shrug. "I guess I've gotten used to the whole what's-mine-is-yours way of things. Sorry man, I meant no disrespect." He looked at Jane where she stood in the doorway to the bathroom. "Unless … do you think you could handle both of us?"

Grayson's fist met Derek's jaw with a satisfying crack. Derek stumbled back and crashed into the banister, cursing up a blue streak. "Dude! What the—?"

His profane question was cut off as his foot slipped on the top step and he tumbled and thumped his way down the stairs.

Grayson turned to her, his face a whirlwind of emotions. "Are you okay?"

She nodded. Truthfully, she wasn't. Not completely at any rate. She wasn't sure what the hell had just happened.

"I'll be back," he told her. "There's a lot that I need to tell you."

"Obviously," she muttered as he left her standing in nothing but a towel.

She ran over to the window and eased the curtains aside just enough to see the front yard. A silver Mustang she didn't recognize was parked next to her Mazda. The two Grayson's came into view and she saw as the one dressed in flannel threw the one dressed in silk against the hood of the Mustang. She couldn't hear what they said, and her first thought was that it was too damned cold to open the window.

"Oh, screw it." All she needed was a crack to hear the raised masculine voices.

"The whole world already thinks I'm you, I could kill you and take over your life permanently."

"Over my dead body," Jane announced to the silence around her. She wrapped the towel around her body again and headed for the stairs. She barely registered running down the stairs and wrapping her hand around the shotgun that had been propped next to the door.

But there she stood, on the porch, clad in only a towel, holding a shotgun.

Annie Oakley had nothing on Jane Alexander.

It wasn't the first time she'd held a gun—she was actually a pretty good shot—and filling Derek's butt with buckshot wouldn't be the first time she'd put lead into flesh. After all, opening day of the deer hunt meant a day off of school.

The two men were rolling around on the ground, exchanging powerful, cracking punches. Derek stood and bent his leg at the knee. He was going to kick Grayson, she knew it. She would have allowed the fight to continue, if it'd been fair. Derek obviously didn't know the meaning of the word.

The *click-click* of the gun froze the scene before her.

Derek took a step toward her, hands held up. "Come on, honey..."

"Don't *honey* me, asshole! I heard you threaten to kill the man I love and I will not allow that to happen. Get the hell out of here before I decide to give you a new career as a sieve!"

Grayson stood. He was breathing heavy and holding his abs but looked no worse for the wear. With narrowed eyes and clenched teeth, he threw a set of keys at Derek. "Consider this your final payment. Stop dying your hair, shave your face and go back to your old pathetic life. If I so much as catch wind of you infringing on mine, I will put your ass in jail."

Derek sputtered something, but in the end had no retort. He cursed vilely. "You haven't seen the last of me."

"Yeah. I have. Now get out of here."

With flying middle fingers, Derek got into the car and, sending mud flying, he made his exit. Grayson hooked an arm around her waist and, pulling her close, kissed her hard on the mouth.

"I need to make sure he leaves. Give me a minute and then we'll talk, okay?"

She nodded, feeling a little detached and kind of cold. The adrenaline had worn off and she had the fleeting thought that it was all too bizarre to be real.

"You sure you're okay?" he asked, kissing the tip of her nose.

"I'm okay." She sounded robotic.

"We'll talk ... then you will be." He turned toward his Jeep but stopped. "One more thing. I need you to do me a favor—" She nodded again. "Have clothes on when I get back or I won't be able to think—about anything else but ... yeah, be dressed."

She grinned like a fool as he jumped into his Jeep and tore off after his look-alike. Remembering the events of the last few minutes confused Jane. Her mind spun out of control. She'd witnessed the entire disconcerting episode but couldn't quite believe what she'd seen. For a split second when she'd seen Grayson—or Derek, she guessed— standing in the doorway, her heart had fluttered with anticipation. Then her heart had fallen to her toes and lurched to a halt. Her subconscious had known it wasn't Grayson. It'd taken a few seconds for her brain to catch up. Even now, she couldn't put her finger on exactly what gave him away.

Which brought her thoughts full circle—what the heck?

There were two Grayson's. Obviously. But why?

It didn't make sense.

As she dressed in yoga pants and an oversized sweatshirt, Jane wondered if anything Grayson could say would explain away what she'd just witnessed. Hell, she'd been willing to commit murder to keep Grayson safe.

She brushed out her hair and pulled it into a sloppy ponytail. She didn't apply make-up. What was the point? She was who she was, and if Grayson truly loved her, like he said, then he'd better get used to seeing her *au naturel.*

He was in the kitchen when she came down the stairs. He turned around and stopped, just watching her. The look on his face was contrite and worried and a hundred other emotions all warring for dominance.

"Where should we do this?" His voice was short and he held up his hands. "Rewind. Let me try that again. I don't want you to be on the defensive at all. I want you to be completely comfortable." He closed his eyes and heaved a sigh, then opened his eyes again and attempted a smile. "Where would you like to do this?"

She smiled a little. "Where would *you* be most comfortable?"

He took her by the hand and walked into the living room, rearranging the chairs by pulling hers to a stop directly in front of his. She sat in what had become her chair and he sat in his, her knees inside his. He sucked in a deep breath and blew it out slowly. "What do you want to know first?"

She didn't pause for a second before blurting, "Who the hell is he?"

"His name is Derek Reese. That doesn't tell you anything, so I'll start with the *why.*" He didn't wait, just plowed on. "I wanted to play ball. I didn't want to be followed around by the paparazzi. Not that they really cared about Grayson Pierce. I was a nobody. It seemed that the media was annoyed by my squeaky-clean persona. My agent said that I needed to get drunk. I don't drink. Never have."

She knew that was true. It'd been a huge selling point for every mother in the county. As if Grayson just being Grayson wasn't enough.

"I was told that I needed to date anything in a skirt. To womanize and get myself on the cover of the tabloids with a popular woman." He laughed and shook his head. "It wasn't until our picture showed up that I—me, Grayson Pierce—did what they wanted. And then I was mortified. I was worried for you." His long, blunt-tipped fingers shook as they plowed through his hair. "I don't want you in my life because of the image our relationship will give the world.

"Janie, my heart has been yours for as long as I can remember. I will do everything within my power to protect you and your reputation."

"That's all fine and good, Grayson, but you forget … I've known you for too long. I know what the name Pierce means to you. You wouldn't just let some loser smear it to get your name on the latest and greatest *shoe*."

"You're absolutely right." He smiled and lifted her hands to kiss her fingers. "I told them no way. I insisted that I would do things my way. It worked out just fine. For a while. Until the paparazzi figured out where I grew up. Until they swarmed Salina like locusts."

"Where are the seagulls when you need them?" They both laughed, remembering the story from their Utah History class; Pioneers planted crops. Locusts swarmed and ate the crops that meant the people would starve. They prayed and seagulls came and ate the disgusting bugs.

"No kidding. I don't like being the center of attention but was happy to be thrust in the spotlight if it meant I could do what I love." His face grew weary. "When they camped out on my mother's front lawn, they'd gone too far."

Damn her, but that explanation made perfect sense. Grayson would do anything for his mother, including being a total ass in front of the world. And that knowledge made her fall even harder for him.

Her brows narrowed, as did her eyes. "Why... if you've really loved me since high school, then why..." Her throat tightened. "Why didn't you track me down before?"

He took a deep breath, gathering her hands in his. "Janie, you broke my heart."

Her heart lurched and tears stung her eyes.

"There now." He rubbed a thumb on her cheek. "I'm not trying to guilt-trip you. I'm just being honest." He leaned forward and kissed the tip of her nose. "For a few years, I avoided you because of my ego and I was afraid..." His voice cracked. "I was afraid you'd shoot me down. When I saw you in the locker room—"

He tugged her forward and his lips met hers. His kiss was passionate; hard and gentle. His tongue licked over the seam of her lips and thrust into her mouth. Her arms flew around his neck and held on tight. She met him kiss for kiss, devouring every bit of his passion. Hard fingers plowed through her hair, biting into her scalp. She moaned into his mouth and tried to keep some semblance of sanity.

She had to stop this now or she'd have to ask the rest of her questions naked. "Wait," she panted.

He stopped abruptly. His breath sawed from his lungs, hitting her face in warm minty puffs. "I'm sorry."

"Oh, for hell's sake ... don't be sorry!" She laughed and pressed a quick chaste kiss to his lips. "I'm just not done talking yet."

They sat there, breathing heavy and staring at each other. Finally she asked, "Tell me about when you saw me in the locker room."

His eyes twinkled, his hands tightened on hers. "When I saw you, I wanted to grab a hold of you and never let go. That's why I had to come and see

you that night. And when you opened the door—"
He laughed and brought her knuckles to his lips.
"—I couldn't help myself. I had to hold you."

She felt his kiss in every nerve-ending. Heat
flooded her bloodstream. She reached up and
cupped his jaw in her palm. "So what now?" she
asked breathlessly.

"I don't know." He sighed deeply and closed his
eyes, keeping them pinched, he asked, "Can I hold
you now?"

She didn't have to be asked twice, because the
truth was she needed to be held. She needed to
feel the comfort that only being close to him could
offer. He opened his eyes and seemed shocked as
she climbed into his lap. "Don't ever let me go."

"Never." His embrace was tender. They were
quiet, just listening to the other breathe. She
leaned back to study his face. Her fingertips
moved slowly over his goatee and eased them back
to rest over his scar. "I'm sorry about this."

He chuckled and she both felt and heard the
deep, dark rumble. "Don't be. It was an accident."

"I know."

Junior year, she'd been his tutor. He'd dropped
his pencil, they'd both bent to pick it up and the
top of her head met his lip. It split open and blood
had spurted in an arc. Luckily it hadn't needed
stitches and the scar it'd left was sexy as hell, as
far as she was concerned. Not to mention that
more than once she'd had the overwhelming desire
to kiss it better.

She'd replayed the scene again and again over
the years and had wished that they'd met lip to lip
but, alas…

"Well, I never said that I was sorry and I should
have. Because I am." She snuggled back into his
hold and just absorbed him into herself. It felt

wonderful and perfect and scary. "How can you possibly love me? You don't even know me."

"Oh, I know you, Janie. And I *do* love you." He stood and gently deposited her in her chair. She wasn't sure how many hours they'd spent watching television and couldn't understand how she'd missed the bookcases on the ends of the table that supported the TV. He pulled a photo album out and brought it over, gathering her in his arms before settling in the chair again.

He opened the album. On the first page was a picture of her. It was from graduation. She was the out of focus and it was the unblurred person watching her in the foreground that caught her attention. Grayson was watching her, adoration obvious on his face.

The next page was an article she'd written for the *Daily Trojan*, her college newspaper.

Page after page Jane saw herself as an outsider looking in.

"This isn't technically my handiwork."

"Your mom?"

"Yeah, she always thought we were perfect for each other. She sent me copies of everything in this book. No matter where I was or what I was doing in my life, Mom made sure that you were always in my thoughts. Not that I minded," he added with a grin. He turned the page, revealing a publicity photo from KHB. "So, I know exactly who you are, Janie. You are the woman I love with everything that I am."

She couldn't believe what she was hearing. Yet, she couldn't *not* believe it. It all made sense. Knowing Maude Pierce and her determined attitude when it came to her son, Jane had no doubt that everything Grayson told her was the absolute truth.

"Now I have a question for you," he said, his fingers playing with her ponytail.

"Really? It seems you know everything about me." She dropped her eyes to look at the book showcasing her life as evidence.

He smiled. "Yes, except the most important thing. I want to know what's in here." He placed his large palm flat against her chest, directly over her heart.

She gulped, her throat constricted. Her fingers wrapped around his hand, holding it to her heart. Closing her eyes, she opened her mouth and launched the truth into the air.

"I am crazy about you. Head-over-heels, can't-sleep-at-night-without-dreaming-of-you, honest-to-goodness in love with you."

He yanked her to him, hugging her so forcefully that the air flew from her lungs. And so relentlessly that she couldn't breathe. "Then I have one more question." He released her just enough to be able to look at her eye to eye. "Will you marry me?"

"No."

A deflated expression crossed his features before he schooled them. "Can I ask why?"

She put her hands on his cheeks, cradling his face. She leaned down and kissed him ever so gently. "Grayson, I love you." She laughed. "Wow! You're right; it does feel good to say it out loud." She kissed him again. "I love you so much, but I love the guy I knew way back when. I need to know who you are now. I need to know that who you are is really who you are."

He looked at her, completely perplexed.

"Ya know, the whole time I've known you—the adult you—I've gotten this whole back and forth insanity—"

"That wasn't me."

"I know." She kissed him. "Really, I do know that deep down in my heart, but my head is going to take a little longer to convince."

"But you love me?"

"Yes."

"Then sit back and enjoy the ride because I can't wait to show you the man I really am."

She laughed as his lips met hers. "One more thing."

"Okay."

"I don't want anyone to say that I'm using you—or our relationship—to further my career."

"Nobody will—" He stopped himself, knowing that even as she opened her mouth to protest that her contradiction would be the truth. He held up a hand. "Fair enough. We'll take it slow. We'll introduce our love to the world slowly, so no one can make accusations that will have any merit. Deal?" He stuck out his hand.

She brushed it aside and said "deal" just before sealing their deal with a passionate kiss.

He scooped her into his arms and all but sprinted up the stairs. His bedroom was next to hers—the one he'd given her, she corrected. Her bedroom had a more feminine feel. This one was wholly masculine; from the enormous lodge-pole, king-sized bed and matching dresser to the dark browns and forest greens and the bear rug on the floor.

With a sensual movement of his hand, he removed the band from her hair. He kissed down her neck before coming back to meet her lips with ferocity. The insecure little girl buried deep inside her wanted to pull away. But she *wasn't* that little girl anymore. Jane was now in the arms of the man she loved, the man who loved her and she wasn't going to deny herself anything anymore.

"I know I said we'd go slow..." he said between kisses.

"Don't you dare!" And she kissed him, bruising his lips for even suggesting such a thing.

Giving herself to Grayson with no reservations, they made love until dawn colored the horizon.

14

GRAYSON AWOKE TO THE SOFT WHISPERS OF breath blowing over his chest ... and was content for the first time in years. He'd slept so deeply that he hadn't even dreamt.

Dreams? HA! His thoughts laughed at that. He had no use for dreams anymore. Back in the day he'd had two dreams; play professional baseball and marry Jane Alexander.

Jane hadn't agreed to marry him yet, but she would. After her eager lovemaking last night Grayson knew it was only a matter of time. The connection between them had been like nothing he'd ever experienced. Grayson hadn't been a virgin when taking Jane to his bed last night, but he had to admit that his knowledge was limited to only a few encounters. And being with Jane had blown all those other experiences out of the water. Nothing could compare. Sex really was better when you loved the woman you were with.

She was lying with her head on his chest and one leg on his thigh. His arm drew her even tighter, using his hand on her bottom to fit them flush. She sighed, her breath blowing the wisps of hair that darkened the space between his pecs. Her arms snaked across his chest and she hugged him to her. There were few ways she could be any closer to him. He smiled, loving the feel of her against him. It was a feeling he was sure he would never tire of.

Even as he held her, feeling content, fear and worry crept into his thoughts, clawing through the bliss. The dread could be summed up in one word: Derek.

Grayson closed his eyes and refused to let his evil alter-ego into this moment. He bent to kiss the top of her head and let his fingers toy with the ends of her hair. He really was a lucky bastard. The smile on his lips widened as he thought of just how lucky he was. He was ready to take his name off the 'eligible bachelor' list. Jane wasn't ready to announce that they were together to the world.

When he did the interview with her, he would say he was off the market. Let her do what she would with the information. Maybe the declaration would end up on the editing room floor, but he would throw it out and see how Jane handled it.

As for today, as soon as Jane woke he would make love to her. They would shower—and maybe make love there, too—and then they would take a trip to visit the 5 and Dime. He grinned. His mother was going to freak. Her greatest desire for her son was that he be happy and she didn't believe he could do that without Jane in his life.

Now that he'd had a taste of what life would be like with Jane in it, Grayson had to admit that his mother was absolutely right. He just wasn't sure if he would admit that to her.

JANE COULD DEFINITELY GET USED TO THIS. She smiled, savoring the scents and sensations of waking up in Grayson's arms. He smelled like masculinity epitomized, so good that she flicked out her tongue to taste his skin.

He flinched and she giggled. "Are you ticklish?"
"Nope."

She kissed him on his side, near his ribs and he chuckled softly, his muscles tensing.

"Are you sure about that?" she asked.

"Okay, maybe a little." He took hold of her hand and moved it lower. "If you're hell-bent on tickling me, I've got a much better place for you to tickle."

"You're incorrigible."

He chuckled softly. Quick as lightning, he flipped her on her back and hovered over her, the muscles of his arms flexed with the effort of holding himself up. His eyes flashed with mis-chief. His brow rose in suggestion. His lips lifted for a moment before that smirk met her lips. He pulled back and his eyes smoldered, the playful Grayson gone. Heated, intense, passionate Grayson taking his place.

"I may be incorrigible, but you're beautiful. And you're mine. And I have a lot of time to make up for. Get ready, baby doll, I have a busy morning planned."

She smiled and leading his lips to hers murmured, "You'd better get to work then."

MAUDE PIERCE HAD BEEN WORKING AT THE 5 and Dime for nearly thirty years. She worked the early shift, opening the store at nine and working until noon. She didn't really *have* to work at all. The three hours a day was her way of visiting with her friends and catching up on the gossip. She knew that Grayson had a woman at his ranch.

She tried not to be irritated by the fact that he hadn't bothered to tell her or to bring the girl by so that Maude could meet her. He *was* a grown man after all. But she was his mother. The least he could do was give her a heads-up so she didn't have to hear the rumors through the gossip of the town.

While straightening the shelves near the rear of the store the tiny bell attached to the door signaled that someone had entered. She glanced up out of habit but couldn't see because of the height of the shelves. They weren't all that tall but they were just enough taller than she was to hinder her seeing the door.

"I'll be right there," she called.

"It's me," came the reply.

"Grayson!" she yelled. She couldn't help the smile that formed on her lips. Grayson's presence did that. He was such a good boy, taking care of his mother. She rushed around the shelves and stopped short. He wasn't alone. Instead of feeling let down, her heart soared. "Jane."

Jane Alexander had been Maude's pick for Grayson from the time the girl hit puberty. Maude had known that she would be a beauty. Maude loved being right. Unlike the girls who had the world by the tail in high school, Jane used the challenges that came in high school to develop a strong perseverance that would be a compliment to Grayson's drive.

Maude had watched while Jane was teased and tormented. Maude heard the whispers from Grayson's friends, and Maude smiled when Grayson defended the sweet girl in the braces with frizzy hair.

"Hello, Mrs. Pierce," Jane said, stepping forward to meet the hug Maude was prepared to give her. "It's so good to see you."

"It's been too long, sweet girl." Maude patted Jane on the back and sighed. Whatever the reason for Jane coming home Maude didn't care. She was back where she belonged, and judging by the smile of Grayson's face and the adoration in his eyes, things were good between them. Giddiness rushed through Maude, nearly causing a hot flash. She giggled and smothered it with her fingers when Grayson shot a look at her.

"So Jane, what brings you to Salina?"

Color flushed her cheeks and Grayson chuckled softly. He eased next to her and wrapped an arm around her waist. Jane melted into his side and looked up at him. Was that love in her eyes? Did Maude dare hope?

"Your son made me an offer I couldn't refuse." Jane laughed lightly and playfully jabbed an elbow into Grayson's side.

Maude raised a brow. "Oh? What kind of offer?" she asked, purposely dropping her gaze to Jane's bare ring finger.

It was Grayson's turn to flush. Jane shook her head and stuffed her left hand into her pocket. "I'm a sportscaster now and—"

"I know, dear. At KHB. I just love that Kate Spencer. Is she as pretty in person as she is on television?"

Jane smiled. "Even prettier. Kate is a very sweet person."

That made Maude happy. So many times people weren't who they appeared to be. Take Grayson for example. She hated how the media portrayed him. She guessed she understood his reasoning for hiring that Derek idiot. Maude hated the idea, but would much rather have some other man being an ass—She inwardly sighed at the curse word, but it was the only appropriate word when considering Derek's antics.—than her son doing the acts himself.

Maude shook her head to clear it and asked her question again, "What kind of offer did Grayson make you?"

"An exclusive." Jane once again glanced up at Grayson and smiled.

Maude wondered if Grayson would tell Jane about Derek. As far as she knew the only people who knew were Grayson, his agent, his coach and his mother.

Grayson leaned down to brush his lips on Jane's forehead and Maude nearly sighed out loud. Jane's eyes drifted closed and her sigh was audible. Maude waited, unwilling to interrupt their sweet moment, until Grayson lifted his gaze back to her. She smiled approvingly, knowing that Grayson would know exactly what she was thinking. *Well done, son.*

His smile answered, *I'm glad you approve.*

Maude realized that Jane was looking from Grayson to Maude and back again. Maude asked her son, "Tell me ... you're giving her an exclusive. What is she giving you?"

"A week," they said in unison. They laughed and Grayson pulled her into a hug. Maude wanted to do a happy dance, seeing the love that was so obvious between them.

Jane was still laughing when her feet met the floor. She met Maude's questioning glance and said, "He said if I would come spend a week with him—without my computer and phone," she added with a glare at Grayson, to which he grinned. "At the end of the week he would grant me an all access interview."

"How many more days in the week?" Maude asked.

"Two," Jane answered, sounding a little melancholy.

A gentle jingle of the bell announced another customer and Maude looked up to see who'd come in. "Give me a bit," she said.

"No problem, Mom," Grayson said, not looking at her as she walked up to the front of the store.

"SHE LOVES YOU," GRAYSON WHISPERED INTO Jane's ear.

"It's good to be loved by a Pierce."

He pulled her into his arms until she fit tightly against his chest. She could hear his heartbeat thumping steadily in his chest. He dipped his head and kissed the sensitive spot just below her ear.

"When I get you home," he purred the seductive threat, "I'll show you exactly how good it is to be loved by a Pierce."

"Promises. Promises." She attempted to tease him, but the words came out as a breathless, suggestive whisper. Her legs were the consistency of Jell-O and she was grateful for Grayson's strong hold on her. She wondered if anyone would notice if they just started making out in the rear aisle of the 5 and Dime.

Grayson's lips met hers in a bruising kiss. His tongue slipped between her lips and she answered his call. His hands dropped down her back and gripped her rear hard, fitting her groin firmly to his. She moaned ... then groaned when Maude cleared her throat from behind them.

Her cheeks flamed with heat and she knew they were the color of the Christmas bows on the shelf next to her. She buried her face in Grayson's chest. His arms held her to him, offering support. Instead of embarrassment though, the man had the audacity to think the situation was funny. His amusement was a deep rumble beneath her ear and he shook as she clung to him.

Jane slapped at his chest and glared up at him. Feeling like a total idiot, she turned to face the mother of the man whose tongue she was just having for lunch. Instead of reproach though, Maude's face was ablaze with approval.

"I would say 'get a room' but I'd prefer you were married before you—" She dropped her voice and stepped closer. "—have sex."

"Mom," Grayson snapped.

She lifted her narrow shoulders in a shrug. "What? Life happens in a particular order; birth, puberty, marriage, sex, babies, death. There are a few more things that happen in there, but you get the idea. I love that you are in love—" She paused when Jane choked. "Oh please, I can see it as plain as the nose on my face. Are you going to deny it?"

"No," Grayson said honestly. "I love Jane Alexander," Grayson shouted, the words bouncing off the bricks of the little store. "But Mom, don't push this. You and I can see it, but Jane's not ready to admit her feelings yet."

"What if I don't *have* those feelings?" she teased.

"You do." Grayson dropped a kiss to the top of her head and pulled her against his side. "It's okay, love. No pressure. Love me in silence if that makes you more comfortable. But don't ask me to hide my feelings for you." He turned her in his arms and dropped his forehead to hers. "I love you, baby. I will never tire of saying it, nor tire of you hearing it. I. Love. You."

The only answer she could offer was to stretch up on her tiptoes and kiss him. She did love him. There was no denying it. And she hoped that he never tired of saying it because she wanted to hear those words from his lips every day, every minute for the rest of her life.

Suddenly, she remembered the audience that had interrupted them. She stiffened in his hold and jerked her head around to see … an empty aisle where Maude had left them to their moment.

Grayson took her by the hand and led her to the front of the store. "Mom gets off in ten minutes. Are you up for lunch at her house?"

"Um. I guess."

"It'll be fine. Truth is I should be the nervous one. You know the scrapbook she made for you?" When she nodded he continued, "I've got one for every year of my life. Would you like to see what little Grayson looked like on the day I was born?"

Jane burst out laughing. "Has he changed much?"

SWEAT DRIPPED DOWN GRAYSON' PITS AND HE had to keep wiping his palms on his jeans. When he'd made the suggestion of spending the afternoon with his mom, it'd sounded like a good idea to let the two most important women in his life bond.

Yeah, well, he was seriously reconsidering the wisdom in that!

The two of them were sitting on the leather couch in his mother's living room. Their heads were together over a scrapbook. They'd been going through them for three hours. Each one containing embarrassing pictures, but it was the mortifying stories that they shared that had him wanting to dig a hole and crawl inside.

Jane laughed, pointing to a picture from when he was six. "He really stuck a Lego up his nose?"

"Yeah," Mom answered, amused. "See that bump? That's it. I had to take him to the hospital to get it out." She shook her head and glanced up at Grayson. "He cried like a total baby."

"Do you think he'd cry now?" Jane asked, stifling a giggle with her long, manicured fingers.

He narrowed his eyes at her, not at all amused. "I'm not stupid enough to stick it up my nose to begin with."

Jane turned the page and laughed. And laughed. And held her sides and laughed some more. She fell back against the pillows and wiped at her eyes. "What happened?"

He knew exactly which picture she found so amusing and bit his lip to keep from laughing himself. He didn't want to encourage her.

Mom pointed to the picture of Grayson with his face painted in various shades of blue and green and purple. "That was Grayson's Picasso stage. I found him in his bedroom with markers around him on the floor. He had my mirror propped against the wall and had painted his face. When I asked why he'd done it, he informed me that he hadn't."

The two women laughed while Grayson glowered at them.

"I told him that he was the only one there and then he told me that a phantom marker guy did it. And that I'd just missed him. If I hurried maybe I could catch him in the yard, 'cause he just jumped out the window." Mom shrugged. "I *might* have believed him if he hadn't had the same colors smudged all over his chubby little hands."

"So what happened?" Jane asked him, tears of amusement shone on her lashes.

"It wouldn't come off," he groaned. "I had to walk around for days until it wore off."

"How did I miss it?"

"It was summer," he said with a shrug. "And we were in first grade. You probably wouldn't have remembered it anyway."

"Oh, I would have remembered *that*." She looked down at the picture and another fit of laughter bubbled out of her. Seeing her so carefree made Grayson's heart fill to nearly bursting. He had to admit that her laugh was the greatest sound in the world. Actually, no ... the greatest sound she made came in height of passion when she screamed out his name.

Mom slid the album into Jane's lap and stood. "Are you hungry? I can throw something together."

Grayson shook his head. "We're good. I wanted to take Jane out tonight."

"You want to join us?" Jane asked. Damn her for being polite.

Mom smiled, appreciating the offer. The look she shot him said that she knew she wasn't really invited. And that she was totally okay with that. "I'm fine. It's Grey's Anatomy tonight. I can't miss McSteamy." She raised a brow suggestively. Grayson's stomach twisted and he fought the urge to be sick. He didn't like the thought of his mother having those kinds of thoughts. By the twinkle in her eyes, she knew how he felt about her statement. "You kids have fun."

She tugged him into a hug and put a kiss on his cheek. "Hold on to her, Grayson."

"I plan to, Mom. I can't live another day without her."

Mom then hugged Jane. "Don't be a stranger, Jane."

15

WHEN THEY WERE BOTH IN THE JEEP WITH seatbelts fastened, Grayson started the engine. "I was thinking we'd go to Mom's Café. Are you okay with that?"

"Absolutely." Her stomach rumbled its own vote of approval. "I already know what I'm going to have."

"Me too," Grayson answered.

"Chicken fried steak," they said together and then laughed.

Mom's Café had been around since nearly the beginning of time. The place was an old brick building that showed signs of wear and tear on its century old structure. Renovations were done, but rarely and only when desperation called for them, those repairs keeping with the 'old' ambience.

Grayson held Jane's hand as they pushed through the door. A bell announced their arrival and Sally Montgomery looked up from her post behind the counter. She hadn't changed a bit. The elderly woman was almost as big around as she was tall with an apron tied around her middle. Her bright blue eyes widened behind her thick lenses.

"Grayson, it's good to see you again." Those blue eyes narrowed and her mouth fell open a bit. "As I live and breathe. Jane Alexander, you are the most beautiful girl. How are your parents?"

"They're good."

"Good to hear." Her eyes swept over Jane from head to toe and an approving smile graced her lips. "It is so good to see you, dear ... and with Grayson." Her grin grew and she turned to pick up menus. "I'll give you a secluded table in the back."

"We'd appreciate that," Grayson told her.

His hand came to rest on Jane's lower back and she relaxed against it. Jane craved the calm that his touch could bring. His touch could also bring on another slew of emotions, but right now was not the time to think about that.

"Here you go," Sally said, placing the menus on the table. "I have to say that it's a pleasure to see you two nights in a row."

Grayson stiffened as he slid into the bench. Jane dropped down into her seat across from him and tried to remember to breathe. There was no way that Grayson was at Mom's last night. Which meant...

"Can I get you something to drink?"

Before Jane could answer, Grayson said, "A Coke and a Diet Coke with lemon. Thanks, Sally."

"You betcha," she said with a wink and disappeared through a curtain into the kitchen.

Grayson smiled at Jane and took her hand in his. He squeezed it then turned it over to run his fingertips over the lines of her palm. "Did you know—"

"Shouldn't we talk about ... ya know?"

"No. It's fine."

"It's not fine, Grayson." Jane's blood pounded in her temples.

"Jane, don't let him ruin tonight. It's okay."   .

She wasn't so sure, but as he continued to trace the lines on her palm, she relaxed.

"As I was saying before ... did you know that I took palm reading in college?"

Jane felt the edges of her mouth quirking and her brow raise. "Really? Wow. Where did you go to school that they had *that* class."

"It was an elective."

Sally came back with their drinks and slid them onto the table. "Do you know what you want?"

"Two chicken fried steaks."

"Mashed potatoes and steamed veggies okay?"

When Jane nodded, Grayson answered, "Perfect. Thanks."

As Sally walked away Jane turned the conversation back to the topic of palm reading. She didn't buy that he had actually attended a class on the subject, but decided she would play along. "What does my palm tell you?"

"This line," he said, pointing to the line that ran parallel to the top of her palm, "is the love line. You tend to hold your feelings in a tight grip." She felt herself bristle and barely resisted the urge to yank her hand away. He must have sensed her apprehension because he tightened his hold just a bit, running his fingertip over the line, a grin on his handsome face. "But it seems that you're content with your current romantic situation. I'd like to think I have something to do with that."

"Oh, please," she snorted. "Like you can tell I'm happy in my current romantic situation by a wrinkle on the palm of my hand. Wouldn't it be more likely that some other romantic situation made me content?"

He frowned and Jane wondered if the flash in his eyes was jealousy. Was it bad that she kinda liked the idea of him jealous over some past love? She bit her lip to keep from smiling as his frown deepened.

"Have there been many men who have made you feel content?"

"A few," she lied. There'd been one guy, one relationship in college that resembled something remotely serious. It had lasted just long enough for him to get what he wanted, leaving her in a devastated puddle of tears.

"By your heartbroken expression I'm gonna guess those relationships didn't end well."

"Hell no, it didn't end well. You broke my heart." She wasn't sure where the words came from. She hadn't been thinking of Grayson at all. At least not in the you-crushed-my-world kinda way.

He lifted her palm and pressed a kiss to it. "I'm sorry for that, Jane. I will never be able to apologize enough for that."

Now who was the jerk?

"I know. Really, Grayson, I know. I'm the one who should be sorry. You're not the only one who broke my heart. Although I have to admit that the scar you placed there has only now begun to heal."

Her eyes began to sting with tears that wanted to fall and she blinked hard. He half stood and leaned across the table to kiss her lightly. "Forgive me?"

Her insides went all warm and gooey over hearing the words she knew to be the utmost truth. She felt her expression go all wistful and her entire body warmed from the inside out. "You're forgiven."

He grinned ... a little smugly. "Let's make a deal. No talking about former relationships."

"Why?" she asked, lifting a brow. "Whatcha hiding, Pierce?"

"Nothin', honestly. Derek had all the fun. I wasn't interested."

"Because of me?" Her voice rose at the end in hopeful question.

He smiled again. "Because of you."

"Yeah, well, I haven't exactly dated up a blue streak these last fifteen years."

That declaration made his smile spread from ear to ear and Jane rolled her eyes, snorting a bit. He chuckled. "I can't say I'm disappointed to hear that."

"And I can't say that I'm disappointed to hear that you're not the asshole, party-animal the world thinks you are."

"Okay, so ... now we know all that we need to know about our prior relationships. I'm going to pretend that another guy has never so much as kissed your lips and you can pretend that I'm still a virgin."

She laughed. "I thought I made a man out of you."

"Baby doll, you've more than made a man out of me. And I am eternally grateful."

They were both still laughing when Sally came out, a plate in each hand. "It's good to see two young people so much in love. Especially you two. Enjoy." She slid the plates in front of them and walked away.

"What do you think she meant by *especially you two*?" Jane asked Grayson.

He shrugged. "I'm gonna guess it's because she's known us since we were in diapers and I'm grinning like a fool and you're all dreamy-eyed."

That made her grin like a fool. "I love you."

"Love you, too." He picked up his fork and scooped some potatoes. "Hurry and eat. I've got big plans for tonight."

"Do you now?"

His eyes darkened to the shade of dark chocolate and Jane could see the lust smoldering in them. "Those plans wouldn't have anything to do with getting me naked, would they?"

"Now who's the fortune teller?" he asked with a laugh. "Eat."

GRAYSON PAID THE BILL AND HELPED JANE shrug into her coat. His heart was already pounding in anticipation. And it wasn't the only part of him throbbing. Eating had been the last thing on his mind as he sat across the table in Mom's Café—or eating *food* had been the last thing on his mind. Staring at Jane he had all kinds of thoughts about what he really wanted to devour.

They made their way to the door and Sally asked, "How was everything?"

"Yummy," Jane answered. "Just like I remembered."

"Good. That's real good," Sally said. "Don't let it be so long before you come back. And be sure to tell your folks hello for me."

"Will do. Goodnight, Sally."

Grayson waved in farewell and pushed the door open, holding it for Jane to exit. They walked hand-in-hand to the Jeep. Twilight had faded to dusk and dusk to night as they'd enjoyed their dinner. Stars twinkled overhead. Grayson opened the passenger door and she slid inside. He had to remind himself not to race around the vehicle and forced his feet to move at a normal saunter.

Their breath puffed in clouds inside the Jeep, and Grayson shivered. "Damn, it's cold."

"According to Molly we're supposed to get a humdinger of a storm tomorrow night."

A slow, lazy smile touched his lips. He had heard that same weather report and had loads of ideas what to do if they got snowed in. In fact, he was hoping for just that. *Let it snow!*

"Where we goin'?" she asked when he pulled away from the curb.

"It's a surprise. Speaking of which—" He eased back to the curb and tugged a silk blindfold from the pocket of his jacket.

"Oh no you don't," she stammered, shaking her head. "I'm not letting you blindfold me."

He didn't have to feign hurt feelings. "Don't you trust me?"

"Of course I—" He recognized the understanding in her expression as soon as she stopped speaking. She let out a long sigh. She leaned toward him, closing her eyes. "You're right. I trust you."

He wrapped the black silk around her head, covering her eyes. After tying it in the back and waving a hand in front of her face to make sure she couldn't see, he kissed her. Nothing too intense, just a quick peck on her lips. Leaning back just enough so that he could see her entire face, he just studied her face. Her breath was warm and damp on his cheek. He kissed her again. He couldn't resist.

"I love you, Janie."

Without waiting for a response, although he got a quiet, satisfied sigh from her, he paused just long enough for a truck to pass and pressed his foot down on the gas pedal. Mud spat from the back end and it slid a bit before the tires grabbed hold of the asphalt and the Jeep jerked forward, quickly gaining momentum.

"I like a good surprise as much as the next girl," Jane said quietly, "but can I get a hint?"

"Do you like surprises?"

"Usually." She rubbed at the blindfold but didn't try to remove it. "I guess it's not being able to see that's bugging me."

"Good to know. I won't do that again. But will you please humor me this time?"

"If you give me a hint."

"You've never done it."

"Ever?"

"That's what you said." He hoped that he hadn't said too much. He wanted their destination to be a bit of a shock. Or maybe it was what he wanted to *do* when he got there that he wanted to leave her completely flabbergasted.

JANE FELT THE MOMENT THAT THEY WENT from the smooth asphalt to dirt. Even with her mind racing, memorizing and analyzing the twists and turns, she still couldn't figure out where they were headed. Oh good grief, it wasn't like Salina and the surrounding areas were a metropolis and she'd grown up there. She knew nearly every inch like the back of her hand.

A few more bumps in the road had her grabbing hold of her seatbelt and gasping when it tightened to hold her in place. She hated not being able to see, not able to predict the next swerve or rut in the road. Her stomach protested almost as much as her mind. She hoped when they got where they were going that she wouldn't have to vomit all over Grayson's shoes.

His hand took hold of hers where it was white-knuckling the seatbelt. "We're almost there. Only a few more minutes."

"Good. Not being able to see is making me nauseous."

"No puking. That would put a serious damper what I have planned."

"We wouldn't want that, would we?" she snapped, irritated by his amusement over the situation.

Nonplussed, he chuckled. "No love, we wouldn't want that."

He was quiet and after another three bumps that had her shoulder aching—and probably bruised—where it met the belt that was supposed to keep her safe, the Jeep eased to a stop. Jane blew out a relieved breath. Her hands went to the blindfold. "Can I—"

"One more second," he cut her off.

She heard a pop she recognized as a seatbelt being released. Since she was still firmly secured to her seat, it must have been his. Then she heard a soft click—the headlights being turned off? His fingers ruffled at the back of her head. When he spoke it was right next to her ear.

"Keep your eyes closed. Just for a second." His arm brushed her stomach as he reached to release her seatbelt.

She did as he asked, kept her eyes clamped tight, breathing in and out slowly to keep her nerves under control. The Jeep was still on and warm air swirled around her. First thing she was going to do was take her jacket off. Unless they were getting out.

The leather of Grayson's seat squeaked and Jane imagined him shifting behind the wheel. He blew out a breath and said, "Okay, Jane. Look."

It was her turn to breathe. She slowly cracked first one lid then the other. Her brows furrowed as she stared out the windshield. It was dark, except for the moonlight reflecting off the water of ... Redmond Lake.

"You said you've never been here to watch the submarine races. I thought it would be fun for us to see how fast those suckers can go."

Jane laughed a little. She was nervous. She'd never made out with a guy in a car ... in the middle of nowhere. "You mean you haven't ever ... watched the ... ya know."

"Jane, I have never kissed—" He paused and turned to look at her. "I don't think I've even kissed a girl here. But I can't swear to that. I do know that I have never watched the submarine races. There was never anyone—besides you—that I wanted to do that with. Will you—"

She cut him off by launching herself across the console. Her lips crashed into his. Desperation overcame her. She kissed and tasted. His arms wrapped around her and guided her into his lap. She straddled him, her knees on both sides of his thighs, her butt resting on the steering wheel. His big hands rubbed at her rump, both pressing her against him and seriously turning her on.

If she thought she was warm before she was now going to spontaneously combust. She jerked and tugged at her jacket. His eager hands helped peel the heavy coat from her shoulders. Grayson tossed it in the backseat and took her face between his hands. His head angled and his mouth covered hers. His tongue plunged deep into her mouth, giving her an idea of exactly what Grayson had planned. Jane knew it was going to happen right here in the backseat of the Jeep or later in his enormous lodge pole bed, with another part of Grayson's body making the same motions.

Anticipation made Jane shiver.

"Are you cold?" he asked breathlessly.

"No way." She reached out and grabbed his vest. With a swift tug the snaps popped giving her access to his flannel shirt. His eyes were hooded as he watched her prepare to unbutton his shirt. It took every ounce of control she had to keep from just yanking it open. As desperate as she was Grayson nearly thrummed under her.

She undid the top button, letting her fingers brush his chest as she moved down to the next. He sucked in a breath, but didn't react further. Two buttons. Three. And she kept torturing them both until she folded the shirt away, exposing the exquisite muscles of his chest and abdomen. She reached out, letting her fingers stroke the dark hair that dusted his pecs.

He leaned forward to kiss her, trapping her hands between them. His fingers slipped under the hem of her sweater and rubbed at her lower back. They moved forward around her waist and eased up her belly. Cold air hit her stomach and before she could so much as gasp or blink, her sweater was over her head and fluttering to rest in the back seat.

His lips met hers for only a moment before moving to her neck. She tipped her head to allow him better access. Every nerve-ending tingled. His teeth nibbled on her lobe and she nearly came apart by just that simple contact. His tongue flicked out and licked down her neck to nuzzle the sensitive area under her ear.

He sucked and nibbled and licked and Jane threw her head back, drowning in the ecstasy of his attentions. As he pressed his lips to the curve of her breast just above her bra, she couldn't breathe.

She reached down for the button of his jeans ... and froze.

So had Grayson.

There was a noise that didn't belong—a tapping sound.

As she opened her eyes she noticed that light flooded the cab, coming through the driver's window, completely illuminating them. She pressed herself against Grayson. If there hadn't been a cop at the window she would have enjoyed the feel of Grayson's bare chest pressed so tightly to her nearly naked one.

Icy air rolled into the cab as Grayson rolled down the window. "Evening, Deputy Brannock."

A hard, mocking bark of laughter sounded. "Well, well, well. Whatcha doin', Grayson?"

"Come on, Brady, you're a smart guy. You know exactly what I'm doing."

"Yeah, I do. What I'd like to know is *who*." He lowered the light so that it wasn't directly in their eyes.

"The *who* doesn't matter," Grayson snapped. The muscles under Jane tensed and she kissed his neck to ease him tension. He rubbed at her back, easing her as well. While his left arm held her close the right one plunged into the backseat. He shifted under her and she watched as he dug around the back seat, finally coming up with her sweater. He handed it to her and she did her best to slip it over her head without showing off her chest to the cop.

Brady Brannock was a year—or maybe it was two—younger than she and Grayson. He'd been a nice enough kid and even now, in the most embarrassing moment of Jane's life, he was amused.

If she'd been the one with the flashlight, she would have laughed herself silly.

The sweater fell into place and Jane fluffed her hair. "Hi, Brady."

Brady grinned, his gaze darting from Grayson to Jane to Grayson. He nodded, like he approved. Did the whole frickin' town like the idea of Grayson bopping Jane? Jane had to admit she did.

"I'll be damned," Brady said. He raised a hand in a lame wave. "It's good to see you, Jane."

"You too," she said. Grayson chuckled, the rumble vibrating deep in his chest.

"You two do know that it's not cool to be out here, right?" Brady stated with censure in his voice. He didn't wait for a response. "I should give you a ticket for loitering, public indecency ... I could probably stack up the citations."

"But you're not going to."

"No," Brady said quietly, "I'm not. The laws are more for minors looking to get lucky, who are too stupid to be safe about it." Brady shook his head. "Why don't you just get out of here?"

Grayson nodded. "Will do."

"I'm going to leave, but expect that you'll go somewhere more appropriate for this kind of ... extra-curricular activity."

"We sure will, *Officer*," Grayson said, smiling.

Brady leaned in the window and whispered, knowing that Jane could hear him, "You are being safe, right?"

Jane and Grayson both sat in stunned silence, her hips still straddling his, until the headlights from Brady's SUV flashed around and lit the road in the other direction. Grayson started to laugh. So did Jane.

"I have never been so embarrassed," she said through her giggles.

"At least your bra was still on," Grayson noted, his gaze dropping to her chest as if he could see the bra through her sweater. "If he'd been a few seconds later, you would have flashed Brady."

"Yeah, that would have been worse." Her sweater was on backward and after she slid back into her own seat she hurried to turn it around. "It's bad enough that the whole town will know ... Crap! The whole world's gonna know about this, huh?"

His head was bent, his hands focused on buttoning his shirt. "That's not how it works, Jane. The whole town might know by tomorrow morning, but they won't tell anyone."

"Yeah, right."

He turned the lights on and put the Jeep into gear. The bumps were easier to take when she could see them coming. "Jane, the town knows who I am. They don't know about Derek. Hell, they probably think that the paparazzi are just out to get me. You'd be hard-pressed to get information out of them." She raised her brows and he laughed. "Okay, so maybe *you* could. But only because they know you."

"I do plan on interviewing some of them for my story."

"Your story?"

"Yeah, my exclusive. You haven't forgotten, have you?"

"No, I haven't forgotten. I guess I was hoping you had."

Butterflies bubbled in her stomach and it had nothing to do with the lurch of the Jeep's tires grabbing hold of the asphalt. "Do you not want to?"

He took her hand from where it rested in her lap. "Jane, a promise is a promise."

"Good. 'Cause the interview is tomorrow."

"Really? It's supposed to be kinda miserable. Is Nate okay to drive in the storm Molly's predicting?"

She looked at her lap, unable to look him at his face. "Actually, Nate's been in Richfield all week. Him and his family." Grayson didn't react, other than to tighten his hold on her hand. "Dale gave me a panic button that would call Nate if I needed to get out."

"Really?" He was wounded.

Turning in her seat she watched his profile. His face was so strong, so masculine, and right now the jumping muscle in his jaw was totally hot. She reached up to gently press her fingertips to it. He flinched but didn't pull away.

"It never came out of my suitcase," she said quietly.

"No, but you felt the need to bring it," he bit out, his eyes narrowing as he stared out the windshield.

She sat back, her back to the door. "I didn't know you. From everything I *did* know about you—the you that Derek portrayed—I wasn't sure I could trust that man. And I sure as hell couldn't love him. But you're not *that* man, Grayson. You're everything I could have dreamed and more."

The muscle jumped again, but Jane didn't miss how the corner of his mouth tipped just a bit.

"The way I see it," she said, turning in her seat to face forward, "you have about fifteen minutes to get over yourself ... because I fully intend on picking up where we left off as soon as I get you home."

He looked at her then, and there was no mistaking that his pouting was over.

16

Jane moaned and stretched, relishing in the sensations around her. She knew she'd said it before, just as she knew she would say it again and again; she could seriously get used to sleeping with Grayson. Although the sex was spectacular, she meant the actual act of ... *sleeping*.

The way he was possessive of her even when he was out cold was endearing. He made her feel loved because he wanted to sleep on her side of the bed, his front to her back with his arm draped heavily over her side.

Who was she kidding? She was already used to this sleeping arrangement and when she had to return to her own very cold, very lonely bed she wasn't sure what she was going to do. She did know she would miss it. Miss him.

Grayson's hand moved up her belly and came to rest on her breast. He cradled her gently against him. "Good morning, my love."

"Morning," she sighed as he kissed her nape. "I've been thinking," she blurted before his kisses removed all thoughts from her brain.

"Uhm-hm," he murmured in her ear, pressing his lips to it.

She swallowed and tried to remember what she'd been about to say. "Um ... about the interview today."

"What about it?" He continued his exploration with his lips.

She moved away from him, but only enough to deter his powers of distraction. "I'd like to discuss my questions. That way if there are any you don't want to answer then we can toss them out."

"I trust you, Janie. Ask me anything you want." He reached for her. "Now come here. I'm cold."

She laughed. "Is it true that a man's shoe size is an indication of the size of his—"

He cut her off by flipping her onto her back and pressing that part of himself to a very intimate part of her. "You tell me."

MAKING LOVE TO JANE WAS QUICKLY BEcoming Grayson's most favorite pastime in the entire world.

Given that he spent nine months of the year playing America's favorite pastime *that* was really-ly saying something.

This morning he'd awoken to her stretching and moaning, grinding her perfect round butt against him. It was more than he could take. She wanted to discuss serious topics, but he didn't seem to have enough blood in his brain for so much as reciting the alphabet.

After some morning action and a shower— separately, she'd insisted—they were sitting in the recliners. She had her notebook and a pen. He had a can of Coke.

"Is there anything you want off limits?" she asked.

"My mom talks too much," he answered without a second thought.

"I'll keep that in mind. Anything else?"

"Maybe I should ask *you* if there is anything off limits. I mean … what about you and me?"

"Off limits."

Her answer came a little too quickly for his comfort, but he tried to force a smile. This interview was her deal, not his. And besides, they'd announce their relationship to the world at some point. It wasn't like Grayson Pierce could get married and no one know about it.

The house phone rang—which meant someone was at the gate. Grayson swallowed hard and tried to pretend his heart was pulling a double-time. The night Derek left Grayson had changed the gate code, so the guy couldn't get in without being allowed inside. But knowing that Derek was out in the world made him nervous.

He smiled at Jane and picked the phone. "'Lo?"

"It's Nate. Open up."

Relief washed over him. "When you get to the fork in the road, keep going straight. We'll see you in a minute." He pressed the code into the keypad and hung up.

"Nate?"

"Yep, they'll be here soon. Are we telling *him* about us?" He didn't want to admit that he was relieved when Jane nodded.

"We probably should. Nate Hughes may be a lot of things but stupid isn't one of them," Jane said with a smile.

She walked over to the door and peeked out the little window at the side, watching for the car to pull up. Grayson could tell that she was excited to see her photographer. He knew that the two of them were tight. At first their relationship had bothered him, made his jealous as hell. But now he saw it for what it was; Jane the little sister to Nate's overbearing, I'll-kick-your-ass-if-you-hurt-her big brother.

Jane flung the door open, cold air rolling in like waves of ice. She raced out onto the porch in her stocking feet and Grayson cringed. It was too damned cold for her to be shoeless. He sauntered over to the door, plucked her jacket off the coat tree and walked out to stand behind her. He draped the jacket over her shoulders. She glanced up at him with love in her eyes and whispered a thank you.

Nate stepped out of the Toyota 4-Runner and walked around to the passenger side where a long-legged, model-beautiful blonde stepped out. She waved at Jane and pointed to the backseat. "We just need to get Gracie."

"Gracie?" Grayson whispered.

"Their little girl," Jane whispered back. "She looks just like a miniature Roxie."

Nate carefully pulled a tiny body from the back-seat. The head fell limply against his shoulder, blond curls bouncing as Nate walked. Little Gracie was out cold it seemed. Roxie rushed up onto the porch and captured Jane in a bear hug. Her judg-mental eyes flicked to Grayson as she quietly asked Jane, "How was your week?"

Jane's green eyes met his and she smiled. She held his gaze as she said, "Oh Roxie, it's been a very, very good week."

This time when Roxie's blue eyes caught Gray-son's they were soft and gentle and ... accepting. She stepped past Jane and stuck out her hand. "I'm Roxie Hughes. This big lug belongs to me." Nate grinned.

"Nice to meet you, Roxie." Grayson pumped her hand gently. "I'm Grayson. Welcome to my home. Let's get inside before we freeze to death."

"That's what I'm talking about." Nate still stood on the dirt, his load stirring as the biting winter wind swirled around them.

The defrosting began when Nate settled into the recliner nearest the fireplace. Jane and Roxie went into the kitchen to grab a few refreshments. Nate tossed a quick look at the kitchen and said, "I'm guessing since my alarm didn't go off that you've been good to her."

"Protecting Jane is my first priority."

"From yourself?" Nate asked in a badass tone that made Grayson respect the hell out of him.

"I'm the last person Jane needs protection against," Grayson said.

"Uhm-hm." Nate looked skeptical with one brow raised and his mouth in a disbelieving scowl. The formidable act was seriously undermined by the gentle way he held his daughter. But it was still uncomfortable being questioned.

The women chose that moment to come back and Grayson was so relieved he could have kissed Jane. Roxie walked over to Nate and handed him a can of Coke. In her other hand was one of those spill-proof cups. Grayson guessed it was for Gracie.

Roxie took her small clone from Nate, whispering in the little girl's ear. "It's okay, baby girl. Mommy's got you. Would you like some milk?"

The child snuggled into her mother's shoulder and, closing her eyes, went back to sleep. Roxie handed the cup of milk to Nate and looked at Grayson. "Do you have somewhere I can lay her down?"

"Um ... yeah," he stammered.

Thankfully, Jane jumped in. "Come on. You can use the guest room."

Grayson watched Jane lead Roxie up the stairs. He liked that she'd called the room he'd given her to use *the guest room*. That's what it was. Her clothes were still in suitcases in that room but she slept in his bed and showered in his bathroom ... and Grayson couldn't fight the sense of accomplishment that flowed through him. He liked living with Jane. Liked sleeping with Jane. Liked waking up to Jane's smiling face. And most of all he liked making love to Jane. He wasn't sure how he was going to deal with the separation that was coming. Tomorrow.

His stomach lurched.

Nate cleared his throat and Grayson realized that he was still staring at the door where Jane had disappeared. What an idiot!

"What'd you do this week?" Nate asked, still in his interrogation mode.

Grayson gave Nate the short version, the very short version of events. He'd leave most of the story for Jane to tell.

Nate narrowed his eyes. "Did you make her cry?"

"Maybe." Grayson could hear the irritation in his voice and willed his blood to cool.

Nate cracked his knuckles, glaring at Grayson. Grayson glared right back. Nate's macho-man shit was getting old. Fast.

Grayson was just about to insist that Nate lose the attitude or get the hell out when Jane said his name. Grayson didn't take his eyes from Nate's. The two of them locked in some kind of tractor-beam stare-down.

Jane's hand slipped around his waist, leaning into him but Grayson refused to break the challenge in Nate's stare. Nate cried uncle first when Roxie called his name. He blinked and looked up at her, repentant.

Grayson bent to kiss Jane on the top of the head, her hair soft tickling his lips, and whispered, "Call off your guard dog."

She giggled a little. But before he could get offended she leaned up on her toes and kissed his cheek. "Nate. Roxie," Jane said, "a lot has happened this week. I don't know exactly where to begin to tell you about it. And maybe I shouldn't tell you about it at all, except that you both should know that Grayson and I ... I mean, me and Grayson ... We..." She shook her head, rubbing at her forehead with her fingertips.

"Is it that hard to tell them you love me?" Grayson snapped, insulted. His short, clipped words had more to do with Nate than with Jane. He was just about to apologize when Jane went up on her toes again. This time her lips met his. He hadn't expected a kiss at all, and certainly hadn't expected the long, leisurely caress of her mouth. When she drew back she smiled, her eyes were soft with desire.

Without breaking their gaze, Jane told their audience, "I love him. I am crazy in love with Grayson Pierce."

Roxie gasped then squealed and clapped her hands together once. "That is so awesome!"

"Jane?" Nate asked.

"It's okay, Nate. I don't need a bodyguard, at least not against Grayson. I appreciate your concern. You're a great friend. The big brother I never had. I need you to cut Grayson a break. Because I love him."

"What about *him*?" Nate jerked his head in Grayson's direction. "He love you back?"

Grayson wasn't normally a wear-your-feelings-on-your-sleeve kinda guy, but it seemed like the moment to lay his cards on the table. He kissed Jane on the forehead. "I have loved Jane since I figured out what true love was. Maybe even before that. It just took me too damned long to convince her of it. She won't ever wonder again."

Nate stood, crossing the room to stand directly in front of Grayson and Jane. He looked from Jane to Grayson and nodded, then stuck out his hand. "I'm glad."

Grayson gripped his hand, squeezing a little harder than necessary. Nate grinned and his grasp tightened. He yanked, pulling Grayson closer, and whispered, "You're whipped, man." His eyes darted to Roxie and he grinned. "Welcome to the club."

ONCE NATE WAS CONVINCED THAT GRAYSON wasn't out to break Jane's heart, he went outside to get the camera and tripod from the back of his 4-Runner. He got everything set up. "Okay, let's do this."

Jane settled in a recliner and Grayson took another. She asked. He answered. That was how things went for about the next twenty minutes. Nate unclipped the camera and glanced at Jane.

"What do you want for b-roll?" Nate asked, camera on his shoulder.

"What do you want us to show everybody?" she asked Grayson.

Grayson shrugged. "Believe it or not this is my first real interview. I've never allowed a reporter in my home. What kinds of things do you usually show?"

She looked from the cozy room with its masculine appeal and immensely decorated tree to the beams across the ceiling to the stairs where the railing was covered in garland.

"We could make every woman drool by showing where you sleep," she said with a laugh.

He laughed and lifted his shoulder again. "Whatever."

Nate headed toward the stairs. Grayson took Jane's hand and they followed him. She hadn't even realized her hands were cold until his warm one encased hers. "You know," he whispered into her ear, "there's never been another woman in that bed."

His words surprised her and the emotion must have shown on her face. He kissed the top of her head as they started up the stairs. "There will never be another. You're it for me, Janie."

She smiled up at him. She stopped on a step and put her hand on his chest, making him stop one step down. They were nearly eye-to-eye and she kissed the tip of his nose. "You're it for me too, Grayson."

He wrapped his arms around her and rested his forehead against her breasts. She listened to him breathe and the thumping of her own heart for what seemed like an eternity. It must have seemed like forever to Nate too, because he cleared his throat from the top of the stairs.

"I hate to interrupt." He cleared his throat again. "I doubt you'd be real happy about me just poking around your house. You wanna show me what you two lovebirds want to put on TV?"

The tour of the upstairs was quick and didn't include the room where Gracie was sawing logs. They trudged down the stairs where Roxie was seated in a recliner. She stood and came over. "Did you guys get everything you needed? It's started snowing and, if we're gonna make it home, we'd better get on the road."

By the look on his face, Nate was giving Jane the final say. She'd wanted to get more footage; maybe Grayson with the horses or riding his ATV or just ... she didn't know. There was no doubt she could make the story with what they had, but she wanted more.

"We're gonna have to stay a little longer," Nate told Roxie. "It'll be okay. We've got four-wheel-drive."

"You're welcome to stay here," Jane said, feeling a bit guilty for Nate's decision. As soon as the words were out of her mouth she realized two things: Nate could read her like a book and she'd just invited people to stay in a home where she didn't pay the mortgage.

Before she could retract the invitation Grayson put his hand on the small of her back and said, "Stay. The roads are going to be hell. It's only supposed to get worse in the next few hours and it's supposed to clear out by tomorrow afternoon. You can leave then."

Roxie needed convincing. "I don't know. We don't want to impose."

"You're not," Jane said. "You can use the room where Gracie's sleeping. It's not like I've been using it anyway." She felt her cheeks blush.

Nate chuckled, not missing a thing. He stepped next to Roxie and put his arm around her waist. It was obvious that Roxie didn't want to stay and even more obvious that Nate could read her easier than he could read Jane.

"We appreciate the offer," Nate said, "but we're gonna head out anyway. We've been away from home for long enough. Gracie doesn't sleep well when she's not in her own bed and it's taking its toll."

"I guess I can understand that," Jane said, both bummed and relieved. She'd just gotten Grayson to herself and she wasn't ready to share him yet. "Can I keep the camera to get some more for the story?"

"You'll be back on Monday?"

"Yep."

Nate tipped his head and shrugged an enormous shoulder. "I guess that would be okay. I'll pick you up Monday morning."

It only took a few minutes for Nate and Roxie to gather everything they'd come with—sans the camera. Grayson stood at Jane's back, his body heat warming her. They waved from the porch until they couldn't see the vehicle anymore. He turned Jane in his arms and took her face between his hands, kissing her soundly.

He pulled back so that they could breathe and ushered her inside. "I have to admit that I'm not upset they left."

"Me either. The invitation just kind of flew out of my mouth before my brain could stop it. Are you mad that I extended your hospitality without asking first?"

"Not at all. My home is your home. In fact I have something for you." He reached into his pocket.

"Another surprise?" She laughed softly.

"I hope it's something you'll use ... a lot." He held up a key in front of her eyes and for a moment she couldn't breathe. "I wanted to make this more romantic."

She felt tears sting her eyes and blinked. "This is perfectly romantic."

"Are you okay having a key to my place on your key ring?"

"As long as you're okay with tampons under your bathroom sink."

Her comment stunned him, she could tell. His lip quirked like he wanted to laugh but the mortification in his eyes made her wonder if he was going to snatch the key back and push her out into the coming snowstorm.

"Um, I guess that comes with the territory."

"Yep. Are you okay with feminine products in your house?"

He smiled then. "As long as you don't expect me to buy them."

THE NEXT MORNING SUNSHINE STREAKED through the slits in the blinds. Jane wondered how much snow had come down last night and how hard it was going to be to get off Grayson's property. His roads weren't paved, just hard packed dirt and a layer of cinders. Now they would be covered with snow and mud.

She knew the moment he awoke because his fingers started to move ever so slowly, teasingly over her skin. They moved up and down her arm. His lips kissed the nape of her neck and goose bumps spread over her body.

He chuckled softly. "Good morning."

"Morning," she sighed, rolling onto her back.

His tortuous strokes then moved to her stomach, making a trail up around her nipple before his hand closed and kneaded her breast.

"I've been thinking," he said as his palm moved up to cradle her face.

"You didn't hurt yourself, did you?" She giggled when he jabbed a finger into her side.

He kissed her, gentle at first then more determined, like he was branding her. "I can't live without you," he said breathlessly.

"Well, it's a good thing you don't have to." She was a little breathless herself. "I'm not going anywhere. Er ... I guess I am. But I'm just going home. My heart is yours."

"That's the problem. Not your heart, your leaving. I hate the idea of you leaving, even if it is only to go back to your job."

"I'm not quitting my job," she said adamantly.

He popped himself up on an elbow and looked down at her, his fingers continuing their unconscious movements. "I'm not asking you to. What I'm proposing—" He grinned when she scowled. "—is that I come with you. Would you mind having my toothbrush on your bathroom counter?"

Wow! She'd never imagined having this conversation. As much as she disliked the idea of leaving Grayson's sanctuary, she hadn't wanted to play the part of needy girlfriend and ask him to drop his life and follow her just so that he can hold the couch down while she went about doing her thing.

"Jane?" She could hear the doubt in his voice and hated that she'd made even a moment of uncertainty creep into his mind.

"I'm okay." Tipping her head, she kissed him. "I can't think of a better place for your toothbrush."

"Phew." He made a dramatic point of sweeping his hand over his forehead.

She laughed. "As much as I'd love to make love this morning, I have to pack and get ready. I'm not even sure I can get my car out of your driveway."

"I've got a tow chain and a winch. We can get it out."

She looked at him skeptically.

"Worst case scenario, we leave it here," he announced like it was the most obvious answer to the problem.

Jane didn't like that idea. At all. She needed her car. Her brows furrowed and she clamped her top teeth down on her bottom lip.

His right brow arched and he smirked. His hand smoothed her hair back from her forehead and he leaned down to kiss it. "Worst case scenario, we'll leave your car here ... *and* you can drive the Jeep. I'll take the truck. You'll have a set of wheels to escape if you need some time away from me."

"It's not that I anticipate needing time away from you. I'll need a way to get to work and—"

"Didn't Nate volunteer to pick you up?"

She frowned and narrowed her eyes at him. "That's not an everyday occurrence. He just needs to pick his *camera* up from me Monday morning. Since I'll have ... Ugh!" She yanked the sheets back and instantly regretted the action when cold air doused her naked body. Since she'd already started the whole dramatic exit thing ... well, hell.

"Why are we even having this conversation?" she snapped. "I want my car ... because it's my car." She stomped across the room, making sure that her feet made noise as they slapped against the hard wood floor. She wasn't really mad and she was acting like a child. In fact, she was a little embarrassed by her actions.

When he whistled and started in with the cat-calls she laughed and turned her head to blow him a kiss.

Yes, she was definitely going to enjoy living with him.

17

Ultimately it'd taken some work—and the use of the tow chain—but Jane's car made the trip north. As much as she'd enjoyed her time with Grayson on his remote ranch, she was happy to be home and sleeping in her own bed. What made it even better was that she was no longer sleeping in that bed alone.

And now she didn't have to do anything alone, unless she wanted to.

She poured two glasses of orange juice and popped a couple of pieces of wheat bread into the toaster.

She'd never been one for drinking coffee. She loved the smell, but for whatever reason never developed a taste for it. Turned out that was another thing she and Grayson had in common.

Feeling him before she heard him, she shivered when he stepped even closer and pressed his lips to the back of her neck. "Good morning."

"Morning. Hungry?"

He nibbled at her earlobe. "Very."

His arm moved around her waist and held her against him. Which was good since her knees weren't strong enough to hold her up. She sighed and leaned against him. She wanted to shuck the clothes that she'd put on and peel Grayson's clothes off.

"I can't," she moaned, hating the words.

"I know," he said with a chuckle. "I just love that I made you second guess your decision to go to work today."

She turned in his arms and glared up into his brown eyes that were twinkling like a meteor shower. Not a single bit of him was repentant. Grayson looked good, delicious in his gray sweater and jeans that hugged every delectable inch of his hard body.

"Well, aren't you cocky?"

"Nope. I know I'm *that* good." Before she could get a snappy comeback off her tongue, Grayson laughed and wrapped her in a tight hug. He kissed the top of her head. "I've been wondering—" She tracked his eyes as they purposefully glanced around her home. "—are you a Grinch?"

"No." Even as she said the words, she couldn't dispute the fact that it did appear that she was.

"Have you bought even *one* gift?"

"Yes," she snapped, then admitted the truth, "no. I guess I really should get on that."

"Give me a list."

"What?" She felt her brows pull together and her mouth drop open.

"Give me a list. You have to work. I don't. Let me get your parents something. Who else is on your Christmas list?"

"Just Molly."

"Okay. What were you thinking for your parents?"

She shrugged. There were more reasons than just lack of time; she had no idea what to get for her parents. They were financially secure and went out to buy anything and everything they ever wanted. That and no gift was ever good enough for her mother. Hell, Jane wasn't good enough for her mother. It sucked forever being a disappointment.

"I have no idea," Jane told him, sounding defeated.

"Okay." He kissed her forehead. "I'll come up with something. What about Molly?"

"She's so easy-going, she'd be happy with a bag of M&M's."

He nodded. "Got it."

She reached into her pocket and searched with her fingers for the key she'd put there earlier. "If you're going to go out today, you should probably have a way to lock up and get back in."

"You're right. I probably should." His eyes sparkled, anticipating where her thoughts were going.

She pulled out the key. "Use it in good health."

"I will. And I don't plan of giving it back."

"That's okay," she said with a giggle, "I can just change the locks."

He grabbed her upper arms, his hands holding her like a vise. His lips crashed to hers and made her regret teasing him. He was too good at teasing her right back. His tongue moved across her lips and she opened to allow him to deepen the kiss.

A knock on the front door made her groan. She didn't want to leave Grayson, but was looking forward to editing his interview today. It'd been a long time since she'd been so excited to bring a story to her viewers.

Grayson released his hold on her and strode toward the door. She grabbed a piece of toast and buttered it. Deep voices rumbled from the living room, coming closer. What had started out as a lazy morning was now rushed. She took a bite and chewed, washing it down with a swig of juice.

Bite. Chew. Swallow. Drink.

"Do you want a piece of toast?" she asked Nate when the two men came into the kitchen.

Nate leaned a hip against the table and shook his head. "I'm good, thanks. You ready?"

"Yeah, I just need to grab my jacket and laptop." She guzzled the last of her juice and dabbed at her mouth with a dishcloth. She crossed the kitchen and squeezed between the two men. "Give me two seconds."

"No problem," Nate said. As she headed upstairs, she heard Nate ask, "What are you gonna do today?"

Knowing how Grayson's home was decked out in green and red, Jane wasn't sure she wanted to see her place after he got done working his decorating magic. She shoved her laptop into its padded bag and shrugged into her warm KHB coat.

Grayson and Nate were discussing sports—specifically Christmas Day games—when she came down the stairs. "You're welcome to come over. Roxie makes enough food for an army."

"We'll let you know." Grayson lifted his eyes to Jane's, letting them rake over her from head to boot-covered feet. He smirked, a small lift of one corner.

Jane knew that look.

That look turned her on ... because it meant Grayson had only one thing on his mind. The same thing she did; no clothes, no cares.

Nate cleared his throat. "You ready?"

"Yeah," she said, her eyes still locked with Grayson's. She walked toward the door, intent of avoiding any kind of contact with him. Leaving him home alone today was hard enough without doing so ... aching.

Grayson had other plans. His arm flashed out and captured around the waist as she strode past him. "She'll be right out, Nate."

Nate chuckled, fully understanding that goodbye needed to be said—without an audience. He made a show of lifting his sleeve to look at his watch. "I'm giving you five minutes and then you can get yourself to work."

He shook his coat sleeve back into place, hiked the camera bag up onto his shoulder, and left.

"Mmm. Five minutes," Grayson murmured against her neck.

Hard as she fought to stay strong against his efforts, she melted. She became a puddle right there at Grayson's feet. She loved the way he kissed her, loved his every touch. It set her on fire and made her every bone melt away until she was supported only by Grayson.

She tipped her head and he nuzzled her neck with his lips, biting and tasting. His hands drifted down her back to grip her bottom, pulling her hips to his.

"You feel that?" he asked. "I'm going to be like that all day now."

She kissed his lips, a short peck. "I didn't start this, so don't go blaming me."

"I will blame you. If you weren't so frickin' hot, it wouldn't be so hard—" He grinned, recognizing his own double entendre. "I meant ... all of it, but yeah, that part of me is in a constant state of arousal whenever you're around."

She ground her hips against his and he moaned. She giggled wickedly. "Good to know." She stepped out of his embrace. "I've really got to go. I hate driving in the snow, so Nate's my ride."

"I could take you."

"You take me places, alright. But I think it'd be safer to ride with Nate. At least that way I know I'll get there with all my clothes on."

"Chicken."

"Damn straight." She kissed her fingertips and blew him a kiss, not sure she could tear herself away from him again. "Gotta go."

He came toward her where she stood with her hand on the door handle. She twisted and jerked the door open. A cold blast of winter air rushed in. "One more thing before you go," Grayson said.

She put her hand out to keep him at an arm's length. His heart was strong and steady under her palm. He looked down at her hand and grinned. He took her hand and kissed her fingertips, then her palm, then her wrist. Her heart rate raced and her pulse took off like a horse emerging from the starting gate. Her eyes drooped closed and a soft moan escaped her lips.

"You're killing me," she panted.

"Good."

Her eyes popped open to see his smug smile only inches from her face. "Now to my one thing—" He laughed when she scowled at him. "—where are your Christmas decorations?"

"Um..." She wasn't sure how much she liked the idea of him decorating her place. Not because it was *him* decorating *her* place. But as it turned out, she was kind of a Scrooge. She preferred the comparison with the old miser versus the owner of the ugly ass dog with the single horn on his head.

"You do have Christmas decorations, right?"

"A few. They're on the shelf in my closet," she said. He gave her a perplexed expression and she darted out the door before he could capture her again—and torture them both with his kisses. "I love you," she yelled over her shoulder as she hurried down the walk.

She climbed into the news vehicle and sighed. She could see Grayson where he stood at the end of her walk. He waved and she returned the gesture.

Nate chuckled softly next to her. He pulled away from the curb and eased out of the parking lot.

"What?" she asked, watching Grayson until he was out of sight.

She turned to look at Nate and he shook his head, a cat-that-ate-the-canary grin plastered on his face. "I'm not sure who has it worse."

"What do you mean?"

"After visiting you at Grayson's house, I thought he was the whipped one, but now I'm not so sure."

"You say that like it's a bad thing," she gritted out, irritated and a little offended by Nate's idea of pleasant drive to work conversation.

"It's definitely not a bad thing, Jane." His smile spread until it completely covered his face. "In fact it's a very, very good thing. I'm glad he makes you happy."

She went all warm and gooey inside. She looked in the rear view mirror, knowing full well that Grayson wouldn't be looking back at her. "Me too." She nodded, a smile of her own growing on her face. "Me too."

GRAYSON LET HIS WORRIES ABOUT DEREK GO the way of the wind. Being at Jane's meant that Derek didn't know where they were. Which meant that Jane was safe.

Grayson spent the day doing one of the things he loved best. And when Jane got home he was going to do the thing he loved very most in the world.

He hoped that Jane liked what he'd done with the place. Decorating for Christmas was something that he'd learned to love from the time he could crawl. His mother had instilled that love, and now he was proud to give Clark W. Griswold a run for his money every year.

Festive didn't begin to describe Jane's home now. Red and green and gold covered every inch. He'd gotten the biggest tree her small living room could handle and put so many strands of lights on it that the thing could probably be seen from space. As for the decorations, they were in their boxes on the couch, waiting.

A red table runner ran down the middle of Jane's table. Grayson put the evergreen centerpiece in the middle and admired how nice the red roses and white carnations looked nestled in the dark green pine boughs.

He stood back and admired his work.

It looked good.

The ten sprigs of mistletoe might have been overkill. But any excuse for him to kiss Jane was a good excuse in his book. He heard Jane's key in the lock and nervous jitters skittered through his gut.

All the lights were off except for the tree, which illuminated the entire downstairs. Fighting the urge to race to her and gather her in his arms, he planted his feet and waited for her reaction.

She stepped inside and stomped her feet on the rug by the front door. As her head rose, she gasped. Then she sighed. Her hand moved to her mouth.

Grayson wasn't sure if that was a good or a bad thing. Unable to stay away a moment longer, he took a tentative step toward her then paused until her gaze finally made it around to him. His hands were buried deep in his pockets.

"Do you like it?"

Her voice wobbled a bit. "I have never seen anything so beautiful."

Relieved breath rushed from his lungs in a whoosh. "I thought we could decorate the tree together. Maybe tomorrow morning?"

She turned in a circle taking in the transformation of her home. "Yes, tomorrow morning," she said wistfully.

He walked up behind her and slid his arms around her waist. She leaned back against him and sighed. He rested his chin on top of her head and just let the contented feelings swirl around them.

"You've been busy," she said.

"I got your shopping done too."

"You did," she nearly squealed and turned in his arms. "Oh, I could kiss you for that."

"Nobody's stopping you."

Her head tipped back and she moved up on her tiptoes. Her lips were soft and warm against his cheek. He shouldn't have been disappointed by the chaste contact, but being the honest guy he was, he admitted he was hoping for at least lip to lip.

She must have understood his flash of dissatisfaction because she laughed softly. Her fingers entwined his and she tugged. "Come on, big boy, I'll thank you properly upstairs."

THE NEXT MORNING AFTER THEY'D MADE love and showered—and made love again *in* the shower—Jane stood in front of the tree unsure of what to do. Grayson seemed to have the whole trimming-the-tree thing down.

Bing Crosby crooned from the stereo and a delicious spicy scent wafted from the kitchen.

Grayson pulled one of the bulb boxes open and held a bright red ball out to her. She wrapped her fingers around it gently. The fragile thing was cold in her hand. She stared down at it where it was perched on her palm.

"Jane?"

She looked up at him and blinked.

Sadly, she wasn't sure what to do with the stupid, beautiful ball. Her mother had never let her even *touch* the tree, let alone decorate it. When she'd first gone out on her own in college, Molly stepped into the tree decorating shoes. Once her own place came around, Jane didn't much care for the memories that the tree and Christmas brought to life.

So there you go ... It didn't take three ghosts for Jane to figure out why she hated Christmas. All it took was one glass ball, and the man who loved her.

"It won't break," Grayson said with a smile. He was so close now that she could feel the heat from his body.

When had he moved so close to her? She wasn't sure, but was glad that he had.

He plucked the bulb from her hand and stepped away. He held the hook between his forefinger and thumb. Before she could register the action, he opened his fingers and sent the ball into a freefall.

She gasped and jumped back.

Instead of a crash though, there was a small thud.

No harm. No foul.

Grayson bent at the waist and retrieved the ornament. He held it out to her. "Put it on the tree, love."

With a smile on her face, she moved forward and stood there. Her hand moved to the top right, paused, moved more to the center and froze again. She leaned over and reached out to place it on a bottom branch but stopped, yet again.

Grayson's warm fingers went around hers. "There is no wrong answer here. Pick a branch and stick it there. I don't care if you rearrange the bulbs every day if that's what makes you happy."

"Really?" Good hell, she sounded so disbelieving. She was so screwed up.

"Yes, really. This is your tree, baby doll."

Warmth spread from the tips of her toes right up to the top of her head. She liked that there was no wrong answer. That she couldn't mess up. That if she didn't like it, she could redo it.

This time when her hand reached out with the bulb, she let the hook grab onto a branch. She stood back for a moment and admired the single red ball hanging on the dark green tree and had never seen anything so beautiful.

"You want another one?" Grayson asked, holding onto the hook of a silver ball.

"Yeah. I do." She took the ball and the first branch she reached for was now adorned with the decoration.

One ball after another, Jane and Grayson decorated the tree. It was surprisingly liberating. If she'd known that this would be her reaction to putting ornaments on a tree, she would have done it years ago.

Once it was all done, Jane leaned against Grayson. He wrapped an arm around her waist. "Do you like it?"

"I love it. But I think you were wrong about something."

"Me? Wrong?"

She laughed. "It's possible, Pierce. As wonderful as you are, you're not perfect."

"Wow." He put a hand over his heart and acted offended. "What was I so wrong about?"

"It's not *my* tree." She snuggled in close to him. "It's *our* tree."

18

CHRISTMAS MORNING CAME WITH A LIGHT dusting of snow and a huge dose of excitement. Grayson couldn't wait for Jane to open the presents he'd gotten for her. He could however wait until the end of time to visit her parents. Unfortunately, the end of time was scheduled to happen this afternoon.

Grayson couldn't say that he didn't respect Jane's parents because, well, they were ... her parents. But he did have issues with the baggage Jane carried around.

As a kid Grayson watched the moments when Jane's mistakes were pointed out for the world to see by her own mother. As a teenager Grayson wanted to defend the girl he loved, but couldn't find the cojones to speak up and potentially turn the wrath at himself.

Things were different now; Grayson was a man.

As a man he would defend the woman he loved, consequences be damned.

Jane came back from the kitchen, two coffee mugs in her hands. "I love this punch. Your mom used to make it when we were kids."

"Yep, every Christmas. It's a family recipe. I'm not even sure where it started."

She handed him a mug and sat down on the couch, curling her feet under her bottom. "It's a great tradition that I plan on passing on to my kids."

The words *our kids* almost flew out. Luckily he was able to bite down and keep them on the tip of his tongue. They hadn't discussed what the future had in store. He had offered a future as his wife—and the mother of his children—but she had declined without even a heartbeat of thought.

All he knew was that she was with him in the present—and he didn't plan on doing anything to jeopardize that.

"You wanna do gifts now?" She practically bounced on the seat next to him and he wondered what she'd placed under the tree for him.

"You want to open or give first?" he asked.

"Give!" Not a single moment hesitation.

She handed him her coffee mug which he placed on the end table next to his own. She melted off the couch and scurried to the tree on her knees. She handed him a square package. The shiny silver paper had white snowflakes on it, topped with a red bow so big it dangled over the edges.

He took it from her and shook it. She giggled when it didn't make a sound. He frowned and looked at her. It was the exact size and shape of a CD.

He held it up and very obviously scrutinized the size. "Gee, I wonder what it is."

She slapped at his knee. "Open it, then you won't have to wonder."

The smile on her face and the twinkle of mischievous delight in her eyes made his heart warm and he fell in love with her all over again. He tore open a corner, his eyes on hers. Sliding a finger up the center of the paper revealed a clear CD case.

Was he good, or what?

It wasn't a CD though. It was a DVD.

"What's this? Home movies?" he asked, the thought making tingles of anticipation shiver through his lower regions.

A burst of laughter erupted out of her, making him laugh too. "No. You'd know if those existed. It's your interview."

That made him smile. He looked down at the silver disk again and appreciated what he held in his hands. It signified what she truly thought of him. Her thoughts and feelings would be evident in the pictures and words in the story she shared with the world.

"Can we watch it now?" he asked.

"Sure."

He realized how selfish that made him. "Why don't you open yours and then we'll watch it."

"No, it's okay." She took the DVD from his hands and popped it into the player. She crossed back to him and snuggled up next to him on the couch. Her legs were folded under her and her head rested on his shoulder.

The first frame popped up and she hit play. Her voice filled the room as a picture of him on the field filled the screen.

"Grayson Pierce is known by most as a man who enjoys his cars, his liquor and his women. This reporter was given the chance to find out what the world doesn't know about him."

His face popped up. "I know that fame comes with the fortune, but I prefer anonymity."

The picture panned across the outline of his ranch, enough to give an idea of the beauty but not the location.

"Anonymity he might be able to achieve, but this baseball all-star is far from anonymous. He is a hometown boy, devoted to those he cares about."

Grayson groaned when his mother's face appeared. "When did you...?"

"Shh!"

Maude was smiling. "Grayson's always taken the best care of me he could. When he was five he thought he'd drive to the store and get me some medicine when I was sick with the flu."

The picture of his face covered in ink popped up as his mother continued, "At one point he was determined to become an artist to support us."

The story continued, portraying Grayson in exactly the way he wanted; loving, caring, kind ... decent.

Finally Jane came on screen. She was bundled in her winter clothes, standing on the front porch. "I have to admit that I too bought the façade of the man we've all seen over the years." She stepped off the porch and walked toward the camera, her face getting closer. "But after spending a week, living the real life Grayson lives, I can tell you that he is a wonderful man. Reporting from the home of Grayson Pierce, Utah's very own MVP, this is Jane Alexander, KHB Sports."

The screen went black.

Grayson didn't know what to say. His eyes stung and he blinked. His throat was tight and he cleared it so that he might be able to say something. Jane's body tensed next to his. He guessed she thought he didn't like it, when only the contrary was true.

"Is it okay? I can change it," she stammered. "Dale wants to wait to air it until February ratings anyway. Which part didn't you—"

He interrupted her by pulling her into his lap and kissing her. Her body relaxed against his and she accepted his kiss, returning it with fervor. One of his hands slid up to hold the back of her spine, the other resting on the small of her back.

She moaned and pulled back, searching his eyes. "It was okay?"

"Yeah, okay." His heart was so full of love for the woman in his arms that he was sure it would burst. "You know I love you."

"I've suspected as much," she said with a small laugh. "You aren't mad that I got your mom? Nate and I went back to get the interview with her. That's why I was so late the other night."

He scowled at her, but the expression was only skin deep. "She talks too much."

"Yeah, and no one knows you better than your mother. I couldn't resist putting that adorable picture on TV. It's good to know that if baseball doesn't work out that you have another career to fall back on."

"Another career," he scoffed. "I'm gonna marry a sugar-mama and live off her money."

Her face fell. "Sugar-mama, huh?"

"You're beautiful face is on TV, you must be loaded, right?"

She smiled, but looked around her house. "If you can live like this—" She waved a hand around her small living room. "—then I guess I can be your sugar-mama."

"Good to know." He nodded, grinning like a fool. "Good to know."

He eased her off his lap and knelt next to the tree. "Your turn."

JANE WAS SO RELIEVED THAT HE'D LIKED THE story. She hadn't had to editorialize even one single word in it. Everything she said—and included—she felt … to the very core of her.

It had taken him a moment to speak after it faded to black. Doubt that he liked it hadn't occurred to her in that moment. She knew that his emotions were getting the better of him. And that made her love him even more.

The package he handed her was heavy for its size, about the width of a book but not quite that tall. Just like he had, she lifted it to her ear and shook it. And just like he had, she frowned. The roles continued to be reversed as he laughed at her reaction.

She had been excited to give her the DVD and he was obviously thrilled for her to open this particular box. She had to pretend that she hadn't been digging under the tree. She also had to pretend that she hadn't already shaken this box and known it didn't make a sound. She knew that there was another box under the tree—a box that most likely came from a jeweler.

Would she be engaged before the morning was over?

Because this time if he asked, she would most emphatically say yes.

She tore the paper from the box and held a black box in her hands. There was gold writing on it. Her heart skipped a beat. She'd wanted one of these, but had never seemed to find the money to purchase it.

Pretending not to know what it was she looked up at him, hoping that the question reflected in her gaze. It must have because he said, "Open the lid."

She did. It was beautiful. It was smaller than she'd thought it would be. A Ruger LCP .380. She pulled the tiny gun from its box and put it in the palm of her hand. Jane didn't have big hands, in fact they were maybe a little smaller than average for a woman, but the thing wasn't much bigger than her hand.

"I have us signed up for some time at the shooting range tomorrow."

Bingo!

That was the reason she'd pretended not to know how to shoot. Because he would have to teach her; standing behind her, very closely behind her, and hold her hips in his large hands. She warmed just thinking about it.

"Jane," he said. "If you're completely adverse to the idea, I can take it back."

"No," she said a little too forcefully and hoped he didn't catch her eagerness to keep the gun. "It's probably a good idea for me to have it."

"Only if you know how to use it," he said. "Jane, I have enemies. Not big, bad mafia types, but not everyone likes me. And you're a gorgeous woman in the public eye."

"Molly has a stalker," she blurted.

"What?" he said so calmly that the sudden edge of fury in his voice was palpable.

"He's just some crazy guy who said that he had a vision she would marry him." She shrugged, playing it off, trying to ease the tension in the air. But the truth was the dude scared the hell out of Molly—and Jane. Not that she was going to tell Grayson that. Every muscle in his body was already coiled and ready to strike out. "She's got an order of protection. It's all good."

"It's not all good," he snapped. He sucked in a deep breath and snorted as he blew it out his nose in one big huff. "I'm sorry. I shouldn't have snapped at you. I just worry about you. Does Molly have a gun?"

"No, she doesn't believe in them."

Molly wasn't pretending about that fact either. Molly was a world-peace-would-happen-if-we-all-just-loved-each-other-more kinda girl. Not that Jane was all about the violence, but push her too far, break into her home, hurt the people she loved and she would defend herself. End of discussion.

Grayson shook his head. "Well, I hope that philosophy doesn't come back to haunt her."

"Yeah, me too," Jane agreed with a quiet sigh. A melancholy fog hung in the room and Jane wanted to blow it away. "You got anything else under there for me?"

His eyes narrowed. "You know darn well there is."

"How'd you know?" she asked, totally surprised.

"My mom is the queen of sneaking peeks at the gifts under the tree. I used to hide her presents in my room because I caught her one year rewrapping them." Jane laughed, unsurprised. "I knew then and I knew now ... the first time you did it. And the second. And the third."

"Well, hell." She thought she'd been so sneaky.

With a sexy grin gracing his lips he held the tiny box out to her. "It's not what you think."

"And what exactly do you think I think it is?"

His chuckle was a scoffing one. "Just open it."

She slid a finger beneath the seam to reveal the white square box, a jeweler's silver insignia embossed on the top. "It's not what I think?"

He shook his head, his lips smiling, his eyes sparkling thanks to the white twinkling lights from the tree.

She pulled the lid off and dumped the box upside down to shake the black velvet box out into her hand. "You're sure it's not what I think?

Again he shook his head.

The lid opened with a crack and Jane's eyes widened. It wasn't what she'd thought. She had half expected—okay, more than half—a diamond perched on a band. This was multiple diamonds set into a silver heart-shaped locket. She tugged gently to release it from the safety of the box, to examine it more carefully.

Slipping a nail in between the two halves it popped open. One side held a picture of her and Grayson that his mother had taken. The other side held an inscription: *Jane, I loved you in the past. I love you today. And I will love you every day of our future. ~Grayson*

The words blurred as she read them over again. She wiped at her cheek when the first tear escaped. She launched herself off the couch. Grayson caught her and wrapped his arms around her, holding her close.

"It wasn't what you expected," he whispered.

"No," she answered quietly.

"I wasn't sure you wanted what you expected," he said honestly.

Her heart clenched at his declaration. "I do. Want it, I mean."

He grinned and bent his head to kiss her nose. "I'm glad."

When he didn't produce another box, she was a tad disappointed. But only a really tiny, niggling tad. He took the locket from her hand and helped her put it on. It rested just above her cleavage. It was small enough that she could wear it every day but large enough to be noticed.

"I have something else for you," she announced, scrambling out of his lap.

He took the box from her and she bit her lip in what she hoped was a sexy, come-hither way. He tore into the paper, leaving behind only shreds that could line a hamster cage. The lid flew like a Frisbee across the room, he peeled back the tissue paper, and a low, erotic growl rumbled from his throat. His fingers pinched the straps, lifting it to dangle from them.

The desperate, eager look in his eyes made her giggle. She stood, walked toward the stairs. "I think we have just enough time to try that on."

He was on his feet and chased her up the stairs and into the bedroom. "It's not the trying *on* I'm concerned with, baby."

19

"Hello, Jane." Sheri Alexander opened the door and scanned Jane from head to toe, once again not approving of the girl who stood before her.

Jane met the scrutiny with a smile, refusing to feel bad for wearing jeans. Her mother as always had both feet firmly planted on the opposite end of the spectrum, unsurprisingly dressed to the nines complete with heels and pantyhose—not tights (tights were for children). Her long, flowing black skirt fell to mid calf and her red sweater was cashmere. Her earrings were diamonds and her nails were manicured. She refused to believe she was getting older, dying her hair a shade of unnatural platinum that made her skin look green—not that Jane dared offer an opinion like that—and her face was a slightly wrinkled version of Jane's.

Grayson's hold tightened on Jane's hand. Or maybe it was her hand performing the death-grip. Jane took a deep breath and stepped through the threshold.

"Hi, Mom. You remember Grayson."

Green eyes shifted, narrowed and scrutinized Grayson from dark hair to Skechers brown boots, then finally stared him in the eye. Jane flinched. Grayson didn't. He met the icy gaze with a strained smile. He stuck out his hand which she took in the very tips of her fingers, her nose wrinkling like she'd picked up a dog turd.

"Yes. I remember," she said coolly.

"As do I, Ms. Alexander," he said in a tone only slightly warmer.

Jane wanted to scream. She'd expected this confrontation—she wasn't naïve enough to call it anything else—and hadn't imagined it to go well. But the volatile waves sloshing off her mother were worse than she could have anticipated.

And the barely contained animosity in Grayson's voice made Jane's insides wriggle. His tense stance made her consider turning around and running before the situation could escalate.

"Janie," Dad said. "Welcome home."

Grayson released the hold on her hand to ease an arm around her. He tucked her into his side as his fingers traced lazy circles on the small of her back. Her eyes slid closed and she absorbed the small amount of comfort he could offer her in front of her parents.

"Hi, Dad."

Paul Alexander wrapped Jane in a hug and squeezed her tight. Then holding her at arm's length, he looked at her and smiled an approval she never got from her mother.

He was wearing black dress pants, a starched white shirt and a tie that was the exact shade of red as Sheri's sweater. His hair was thinning and was grayer than the brown that matched Jane's.

Jane stepped back and took comfort in the strength of Grayson standing next to her. When Grayson's arm came around her waist again she bit back a sigh and said to her father, "You remember Grayson?"

Paul extended his hand and took a hard hold of Grayson's, pumping it gently. "Welcome to our home, Grayson."

Grayson smiled at the older man. "Thank you. I'm glad to be here."

Jane sighed, smiling as the two began the discussion of Grayson's career. She felt her mother step up behind her and she tried not to tense. Sheri cleared her throat. When Jane didn't turn around or say anything, Sheri cleared her throat a little louder. Jane was sure that her mother had meant to be subtle, but the noise turned all three heads.

Sheri smiled tightly, her lips thinning to an unflattering line. "Jane, could you help me in the kitchen?"

Alarm raced through Jane's bloodstream. Her heart lurched against her ribcage. She was pretty sure that her face registered the terror on her face, verified when her mother's lips lifted in a victorious grin.

Sheri took Jane's arm ... and Jane became a dead-woman-walking as they crossed the living room. She chanced a panicked look over her shoulder to see Grayson's smiling face. He dropped his head in a supportive nod before he winked and mouthed the words *I love you.*

When Jane smiled back, she felt a bit of the anxiety drain from her body.

"I can't believe you'd bring him here," Sheri snapped when the kitchen door swung closed.

"Why wouldn't I bring him here?" Jane asked nonchalantly, surprised that her blood pressure hadn't risen.

Sheri snorted, picking up the whisk to beat the gravy into submission. "Did you forget what he did to you?"

"I've forgiven him." Jane shrugged.

Sheri stopped beating the gravy to death and turned to face Jane. "Well, I haven't."

"This isn't about you, Mom."

"This isn't—? I picked up the pieces of your heart, Jane. I held you while you cried. *I* did that."

Actually, her mother told her to stop crying, that Grayson was too good for her anyway. She'd picked up the pieces … only to crush them further.

"It's *my* heart, Mom." The blood vessels in Jane's temples pulsed.

"Well, I'm not going to do it again. When he breaks your heart, I'm not going to be here to comfort you."

"I guess I've been warned," Jane said flatly. "What can I do to help?" She hoped beyond hope that the change of subject would detour her mother.

"You can get the butter out of the fridge." Sheri used the whisk to point. "I'd suggest you don't have any. You're looking a little chubby through the cheeks." Her eyes pointedly dropped to Jane's midsection. "How much weight have you put on?"

Knife to the heart.

Jane blinked and turned to jerk the fridge open, only to bury her head inside. Fluttering her eyelids held the tears at bay—barely. She was just about to begin the search for the butter when the door whipped out of her hold.

Her mother glared at her. "It's not that hard."

The low intonation of male voices came closer and Jane had never been more grateful for a reprieve. Dad came through the door first, holding it until Grayson's palm finished the job. He was still talking about Xavier's great season when his eyes sought out hers. There was a second where her hurt feelings floated through the air between them before Grayson crossed the kitchen in three steps and took Jane in his arms.

She gasped when he lowered his head and kissed her. Nothing too sexy, but sexy enough to have make her cheeks flame.

"I'm sorry," he said when he lifted his head.

Both of her parents' jaws hung open, their eyes wide as the plates her mother held.

He grinned at them. "Sometimes I just can't help myself. I just love your daughter so much."

Dad chuckled softly and nodded, looking more than a little pleased at the idea of her and Grayson together. "I'm glad to hear that."

"Well ... isn't that nice?" her mother snapped.

Dad's eyes narrowed in an icy glare that was met by Mom's arctic one.

Jane prepared herself for an argument that would end with dishes being thrown against the wall. Instead, after an uncomfortable couple of seconds, those dishes pushed into Jane's hands.

Her mother's voice was cold when she informed the room that, "All of my hard work is going to be ruined if we don't eat soon."

And with that the confrontation had been averted. At least for the moment.

They all proceeded into the dining room and Grayson sat down next to Jane. He put a hand on her knee and squeezed lightly. She glanced at him and smiled. In the few minutes Jane spent captive in her mother's kitchen her emotional thermometer had dropped until all the color was resting in the little ball at the bottom. She'd needed what only his love and support could offer.

And he gave it to her.

Dinner progressed with minimal backhanded compliments. Jane helped her mother clear the table—as did Grayson, which was unheard of in the Alexander home. Women cooked and cleaned up the dishes while the men vegged out in front of the TV. Sheri tried to shoo Grayson away—no doubt annoyed by his presence—but he wouldn't leave. He stayed close on Jane's hip.

They were alone for a second in the dining room and Grayson tugged her into a hug.

"You okay?" he whispered in her ear.

"Yeah." She leaned against his chest and breathed in the masculine woodsy scent of her man. "Thanks to you."

"I'm not going anywhere, ya know?" he said. "And I'm not going to break your heart."

"You heard her?" she asked in a breathless whisper, completely mortified.

His chin rubbed over the top of her head as he nodded. "I can't promise that I won't piss you off. And I probably can't promise that I won't ever hurt you. But I can promise that it won't be on purpose. I love you, baby."

"I love you, too." She wrapped her arms tighter around his waist and held on. Throughout the day she'd felt like a tiny canoe being tossed on the swells of an angry ocean. Grayson was her anchor. He kept her boat from sinking.

"Your dad pulled me aside and gave me permission."

"Yeah?" she asked, her boat jumping to the top of the highest wave.

"Know that you'll be my wife. I'm not going to tell you when or how that question will be asked formally, but plan on spending the rest of your life with me."

Jane's heart soared.

"You're pregnant, aren't you?"

The question, asked by her mother, caused the sweet happiness of the moment to flee like light being doused into shadow with the flick of a switch.

Grayson turned with his arm around Jane's waist. His hip was in front of her, protecting her. His fingers fisted and released at her side. She could actually hear the grinding of his teeth. He took an audible breath, held it and blew it out—loudly.

"Ms. Alexander," he said low and directly, "you may think that your daughter is unlovable."

"I—"

"You may think that I am not worthy of her love."

"You're not," Sheri snapped, her hands on her hips.

"I happen to agree with you," he said, completely unaffected by the insult. "I have never been more grateful to gain the love of a woman I don't deserve. A woman I love more than anything else in this world."

"You broke her heart!" Sheri shouted, her face turning red.

"And so have you," Grayson shouted back. He stepped away from Jane and stood inches away from Sheri, glaring down at her. "Every time you open your mouth, you spout venom that destroys her a little bit at a time. As of today this woman is my responsibility, a responsibility that I take very seriously. I will protect her, even if I have to protect her from you."

Sheri's mouth opened and closed and opened again—only to close. Her eyes couldn't possibly get any wider. Jane didn't think hers could either, or that her heart could get any fuller. A slight movement caught her eye and she noticed that her father stood off to the side.

Jane didn't miss the slight smile on her father's lips. There weren't many people brave enough to go toe-to-toe with Sheri Alexander.

Her father cleared his throat and said calmly, "I think everyone needs to calm down."

The soft, peaceful voice of reason seemed to snap Grayson out of his rage, even if Mom still had steam pouring out of her ears. Grayson turned and looked at Jane, closed his eyes and crossed to where she stood next to her father. He kissed her lightly on the cheek and she could almost feel the emotion rolling off him.

"I believe there are presents to be opened," Grayson said, his voice still tight.

Paul clapped his hands in a loud pop. "Grayson's right. This isn't the time for—" He stopped, his gaze resting on Sheri, who stood behind Jane and Grayson.

Jane didn't dare turn around to see the expression on her mother's face.

Paul smiled and waved a hand, leading the way. "Come on *everybody*, let's go into the living room."

TENSION WAS SO THICK IN THE AIR, GRAYSON was sure he could have sliced a knife through it and watched as the two halves peeled away. He hated that all of his pent-up frustration with Sheri Alexander came to the equivalent of a mushroom cloud today, of all days.

The last straw had been placed upon his back though. As if the only way he'd marry Jane would be because she was pregnant! The clock had ticked by—thirty-three minutes—and he was still so pissed his blood boiled in his veins.

He sat next to Jane on the couch. Her hand on his thigh, her fingers rubbing gentle, calming circles. It was her touch that kept him grounded. And he could tell that he was steadying her. He wasn't sure why they were still under this roof, but if Jane wanted to stay, then there was no way in hell he was leaving.

"We don't have a gift for you," Sheri told him matter-of-factly, "we didn't expect you."

Jane stiffened next to him. "I told you he was coming, Mother."

"Yes, well, we weren't sure whether or not he was going to actually show up." She bent over to pick up a gift and muttered under her breath, "He's not exactly trustworthy."

His jaw clamped shut. He hadn't realized he was jumping to his feet until Jane stood as well. She took his hand and lifted it to her lips. The tender touch moved through his body like a cool rush of calm. She smiled, love blazing in her eyes.

"Would you mind getting the gift from the car?"

"Sure thing, baby doll." He bent to kiss her and whispered, "Thank you," in her ear.

Jane being Jane, she knew what he needed and provided the opportunity; a few minutes to cool off. He sliced a warning glance at Sheri before he slipped out the door. The icy breeze that greeted him was a slap of reality. As much as he wished to just get in his car and flee, he hurried to grab the gift basket and get back into the house. Because Jane needed him.

"I wasn't sure what size to get, so I got one that I knew would fit," Sheri was saying when he got back inside.

Jane was standing with a t-shirt held up to herself.

Fit who? Grayson thought. The shirt was so big that he might just fit in it—with her. He smiled thinking they'd have to try that when they got home.

"Oh!" Sheri breathed when she realized he'd come back in. "What a beautiful basket! Did you do this, Jane?"

"Actually Grayson did it."

Sheri nodded. "I'm not surprised. Well, actually, I am. I'd never taken *you* for the crafty type."

"There's more to me than you know," he countered without missing a beat.

She took the basket from him and began picking through the sodas and boxes of microwave popcorn and DVD's. "This must have cost you a fortune."

"She can afford it," Grayson said. And he sure as hell could!

"Yes, I guess she can." Sheri sighed. "Would you like to stay for dessert and a movie?"

He shot a quick glance at Jane. She didn't nod, didn't shake her head, didn't really react at all. But she didn't have to. Grayson knew she was done.

He spoke for the both of them. "Thanks for the invitation, but we're gonna head for home."

"Home?" The idea of them sharing a home obviously didn't please Sheri. "What are people going to say?" she asked her daughter not waiting for an answer before asking him, "What is your mother going to say?"

"Would it surprise you to know that my mother is thrilled?"

Sheri waited a second to let that sink in then huffed, "I guess you can wear cream."

"She'll wear white."

"Grayson." Jane walked to his side and eased her fingers through his. He wondered if he'd over-stepped, insisting what color she'd wear. She wasn't one to be told what to do. "What if I want to wear fuchsia?"

Sheri literally swooned. Paul caught her and awkwardly waved a scrap wrapping paper over her face. Grayson didn't miss the humorous glint in the older man's eyes. Jane took their coats from a chair by the door and offered his to him. Grayson opened the door as Sheri's eyelids fluttered.

"Sweetheart," he said a little louder than was necessary, "you can wear fuchsia and I think I'll wear chartreuse."

20

"OKAY, GRIP IT WITH YOUR RIGHT HAND AND wrap your left hand under it for support."

Grayson's hands were warm against hers and his body was hot pressed to her back. She followed his directions. The earplugs muffled the sound of his voice and she knew he was practically shouting but since they were the only ones in the firing range it still felt intimate.

"Good." He rewarded her with a kiss on the cheek. "Take aim and fire when you're ready."

She spread her feet and shifted the gun in her hands to get a better, more comfortable grip. Grayson's help had been ... helpful and hot. However she liked to do things her way. She concentrated on the target that swung from its hooks three yards down range and closed her left eye. Focusing on the target through the sites, she slowly curved her finger. She felt the moment that the trigger caught and registered the shot before split-second it went off.

Firing five more shots in quick succession emptied the magazine and she turned to face Grayson. His mouth hung open and his eyes were the size of saucers. She grinned. He took a step toward her and pushed the button to bring the target forward.

Six perfect shots in the middle of the chest.

He plucked it from the clips and ran a finger over her grouping. "This isn't the first time you've shot a pistol, is it?" His question wasn't accusatory. It was more dumbfounded awe than anything else.

"No." She placed her weapon on the counter and eased up against him. "The truth is that I've wanted one of those little babies for a long time."

That made him smile. He tipped her chin and kissed her lightly on the lips. "Why didn't you tell me?"

"Well—" She wrapped her arms around his waist. "—I wanted you to *teach* me to shoot a gun. I love your hands on me."

A low groan rumbled in his chest and Jane laughed. She could also feel his response to her a little lower and loved that she could make him crazy, loved that she wasn't alone in the need to touch one another.

"I love my hands on *you*." His hands moved down the curve of her spine and rested on her butt. He squeezed and dropped his head to where the muffs protected her ears. He lifted the muff and whispered, "Let's see what else you've got. If you do that again, I'll make it worth your while."

She was about to ask how he was going to do that when his teeth closed over her earlobe. An erotic shiver raced up her spine. Fighting the urge to jump his bones right there in the shooting range, Jane tore herself out of Grayson's hold and began reloading the magazine. The first four bullets slipped into the magazine without much effort but bullets five and six took a little more pressure to get them seated. She put the magazine back in the butt of the gun and waited while Grayson pressed the button that zipped the little paper outline down to the far end of the range.

"Twenty-five feet."

"No problem." She made sure that the muffs were in place and took aim.

Bam!

She paused, took a breath and fired again. She didn't need the break, just the theatrics. It wasn't much fun if the challenge wasn't a challenge. She fired off the last five shots and they formed a group that was no bigger than her fist.

A zipping sound brought the target forward and Grayson yanked it from the pins. "Hot damn! Wyatt Earp has nothin' on you, babe. I'm impressed. Seriously impressed. If I'm ever in a gun fight I want you at my back."

She placed the gun down and used her fingertips to rub up his thigh, getting dangerously close to his groin. "Wouldn't you rather have me at your front?"

He pressed her back until her spine hit the gun rest. "I want you ... to pull my trigger."

She laughed when he held up a weapon that looked like it had come straight out of Wyatt Earp's era. She had to admit that a gun range wasn't the most romantic place on earth. But being here with Grayson made it that way. Just being with him made her blood warm. His touch, his suggestive statements heated her in other places.

"How about we make this interesting?" she asked.

"I'm listening." He cocked his head to the side, one brow raised.

"Back the targets out to forty feet. The one with the best score gets to make the plans for the rest of the day."

"I like that. You're gonna shoot this." He held out the long-barreled revolver.

"That's fine. You're gonna shoot *this*." She gave him the LCP.

His hands dwarfed the tiny gun ... just like she knew they would. He'd have trouble getting off clean, accurate shots because it wasn't the right fit. She was counting on that. She'd seen men try to fire this particular gun and knew that it took the knuckle closest to their hand to pull the trigger.

He narrowed his eyes and she could see the challenge in them. She could also see that he knew that she'd stacked the deck against him.

"Let's see what you've got, Pierce."

He stepped over to the next lane and took aim. Back so far, at the furthest end of the range, the targets were under the heat vent and flapped in the gentle breeze. She let Grayson shoot first. Not bad. At least not as bad as she'd thought—or hoped.

Her turn. The gun she held now was heavy. Inwardly she groaned.

The larger the caliber, the larger the recoil. Personally she hated the reverberation that ricocheted up her arm. Once when she'd gone out shooting with her grandfather she felt a tingling sensation in her upper arm and shoulder a week later. She anticipated having that with this gun.

It was way too big for her hand as she wrapped her fingers around the grip. Like Grayson not having right finger placement on the trigger, Jane didn't either. She had to use the very tip of her finger which didn't offer the kind of control she liked to have.

Deep breath in, long breath out.

She closed her eye and squeezed off a shot. The trigger was light and the gun discharged before she'd anticipated it would. She hit the target— barely. Grayson laughed, a little too mockingly for Jane's taste. She glared at him.

"You shouldn't tease me while I'm holding a gun."

He laughed harder. "I'm not sure you're any kind of threat with that one."

She narrowed her eyes and glared right through him. She would make him pay by making the final five shots count. She would win this bet and have him painting her toenails.

The next shots were indeed better. As the targets zipped closer she wasn't sure who the winner would be. Grayson left his target on the clips and counted. "Forty, eighty, one-twenty, one-sixty, one-ninety, and the bulls-eye makes one-forty. What'd you get, baby doll?"

She'd been counting hers as he did his. "One-thirty," she groaned.

"Yes!" He pumped his arms in the air. "I know exactly what I want you to do."

"What's that?" Yeah, she sounded like sour grapes. She hated to lose! Especially when she lost when doing something that she was really damned good at.

"Oh, come on." He scooped her up against him. "I promise you'll enjoy it too."

The taste of defeat was bitter on her tongue when she swallowed. She inhaled and the masculine scent of him mixed with burned gunpowder filled her nose. The smell and being so close to him melted away the irritation. This time when she asked, "What do you have planned?" there was no edge to the question.

He smiled, looked over his shoulder to make sure no one was watching before he pressed his lips to her neck. She shuddered as his tongue traced over the soft tissue beneath her ear. Once again he removed the muff and whispered exactly what he had planned.

And he was right ... she was going to like it.

SHOOTING WITH JANE—AND THE ADVENTURES afterward—had been the best day ever. It'd been two days ago, but the image of Jane squaring herself to the target and firing off those first six shots, nearly made Grayson lose himself.

She'd pretended not to know how to shoot. She'd been smart if she'd made him the bet *before* he knew what kind of marksman she was. He definitely would have lost then. As it was, he only won by the skin of his teeth—and a stray shot by Jane.

Normally Grayson didn't like to be bested. In this case, however, he enjoyed it.

Grayson loved that she was a crack shot. His girl could outshoot him or any of his friends. He looked forward to the day when he could take her out and show her off.

The little worrying niggle that had been slithering through his stomach had eased some. But not completely.

He was pretty sure that Derek hadn't just gone away. The guy had had a cushy gig playing Grayson. The "job" had given him money and status and publicity—and women.

Freshman year the two had been paired as roommates. Derek had an academic scholarship, Grayson baseball. And Grayson had to admit that they looked a lot alike, eerily so. Especially when Derek went the extra mile to make the impersonation almost flawless. As much as they were similar physically, they were polar opposites when it came to everything else—and Grayson was happy to keep it that way. He wanted to be nothing like Derek.

The first week of school, Grayson walked in on something that made his blood curdle. He'd made Derek promise to leave his side of the room alone, muttered an "at least put a sock on the handle", and left.

He always knocked from then on out.

Derek was a sexual deviant. And that scared Grayson. Because not only was he a perverted sonofabitch, he looked at Jane with lust in his eyes.

In Derek's mind, Grayson was sure, this wasn't over. Derek had had everything that was Grayson's for so long that stopping cold turkey wasn't going to be a pliable option—for Derek.

Seeing that Jane could protect herself, if needs be, relaxed Grayson a bit.

Jane would be home from work soon and Grayson had big plans for the night. He jogged up the stairs and lit the candles. He turned his attention back the new red satin sheets he'd bought. The things were like ice. He considered changing them for flannel ones but decided that if things went according to plan the sheets would be warm soon enough.

He went out into the hall to crank the heat—just in case.

A sound from downstairs caught his attention. He dipped his head to look under the railing. "Jane?" he hollered.

No response came.

The increase in his heart rate should have been a red flag. Looking back, playing Monday-morning-quarterback, he would realize that taking a weapon with him was the best course of action—and would have put a stop to the events about to unfold.

He cautiously took the stairs, pausing on the bottom one. "Jane?"

Still no answer.

His foot had just hit the tile floor when something hard hit him in the back of the head. There was a burst of light just before...

Everything went dark.

DEREK KICKED GRAYSON IN THE SIDE AND didn't get even a gratifying grunt. As if the bastard wasn't irritating enough, he was now bleeding all over the frickin' floor. Derek went into the kitchen and took a dishcloth from the counter. He wrapped it around Grayson's head to help minimize the mess.

He really didn't have time for this crap. Since the romantic sap had been upstairs lighting candles and turning down the bed Derek bet that Jane would be home soon.

And his plan wouldn't work if she came home to find both of them together, not to mention that she'd probably freak out to see all the blood gushing from the back of Grayson's head.

He couldn't have that.

The last time he'd come face-to-face with the woman, she'd recognized that he wasn't Grayson Pierce—the weak, pathetic version of Grayson Pierce. He wasn't sure how she'd known but he was going to test her again.

If she figured it out then he'd spend the night teaching her that submitting to his dominance could take her higher than she'd ever been before.

Slipping his hands under Grayson's shoulders, Derek hefted him to the door that hid the space beneath the stairs. Derek had made sure there was enough room to hide Grayson's body from view until he could dispose of it.

He was just kicking the door closed when he heard a key slip in the lock. With a grin on his face, he ran upstairs to prepare for his brand of seduction.

21

"GRAYSON," JANE CALLED AS SHE OPENED the door.

There was no snow on the ground but it was really, really cold outside. She closed the door and shivered as the warmth of her home enveloped her. She dropped her bag on the floor just inside the door and shucked her coat. Lights were on upstairs and she could see well enough. She tipped her head upward and called his name again. A smile tipped her lips as she thought of him up in her bed eagerly waiting for her to come up and greet him.

She would do just that ... after she grabbed something to drink and a quick bite to eat. The Jazz had had a game tonight, which meant that Jane didn't get dinner. She was starving—for something other than Grayson.

She yanked the fridge door open and stuck her head in to see what leftovers were ... left. Nothing sounded particularly palatable. She grabbed a can of Diet Coke and was turning to pull out a box of crackers when she felt the warm body come up behind her.

The exhaustion of the day consumed her and she leaned back against the support of his body. "Oh, Grayson," she moaned.

His fingertips moved her hair away from her neck and his lips met her skin. She stiffened a bit and her adrenaline spiked. She tried to keep her distress under control. He was too close. He would sense her panic. She would have to be very careful. His hand went around her waist and pulled her back into him.

"How was your day?" he whispered.

"Good. Busy. Yours?" Alarm bells blared behind her ears. She was in trouble. Serious trouble. Even as she contemplated how to handle her current situation there was a question racing through her mind that worried her even more; *Where the hell was Grayson?*

"I've missed you." The words were a low erotic purr in her ear.

"I didn't get dinner," she said. "I'm starved. You want something?"

"You."

Bile rose in her throat as she pasted a smile on her lips. She hoped her lips didn't quiver as she turned in his arms. "Let me feed my belly first," she said.

Her only game plan was to play along and act as though she didn't know that the man in front of her was Derek Reese. It was her only hope of getting a chance to protect herself. She crossed the kitchen, forcing herself to do so without jerky, rushed movements.

Pulling the fridge open again, she removed some leftover cooked chicken, a cube of cream cheese, butter, eggs, milk. She wasn't sure what she was going to make, her mind wasn't on cooking. She went to pantry and took out a box of fettuccine. She had no idea how to make Alfredo sauce but Derek didn't know that and she was sure it would take a while before he realized she was clueless.

She put the cream cheese and butter in a pan. They sizzled and popped. The pop made her jump. She needed to get upstairs. If she could just—

"Can you stir this? Don't let it burn."

"Where are you going?" he asked incredulously.

She lifted her shoulders in what she hoped was a nonchalant shrug. "I just want to change. I'll be right back."

"I could help you change."

Once again she forced herself to smile. "If you help me I won't get to eat."

"You'll get to eat alright."

She laughed and heard an edge of hysterics to the sound. She walked over to where he stood by the table and handed him the wooden spoon. "Stir. I'll be right back."

He smacked her on the butt with the spoon as she left. She yelped and he laughed.

Her bottom still stung when she got to the bedroom. Candles burned and new satin sheets adorned the bed. She was sure that both of those things were Grayson's doing. That gave her a bit of hope.

Hope eclipsed by fear, but she had to hold on to that hope or she was going to lose it!

Breath raced in and out of her lungs in frantic gusts. *Pull it together! Now is not the time to hyperventilate.*

She bent over and put her head between her legs and forced the inhale and exhale to slow. As soon as she was in control again, she would be able to protect herself.

She was just standing up, ready to retrieve her gun from the nightstand drawer when Derek cleared his throat. She jumped and whirled to see him leaned against the door jamb with his arms folded over his chest.

He was shorter than Grayson but only by millimeters. His shoulders were just as wide though. He nearly filled the doorway. Jane swallowed hard. Derek was dangerous enough when they were in

the kitchen but here in her bedroom, he was deadly. As if following her train of thought, his eyes
moved to the bed and he grinned.

"What about dinner?" she asked, a tone of panic
in her voice.

"It can wait." When she opened her mouth to
protest he said, "Don't worry, I turned everything
off. The only fire in this house tonight will be right
here."

Jane's heart was hammering so hard in her
chest that she couldn't hear. Breath puffed in and
out of her lungs in pants. This time she   really
was going to hyperventilate. Her anxiety only got
worse when Derek stepped forward, pulling a piece
of black fabric from his pocket.

"You   promised   you   wouldn't   blindfold   me
again," she muttered, her eyes widening as he
stretched the fabric out between his hands.

"And I won't." His laugh was so sinister she
wondered if he was going to tie her to a railroad
track. "I have big plans for tonight, honey."

As if she needed another verification that this
lunatic wasn't the man she loved, the term of en-
dearment sent her already churning stomach into
convulsions.

He grinned behind his trimmed goatee. "What's
the matter, never done anything this naughty? I
promise you'll like it."

"I don't really like to be hurt."

"This is different." He stalked her, his unwilling
prey. She squeaked when his hand grabbed hold
of her wrist and he began tying the soft fabric
around her wrist. "We're gonna play some games
tonight. Games you'll never forget."

Of that she was sure. She would *never* forget a
moment of this night. They would forever haunt
her.

Hard hands gripped the front of her shirt and tugged hard. Buttons flew, exposing skin and her sensible white, cotton bra. Smooth fingertips moved over the swell of her breasts. She sucked in a breath, trying to put space between her skin and his touch.

"You have the most beautiful tits."

"Thanks," she murmured quietly. If she could keep him talking she might be able to come up with a plan to save herself—and Grayson. *Where is he?*

Derek's hands were rough as he pushed the shirt from her shoulders. It fluttered to the floor at her feet. "*This*—" He tugged at her bra strap, letting it go so that it snapped back to hit her skin. "—doesn't do it for me. Put on something sexy. Now."

His harsh command startled her. With a flinch, she hurried to the closet, grateful he didn't follow her. She changed into a sexy red bra with lace cups. Grayson loved it and the thought caused her heart to stutter. She was about to get raped by a man who wanted everything that belonged to Grayson—including her. She wasn't sure how to stop it either. There was no house phone and her cell was downstairs in her purse.

"I'm waiting," Derek said tersely.

She didn't bother to take off her pants—or even her shoes. If he was going to do this to her, then he was going to have to take it. He was going to have to fight her. When it came down to it, he was going to have one hell of a fight on his hands. Jane would play along for only so long. She would *not* willingly give herself to another man, especially *that* man.

She gritted her teeth and walked out of the closet, through the bathroom, pausing to stand in the archway that separated the two rooms.

He smiled when he saw her. "Much better," he said in a low guttural groan. He lifted a finger and crooked it at her. "Come here. I want to taste you."

Her feet refused to move. Her brain sent the signal, but it was like she'd stepped into cement. Her hesitation didn't impress him. His dark eyes narrowed and he began to remove his belt. He snapped it when it came loose.

"I said, come here."

Again she tried to move, but her feet wouldn't listen. He stood and folded his belt in half, tugging the ends together to make it crack. She jumped.

"Bad behavior gets disciplined. I'd like nothing more than to spank you, but I'm not sure you'd like it." He pointed at her then at the floor at his feet. "Come. Here."

This time her feet did move. He was right; she didn't like the idea of getting "spanked". Heaven knew she didn't like it as a child—and that had only been with a hand ... by someone who loved her.

Her feet trudged over the carpeting which had taken on the consistency of tar. It took effort to place one foot in front of the other. He reached out and took hold of the waistband of her jeans, tugging her to him.

"Why so nervous? We've done this before."

Somewhere behind all the terror was the realization that this guy was totally nuts. She and *Grayson* had made love before, but never had *Derek* touched her in intimate ways. She lifted her eyes to his and searched them for some semblance of sanity. There wasn't a whole lot reflected back at her besides desire and ... *crazy!*

He picked up the ribbon that was tied around her wrist and let it slip through his fingers. "I'm going to tie you up."

No! her thoughts screamed. The rest of her body protested in other ways. She needed to think fast or she was going to be completely at his mercy. The thought horrified her.

Her eyes darted to the nightstand. To her only hope for salvation. He followed her line of sight and grinned. "What's over there?"

He took a step toward it and she grabbed his arm. She prayed for enough bravado to carry off the lie that was about to cross her tongue. "The truth is, baby—" She traced a fingertip over the skin bared by the V in his shirt. He sucked in a breath and groaned. "—I've been meaning to try something with you, too. I am a little bit of a naughty girl and wasn't sure you would go for it."

His lids grew hooded, his eyes dreamy.

"I have a toy in there that I want you to use on me while I'm all tied up and at your mercy." The words tasted vile on her tongue. She hated to lead this psychopath on when what she really wanted to do was knee him in the balls and run for her life.

Heat rolled off him and when he pressed himself against her, she could feel the hardness of him. It frightened her that he was so aroused. But she would use it to her advantage. He grinned down at her, all lecherous teeth. He bent his head to kiss her and she put her fingers to his lips.

"Huh-uh. There will be time for that later. What I need is for you to grab the lubricant from the bathroom."

For someone hell-bent on being dominant he sure took orders well. She stumbled; he'd released her so quickly. As soon as he was out of sight, she raced over to the nightstand. She tugged the drawer open and felt a calm rush of relief at the sight of her savior lying amongst her panties.

She didn't waste a second.

The feel of the metal in her palm was a welcome coolness that relaxed her. Holding the weapon in her right hand, she pulled the slide back with her left, putting a bullet in the chamber. The gun was ready. She was ready. This was going to end as soon as Derek came back. Grayson would have known where to find the lubricant, would have known that he didn't have to even leave the room. Luckily there was another unopened box under the counter.

She could hear drawers being opened and closed, cupboards slamming. The search seemed to be aggravating Derek, which was just fine by her. Her heart was pounding a little faster than normal but she felt calmer than she had since the ordeal had begun with the press of Derek's lips to the back of her neck.

When Derek came out of the bathroom he was buck naked. She had to fight the urge to laugh. Not because he held up the box of KY like he'd struck gold or because his eyes had widened absurdly at the sight of her with a gun in her hand. Derek may have been able pass for Grayson Pierce when fully clothed but no one would ever confuse the two the way God made them.

She bit her lip and gripped the gun tighter in her hand. "Did you really think I wouldn't notice your ... deficiency?"

"I am not deficient," he growled. The lubricant dropped to the floor with a thud and he advanced on her, murder in his eyes.

"Stay back, asshole." She motioned him away with her gun.

"You won't shoot me."

"I wouldn't be so sure, if I were you. It seems to me that I promised you once that I would. And that promise hasn't changed." She narrowed her eyes, letting the animosity she felt for the man to flood the room. "The jig's up, *Derek.*"

Surprisingly he was nonplussed by the fact that he was naked as the day he'd been born, standing at the business end of a gun—held by a really pissed off woman. He shrugged. "When did you figure it out?" he asked calmly.

"The second you kissed my neck."

"No." He shook his head. "You couldn't have known that soon. When did you know?"

"Grayson has calluses on his fingertips. You don't. Grayson's lips are a bit chapped from riding Zeus in the cold. Yours are smooth as a baby's butt." She enjoyed watching his boldness drain into insecurity. "Shall I go on with the differences between you? I could probably do so all night." As she said the last words she let her eyes drop to his manhood.

"Enough!" he shouted. He started for her only to stop. Panic flashed across his face and his eyes were wild as they sought out the window.

Sirens.

She was so relieved she might just cry.

He rushed toward the doorway but Grayson filled the path of his exit. He had her cell phone pressed to his ear. "I don't think so, Derek."

The sight of Grayson alive and well made her eyes burn. The scene before her began to blur and she blinked violently. She couldn't lose it now. Grayson was hurt, blood still oozed from a gash at the back of his head, running down his neck. She needed to maintain control of the situation.

From downstairs a loud crash sounded, quickly followed by the identification of the newcomers.

"Police!" Shouts rose from down below, growing louder as heavy footsteps pounded up the stairs. "Police!"

She looked toward the doorway, relieved that law enforcement was only seconds away. Just as she saw the first dark uniform, Grayson yelled and out of the corner of her eye she saw a flash of movement on the other side of the room.

In the moment that followed, Jane didn't think. She only reacted. Instinct kicked in and she let her gut call the shots. Her grip tightened on the butt of the gun, her finger curling around the trigger.

The shot exploded. The smell of gunpowder filled the air and Jane's ears rang. Her hand fell limply at her side, the gun hitting the floor with a soft thud.

A maelstrom swirled around her and she stood in the eye of the storm. She recognized what was happening but didn't register any of it.

As uniforms filled the room, she let the tears she'd kept at bay cascade over her cheeks, not having the energy to wipe them away. She was petrified. She was numb. The threat was over; Derek lay in a motionless heap near the foot of the bed. He'd almost reached her.

He'd almost gotten to her.

Jane stared at Derek. Was he dead?

Her head swiveled loosely on her neck, finding Grayson just as he dropped to one knee and put a hand to the back of his head.

In the recesses of her mind she heard an officer ask where he could get a towel for Grayson's head. Jane was in the room but she wasn't present. So this is what an out-of-body experience was like, she thought, unamused and totally unimpressed. She heard Grayson respond in the affirmative and watched as he pointed to the bathroom.

An officer stepped up to her like she was dangerous; his hands outstretched, his voice low and calm like he were talking her off the parapet of a building. It was then that she realized she still held the gun.

But she'd dropped it.

She knew she'd dropped it. She heard it—

But as she looked down at her hand, there it was. It wasn't pointed anywhere, just hung lose amongst her fingers.

Well, hell, she was armed. However, in her current state of mind she was far from dangerous.

Numbly, she lifted her hand and relinquished the gun. And then she ... melted. Her muscles just gave out. She crumbled to the ground like a ragdoll and sobbed.

The situation was over.

She was safe. Grayson was safe.

Grayson.

She scrambled over to him on her knees, tripping over a book that had somehow fallen from the nightstand to the floor. With hands that shook she wiped the tears from her cheeks. Grayson's eyes were wild as they searched her for injuries. She kissed his cheeks, his lips, his eyes. He groaned as she grabbed the back of his head to pull him closer.

"I'm sorry. I'm sorry." She took his face between her hands. "Are you okay?"

He smiled, but she could see the pain in his expression and in his eyes. He wasn't fooling her. He wasn't okay. He was alive, but he was far from okay. He needed a doctor. As if they'd read her mind two officers reached down and helped him to his feet.

"There's an ambulance just outside. Let's get downstairs then we can get you on a gurney."

"No gurney," Grayson said ... then hissed in pain as he got to his feet. "I'll walk."

"Okay," one of the officers said. "You'll walk. We'll help keep you upright."

The other officer smiled kindly. "Are you okay?" he asked her.

Yes. And no.

She didn't trust her voice so she just nodded.

He nodded back. "We should probably get you a shirt before we go."

Again she nodded. She'd heard the words but couldn't quite wrap her brain around the fact that she was standing in her bra and that it was cold outside. All she could think about was that Grayson was bleeding, that he could barely stand ... and that the nightmare was over.

The officer came back and put a t-shirt in her hand. "Jane," he said softly, "put the shirt on and we'll get out of here."

She tugged it over her head, shivering at the sensation of warmth on her cold skin. The officer put a hand on her back between her shoulder blades and she jumped. She'd known that he was only guiding her toward the door, but she couldn't stop the flinch at the contact.

"It'll be okay," the man in uniform said from behind her.

Would it?

She couldn't be sure.

The officer was close, his hand on her arm, helping her down the stairs. She didn't brush his hand away because she didn't want to fall. And since her legs weren't working quite right, that was a real possibility.

A thought occurred to her and panic slammed into her. She stopped suddenly, jerking her arm away. He paused on the stair below her. "Jane, are you okay?" More with the danger-to-herself-and-others voice.

"Am I going to jail?" she asked in an unemotional monotone.

Tears welled again as he smiled at her. Recognition sparked somewhere deep in her memory. She knew this officer. She'd met him before, but didn't know his name. Yes, she did. She did know his name … but couldn't remember it.

His eyes were kind as he assured her, "I really don't think so, Jane. It was self-defense."

"You're sure? I shot him." *You have the right to remain silent, stupid!*

"I saw it, Jane. With my own eyes, I saw it. There will be an investigation but, as your friend, I don't think there will be any charges."

So, she did know him.

"Come on, Grayson is waiting for you in the ambulance."

Surprisingly, that gentle urging made her feel better.

Maybe it *would* be okay. As soon as she could hold Grayson in her arms and lose herself in nothing other than him, then maybe … just maybe, she would be okay.

On the periphery of her shell-shocked mind she noticed that lights flashed and neighbors gawked. She noticed that Molly was telling Clayton off, her finger in his face. Jane climbed in beside where Grayson was sitting on the gurney inside the ambulance.

"I'm okay, baby doll. I'm okay."

When he opened his arms she slid into his lap and buried her head against his shoulder. She was tired, so very tired. She felt Grayson kiss the top of her head and she considered that she too might just be okay.

22

It'd been nearly a month since Derek's attack. With cold sweat dotting his skin and the out of control pounding of his heart, Grayson reached out to regain his sanity. Jane rolled into his arms, resting her head on his shoulder.

His breathing slowed. His heart rate returned to normal. But he couldn't find enough peace to sleep. He tightened his hold on Jane.

The nightmare had been the same; the outcome different. Instead of Derek lying dead on the floor, it was Jane's blood staining the floor.

His heart kicked.

He kissed her forehead and tried to think of something happier. But his thoughts refused to leave the events of that night.

When he woke and found himself with a blinding headache in a dark closet he'd panicked. He could hear the soft lilt of her voice upstairs, she sounded in complete control of her emotions. His first instinct was to race to her rescue. He probably would have if his first step hadn't dropped him to his knees.

Her bag was on the floor near the door and he prayed that her cell phone would be in the pocket. It was. He'd dialed 9-1-1, informed the operator of his emergency then stalked up the stairs.

Jane had been stone cold calm with her gun pointed at Derek. The sight had made Grayson's vision blur. More from the stars of pain than the tears of relief, his macho side insisted.

Even now he had to laugh at the lie.

Jane sighed in his arms and tipped her head. He thought she was asleep until her lips pressed against his neck.

"Go back to sleep, my sweet," she whispered. "I'm okay. You're okay. We're okay."

He kissed the top of her head. He'd murmured those exact words to her when the nightmares that haunted her brought her seeking the comfort of his arms.

"I love you, baby doll. I really do."

"I know. Now, sleep."

GRAYSON RUBBED AT HIS GOATEE WHILE he waited to be interviewed—again. Definitely not his favorite thing in the world. But Jane thought it would be a good idea to get his side of the story out to the world. The gossip rags were making Derek out to be a victim. Grayson knew that Jane was right.

Even as his head understood that fact, he tried to convince the rest of his body that he wasn't nervous. He couldn't ignore the butterflies in his stomach or the fact that he was going to wear a hole in the carpet if Jane didn't come out soon.

Sure, he could have called Jane on her cell phone, but she wanted their relationship to be professional. So he would wait in the lobby—like a professional.

There was a whole 'lotta burgundy in this room, he thought as he continued another circuit around the room. He paused to watch the replay of an earlier newscast on a television mounted on the wall, and admired the pictures; large headshots of the major players in the KHB family. Jane's smiling face warmed his heart. She was a beautiful woman. And she was his.

"Grayson," Nate's voice boomed from behind him.

Grayson turned and smiled. He stood and strode over to the other guy. Nate stuck out his hand and Grayson shook it. "It's good to see you, my man. How are Roxie and Gracie?"

"They're good. Come on, Jane's just finishing up." Nate strode toward the large set of glass doors and waved a keycard over an electronic sensor. There was a click and Nate pulled one of the doors open. He extended a hand in a silent *you first* and Grayson walked back into another foyer type area that contained a maze of hallways and a bank of two elevators.

Nate turned to the right and Grayson followed him through another set of glass doors, these ones were open. The newsroom was bustling with people, cubicles and desks dotted the gray flooring. They weaved through the labyrinth, making their way to the back corner.

Molly waved from where she sat in front of a computer, weather maps on the screen. He waved back and smiled. He really liked Molly. She was a good friend to the woman he loved. Her stalker had bothered him from the moment he'd learned about the lunatic, and after what happened with Derek, he was terrified for her.

Jane was at her desk, running a make-up brush over her nose and cheeks. She noticed him in the mirror she was looking in and he saw her eyes brighten. When she turned around though, she was all business.

She stood and stuck out her hand. He shook it, fighting the urge to tug her into his arms and kiss that serious look from her face. "Thank you for coming in, Mr. Pierce."

He cocked a brow and grinned at her. "Please call me Grayson. May I call you Jane?"

Nate laughed and shook his head. The big guy obviously agreed with Grayson; this whole act was ridiculous. Especially since the entire newsroom knew that Grayson's psycho look-alike had attacked both of them in *her* house.

"I believe Nate's got us set up over here," she said, walking over to where a camera rested on a tripod, facing a set of blue leather chairs.

"Where do you want me?" Grayson asked, hoping to take her mind somewhere erotic. He noticed the spark of sexual electricity before she blinked. It was gone when she opened her eyes again.

She motioned to the chair that was directly in front of the camera. He sat and she sat down in the other one. She crossed her legs, the flowing black pant legs flaring out over her feet.

Nate cleared his throat. "I know this isn't your first interview but I just want to remind you not to look directly at the camera."

Grayson nodded, grateful for the reminder. His mind was all kinds of muddled, sitting so close, yet so very, very far away from Jane.

"Rolling," Nate said.

"We're going to run most of this in its entirety. I'd like to edit it as little as possible, okay?" Jane said.

He nodded. "Sounds good." It was about damned time he got to tell his story.

Jane shifted in her seat and Grayson watched as she transformed into Sportscaster Extraordinaire. "Can you tell me about the man named Derek Reese?"

"I met Derek Reese in college. We were roommates. One Halloween he dressed up like me, uniform and all. There was an uncanny resemblance. It was a bit disturbing at the time but I didn't really think much of it." He shrugged. "Then I went to the majors."

"And what happened?"

"Would you believe that I wasn't interesting enough?" he said with a bitter laugh. "As it turns out nobody cares about a country boy, who lives on a ranch and loves his mother. My agent insisted that I needed to be a bad-boy, that in order to get better endorsement deals I needed to smear my squeaky-clean image. I didn't like that idea. At all. But when the paparazzi came home to roost, nearly running my mother off the road, I knew something had to change.

"Believe me, I hated that my name would get drug through the mud. But also realized that there was a solution; a win-win solution; I got to live the life I wanted and everyone else got what they wanted too."

"Enter Derek," she said.

"Yep, Enter Derek." Grayson laughed. "He was more than willing to live my life for me. I set him up in a Vegas apartment, gave him a fancy new set of wheels and he pretended to be me."

"So the party animal we've seen plastered all over the covers of tabloid magazines—"

"Derek."

"The guy convicted of drunk driving?"

"Derek."

"The guy accused of rape in New York."

"Derek."

With each pronunciation of the name, it became more of a curse. His blood was simmering below the surface and he took a deep breath to calm down. Jane seemed to notice it too, her fingers stretching toward his hand. She caught herself, though, pulling her hand back into lap.

"Why come clean now?" Jane asked.

He looked her in the eye and said with complete sincerity, "Because of Derek Reese I nearly lost everything."

"Can you be more specific?" Nate asked from behind the camera.

Grayson made a point to avoid making eye contact with the lens and looked at Nate. "I'm not talking about my career or any other personal items ... they can be replaced." His throat tightened. He lifted his fist to his mouth and cleared his throat.

"Then what did you almost lose?" Nate pressed, already knowing the answer. Grayson didn't doubt that Jane would make her photographer pay for steering the interview in this direction.

Grayson looked Nate in the eye and took the bait. "I nearly lost the woman I love."

Jane gasped then coughed in an attempt to cover it.

Grayson suspected that Nate knew exactly what he was doing. His thoughts were validated when Nate asked, "Anyone we know?"

"One thing all you media types need to learn about Grayson Pierce," Grayson said sarcastically, "is that I keep my private life private. And she wants to be in the spotlight even less than I do."

JANE TOOK CONTROL OF THE INTERVIEW again. "I'm sure that we're not the only ones eager to meet the lucky woman who's captured your heart."

Her heart fluttered when he smiled at her. "She really is something special. I'm sure that everyone will love her as much as I do."

She seriously needed to get off this topic before she jumped across the chair and kissed him. "I guess we should give you the last word. Is there anything that you wish to add?"

He thought for a moment then shook his head. "I don't drink. I would rather drive a four-by-four than a Porsche. I am a one-woman man, who is very much in love with one very special woman. If being who I am means that I'm boring and unmarketable, then ... I'm boring and unmarketable. And I like it that way."

"I can say that I like you that way, too," she said before the filter in her brain could stop the words.

Nate laughed out loud. She was going to kill him. He'd purposely led the interview into territory that was personal. And not just Grayson's personal life, but hers. She turned to glare at him. His laughter cut off abruptly, but humor remained in his expression and sparkling in his eyes.

"I think I hear a phone ringing," Nate said just before grabbing the camera and rushing off to hide in a corner somewhere.

"Coward," she called after him. He raised a hand in a wave, dismissing her as he retreated.

Grayson laughed. His hand covered hers where it gripped the armrest. The contact cooled her temper. "Will this air tonight?"

"Yeah. Then we're going to air the other piece tomorrow night. Dale is beside himself."

He stood and took her hand, helping her to her feet. She gave into the need to feel his arms around her and leaned into his chest. He hugged her to him. The weight of his chin was welcome on the top of her head. She sighed and wrapped her arms around his waist.

His hold tightened. "You know, we're probably going to be linked together in the media."

Jane sighed. "Yeah, I've thought of that."

"And?"

"Grayson, I think I'm pretty okay with speculation about us. I'd just really like to wait to confirm or deny—"

"Deny?'

Jane laughed at his distaste of the word. "Okay, let me rephrase that. I want to wait to *confirm* our relationship until I'm ready."

He kissed the top of her head. "I can live with that."

"I learned a lot from this experience."

"Yeah?"

"I nearly lost the man I love in that attack."

"But you didn't," he said in her ear. "I'm not going anywhere, baby. You're stuck with me for as long as you'll have me."

"How does forever sound?" she whispered.

23

Jane glared into the mirror, knowing full well that Grayson was looking at her reflection. She was pouting like a child. "Tell me."

"No. I'm not going to tell you. It's a surprise." Grayson went into the walk-in closet and returned with a dress bag. He held it out to her, the hanger dangling from his finger. "If you'll wear this, please."

Dressed in tuxedo pants and nothing else, Grayson was pretty damn hot. She watched his muscles flex with each movement and seriously considered nixing whatever he had planned and just watch him strut around in those black pants all night—or at least until she took them off of him. He shook out a crisp white shirt and shrugged one sleeve into it before walking into the bedroom.

She was so lost in the erotic plans of how she was going to remove his pants that she jumped when he called, "Ten minutes, baby doll. We don't want to be late."

She rolled her eyes and swiped the mascara wand over her lashes. He'd been very tight-lipped about what he had planned for their last night before baseball took him from her life for the next few months. On the bright side, the Rockets played their spring training in Arizona instead of

Florida. And his pilot's license would cut the time between visits.

A quick *ziiiip* of the black vinyl bag exposed red chiffon. She slowly, carefully pulled the dress out. It was beautiful; a halter top with flowing fabric that circled around her knees in elegant flutters.

She finished pinning her hair up on top of her head, leaving a few brown curls to kiss her neck and brow. She had to admit she was a little nervous for tonight. She had no idea where they were going. This was Salina; there wasn't a whole lot to do that required tuxedos and elegant gowns. In fact, there wasn't a single thing that she could think of.

After slipping her feet into red platform heels that would bring her to nearly the same height as Grayson—She hoped that she would get a lot of time to take advantage of the vertical increase—she walked down the short hallway and down the stairs where Grayson was waiting at the bottom. He'd donned the shirt and had even added the jacket and a bowtie that was the exact color of her dress.

"Aren't you cute?" Cute wasn't the right word though. The man was breathtakingly gorgeous. Again, she wanted to skip whatever was on the agenda for tonight and take him back upstairs and take her time undressing him.

He looked down at himself. "I do, don't I?"

She stopped on the bottom step and for the first time ever was actually taller than he was. She kinda liked it. She smiled and leaned down to kiss him. He obliged, tilting his chin up to meet her lips with his.

"Now will you tell me where we're going?"

"Not yet." He ran a finger down her neck and picked up the locket just to let it thunk against her breastbone. "You'll know soon enough."

✦ ✦ ✦

JANE WAS QUICKLY LEARNING THAT SHE hated surprises. He'd promised her that he wouldn't blindfold her again, but that didn't mean he wouldn't ask her to close her eyes—with the threat of busting out the blindfold if she peeked.

"Talk to me," she whispered.

His long fingers wrapped around hers and she instantly felt the calming influence his touch evoked. "What would you like me to say?"

"I don't know."

"Okay. Well, how about ... I love you? Or tonight will be perfect? Or you need to relax?"

"Those are all good things." She swallowed hard around the lump in her throat, trying to convince herself that she would not cry. Crying would seriously mess up her make-up and she didn't want to look like a raccoon. "I especially like the 'I love you' part."

"I love you," he said again, squeezing her hand. The car came to a stop and Grayson stated the obvious, "We're here."

"And where is here?"

"Patience, my love."

She loved that he called her his love. She loved that he loved her and wasn't afraid to tell her so. Grayson would be more than happy to stand on the highest rooftop and shout it at the top of his lungs. She, on the other hand, was a little nervous to announce her feelings to the world. Not that she didn't feel them; she just wanted to keep her personal and professional lives separate. Especially given that he was a major sports figure and she was a sportscaster. She'd worked too damned hard for her career to give anyone the impression that she was using Grayson to further it.

His door closed and moments later a cool breeze blew in as her door opened. He took her hand and helped her out of the car. She tried to listen for clues as to where they were; and got mostly nothing. Rocks crunched under her shoes. The surface was flat.

"Stairs," Grayson whispered, his arm moving around her back to steady her. "One more."

Then a door opened with a squeak. Cool air whooshed up around her, chiffon brushing around her knees. She was able to make out a low, steady thumping. Music? Another door squeaked. Yes, definitely music.

"You are the most beautiful woman I have ever known." Grayson's lips brushed her ear, his breath tickling. "I love you."

He was right behind her. She couldn't believe that she had actually kept her promise not to sneak a peek. Her eyes had remained closed. He put his hands on her waist and tapped. "Open your eyes."

She did ... and the scene before her stole her breath away. They were in the high school gym and it had never been so beautiful; crepe paper streamers, pink and white balloons, a DJ was doing his thing at one end and a refreshment table was set up at the other. It was also filled with people.

Most of the Rockets (sans Xavier) were dressed to the nines, some with women on their arms. Nate waved from the refreshment table—exactly where she'd expect him to be hanging out—and nudged Roxie with his elbow. She shot a glare at Nate then smiled at Jane. There were also faces Jane recognized from her high school days. And ... Jane gasped in surprise.

Molly rushed forward, throwing her arms around Jane's neck. The added height difference made the hug awkward and Molly let go after a quick squeeze. "He is so sweet. I can't believe he did this for you. He's a keeper, Jane."

Grayson was standing right next to them and Molly's approval was directed more to Grayson than to Jane. As if she and Grayson hadn't known that Molly adored him. The Christmas gift of a spa-day for Molly and Jane had pretty much sealed that deal. Jane beamed up at Grayson. He kissed the top of her head.

Molly glanced over at where Grayson's teammates were congregated and smiled. "Do you think you could introduce me?"

"You don't want any of them, Molly," Grayson told her. "They're not good enough for you."

"Yeah, well, I sure wish I could find someone who is." Molly sighed and faded into the crowd, every unworthy eye on her.

"I can't believe you did all this."

Grayson grinned. "I am pretty amazing."

Jane laughed. "Yes, you are."

"And what's really good about this prom—" His lips were right at her ear. "—there aren't any teachers gonna stick a biology book between us."

"You mean we can dance as close as we want?"

"Yep." He tugged her close. "I expect to be very close."

Warm, fuzzy feelings fluttered in her stomach but didn't get a chance to grab hold because Maude stepped forward. She took one of Jane's hands and one of Grayson's. She placed them together, holding them joined between her palms.

"I always knew you two were a perfect fit. There was a time when I didn't think it would work out between you and my heart broke. Then you show up on my doorstep—" Her voice cracked with emotion and she paused for a moment to gain control. "You are the daughter I've always wanted."

Now it was Jane who was overcome with emotion. "Thank you, Maude."

"Call me Mom."

"I'd like that, Mom."

Trent stepped up to them. He smiled at Jane. "I'm glad you finally came back into this schmuck's life," he told Jane. "He's been hopeless over you for as long as I can remember."

"Your memory's not that great," Grayson snorted.

"So you're not hopeless for me?" Jane asked, smiling.

"Oh, he is," Maude defended. "I'm his mother and I would know."

Grayson glared at Trent. "You're gettin' me in trouble, man. Get outta here."

Trent laughed and handed Grayson a microphone. As Trent sauntered away, Maude also slid away, leaving Grayson and Jane standing alone in front of the crowd. Grayson put his arm around Jane and tucked her into his side. The smile he gave her was huge and full of love. He looked out at their audience quickly then, lifting the microphone to his lips, spoke as if they were the only two people in the room.

"Every girl deserves to go to prom. Jane never got that—"

Well, hell. She'd wanted that horrible exclusion from her past to stay dead and buried right where it'd been for the last fifteen years.

"—I'm sorry to say that that tragedy is my fault. Thanks to all of you for helping me make it up to her." He dipped her backward and kissed her passionately—obscenely—as the onlookers whistled approvingly. He straightened, lifting her with a flourish. "Woo! I love this woman," he said into the microphone.

More whistling.

Heat rose in Jane's cheeks; not by the statement, but the fact that he'd made it publicly. Not that she was surprised. This forum wasn't exactly a rooftop, but it was nearly everyone they knew personally.

"Let's party!" he shouted.

And did they ever!

The entire group laughed and sang along to the songs that were becoming *classic*. She giggled through the entire Macarena and held Grayson's hand while doing the Electric Slide.

"Last song," the DJ announced and Grayson pulled her against his chest, his hands coming to rest on her hind-end.

He'd certainly made up for her missed prom—and his, technically. Tonight had been perfect, made better by the love that they shared.

"I love you." Her heart was so full of emotion she wanted to cry, wanted to scream, wanted to shout those words from the rooftops. If she'd had a microphone, she might have told all of their friends how she felt about the man holding her.

As they swirled around the dance floor, Grayson pressed a kiss to the skin under her ear. His hands made lazy circles on her back and she melted against him. "I've been thinking."

"About?" she purred, feeling completely content in his arms.

"I know you don't want the public to think that you're with me because of what it might do for your career. And I understand. I do. I get that. And if I were in your shoes, I would feel the same. With that said, I want to make you a deal."

"What kind of deal?" she asked hesitantly. The last deal she'd made with him had landed her in his home for a week—and she'd lost her heart to him.

He grinned and she had to smile, too. "Well ... if the Rockets win the World Series, we have a press conference to tell the world we're together."

"And if they lose?"

He feigned offense, pressing his hand to his heart. "*If*—and that's a big if, baby doll—we lose, then you get to decide when to announce our engagement."

"Our engagement?"

His hand slid between them, into his pocket, to produce a black velvet box. It opened with a click to expose a sparkly rock the size of a marble inside. It was big; an enormous solitaire diamond with channel set diamonds running around the band. And it was beautiful.

As gorgeous as the ring was, it was totally eclipsed by Grayson.

"Marry me, Janie."

She stared at him. Emotion swamped her. She couldn't believe that this wonderful man was offering to love her forever.

"Jane?"

"I only have one thing to say to you, Grayson Pierce," she said, keeping her tone flat.

His face feel and panic flared in his eyes. His Adam's apple bobbed with his swallow.

She smiled as sweetly as she could. "All I have to say is that ... it's about damned time you make it official."

"Is that a yes?" he asked, a chuckle in his voice.

"Abso-frickin'-lutely!"

"She said yes!" he shouted.

Their friends applauded and Grayson wrapped her in a hug, spinning her around.

"The Rockets *are* going to win," he promised her, sealing it with a kiss. "It took a lot of years but I finally won your trust and your heart. And by damn, I will bring that trophy home."

Staring up into his dark eyes she fell in love with him all over again, and didn't have a doubt that he would.

Epilogue

THE CROWD CHEERED.

Tickertape fluttered from the sky like brightly colored snow.

Jane stood shoulder to shoulder amongst the media and grinned up at Grayson where he stood on the podium. Her own microphone was buried in the pile. Nate was right behind her, recording the win for posterity.

A microphone was shoved into Grayson's face and someone asked, "Grayson Pierce, your home run won the World Series. What are you going to do now?"

His eyes twinkled as he looked down at her. His lips spread into the biggest smile she'd ever seen on his face. He threw his head back and laughed out loud.

Before she knew what was happening, his hand had wrapped around her forearm and yanked her up on stage. It was all transpiring so fast that Nate's hand was gone before she comprehended that it was the force pushing her butt upward.

Grayson took her left hand, kissed it and held it up so the diamond caught the light and sparkled brightly.

"I'm going to marry Jane Alexander and take her to Disneyland!"

Turn the page for an excerpt from:

Fade to Black

Two great men,
one impossible choice.
Walking along a mountain of heartache and regret, Kate struggles to find a world where love does
conquer all.

"A true love story, with a dramatic and devastating
twist...no one could have predicted the devastating turn
these characters face within the pages....

Fade to Black is not a book you should miss, if you're
even a little bit of a "romantic." I give it a 5+ stars..."

Well, this is it, Kate thought as she stood outside the five-story building that housed KHB-Salt Lake and would be her new home away from home. Her hands ran down the front of her steel gray slacks, smoothing away any fresh wrinkles. With the matching jacket pulled tight around her, she grabbed her heavy coat and threw her laptop bag over her shoulder.

Nervous energy bubbled in her every cell. She'd heard that this was one of the best stations in Utah, but now that she was here, she couldn't help but second guess her decision to leave the comfortable for the frightening unknown. A frigid autumn breeze kicked up and blew a lock of hair into Kate's face. She tucked it behind her ear, wishing like hell she'd taken the time to actually speak with the people she'd be meeting, for all intents and purposes, for the first time today.

She walked through the foyer, one foot in front of the other, until she stood in front of the reception desk.

"May I help you?" the receptionist asked, her reading glasses perched on the end of her nose.

"Yes, Kate Callahan to see Dale Morris," Kate said with a smile.

"Of course. Just take a seat and I'll let him know you're here." She motioned toward the open room Kate had just walked through.

"Thank you." Kate was much too nervous to actually sit. So instead, she resorted to perusing the lobby. The warm burgundy and gold hues were welcoming, and the low sounds coming from the television, of course tuned to Channel 17, eased some of her tension. Faces of their main anchor people smiled back from pictures that adorned the walls.

"Kate."

She turned. "Dale." She extended her hand toward the man that was the same age as her father, but with more honey blond hair than distinguished gray.

He took Kate's hand in his strong grip and shook it gently. "We're so glad to have you as part of the News17 family."

"Thank you. I'm glad to be here." And she was.

The news business wasn't new to Kate. She was good at it, and could eat, breathe, and sleep breaking news. Unfortunately, the glass ceiling was alive and well in some newsrooms, and she prayed that this one was just as she had heard—shattered. Ambition ate at her. She wanted the anchor chair. To be the face on all the billboards. Maybe even end up in New York.

"Come with me and I'll introduce you around." He motioned to the receptionist. "This is Lydia. Lydia, this is Kate Callahan, our newest reporter."

Her gray curls bounced with her nods as the phone began to ring. "Nice to meet you, Kate," she said before turning to answer the incoming call, "Thank you for calling News17, your extended family, how may I direct your call?"

Kate followed Dale through another set of glass double doors where he called, "Jordan."

Smack dab in the middle of the newsroom was the assignment desk—the hub of every news organization. Three men looked up and Kate couldn't begin to guess begin to guess which one was named Jordan. The red-haired man, who sat behind the desk, waved as he talked away on the phone. The other two stood with their arms resting on the top of the chest high assignment desk. They were waiting for their next task—or shooting the bull.

She recognized both of them, had worked alongside them in the field for two years while she was their competition. Kate hadn't cared then to even learn their names, and this moment was the first time she'd taken the time to notice more than just the cameras they carried around.

One of them looked like a body builder, his sleeve straining against the muscle of his bicep, with blond hair, cut short in the back with longer curly locks on top. He smiled and his dimples nearly swallowed his cheeks.

The second man had light brown hair that looked as though he'd just stepped out of a windstorm. He had a toned physique, under his cream sweater and loose-fitting jeans—much more Kate's type than was his muscled friend. And his eyes.... Kate swallowed hard. His eyes were the color of the Caribbean Ocean sparkling in the bright sun. She shook her head, trying to rid her mind of the sudden urge to go skinny-dipping in the salty water.

The tropical waters focused on Kate's face for only a moment before roaming slowly over her body as though she stood before the group without a stitch on. His lips pulled at the corners, forming a sexy, knowing smile.

Former journalist Morgan Kearns is living the dream! One of her very favorite things is to meet new characters as they step out of her imagination, introduce themselves and keep her up all night telling their stories. Morgan lives in Northern Arizona with her wonderfully supportive husband and her four great kids—and her bulldog, Gus.

Morgan loves to hear from her readers! She can be reached at www.MorganKearns.com.

CPSIA information can be obtained at www.ICGtesting.com
Printed in the USA
LVOW131559060612

284945LV00011B/72/P